Other Mystery Books
by T.K. Sheffield

Pontoon

The Infinity Thieves

Model SUSPECT

T.K. SHEFFIELD

The Backyard Model Mysteries

— Book One —

Making Hay Press

Contact the author at tksheffieldwriter.com

Names: Sheffield, T.K., author.
Title: Model suspect : the backyard model mystery, book one / T.K. Sheffield.
Description: Mukwonago, WI : Making Hay Press, 2023. | Series: Backyard model mystery, bk.1.
Identifiers: ISBN 978-1-949085-92-1 (paperback) | ISBN 978-1-949085-84-6 (ebook) | ISBN 978-1-949085-87-7 (audiobook)
Subjects: LCSH: Murder--Fiction. | Models (Persons)--Fiction. | Internet personalities--Fiction. | Wisconsin--Fiction. | Cozy mysteries. | Mystery fiction. | BISAC: FICTION / Mystery & Detective / Cozy / General. | FICTION / Mystery & Detective / Amateur Sleuth. | FICTION / Mystery & Detective / Women Sleuths. | GSAFD: Mystery fiction.
Classification: LCC PS3619.H44 M63 2023 (print) | LCC PS3619.H44 (ebook) | DDC 813/.6--dc23.

LCCN: 2023914203

Author photo by Udo Spreitzenbarth

Making Hay Press, d.b.a. Making Hay Productions, LLC

To my mother, Joan, who always said,
"Find a way or make one."

Acknowledgments

"As Shakespeare says, if you're going to do a thing you might as well pop right at it and get it over."   ~P.G. Wodehouse

Thank you to those who helped me "pop right at it" and write this book, including my family who never wavered in their belief that I could do it. And to my writer friends Kerri Lukasavitz and Valerie Biel, who encouraged my every word along the way. Also, to the professors of my master's degree program who offered advice, critical feedback, and support. And to my agent, Julie Gwinn, who believed in my voice. Warm hugs to dear friend Joelle, who kept saying how proud she was that I was a published author—and her husband Rob, too! A huge thanks to the friends I've met on social media who enjoy my Wisconsin Backyard. I will keep sharing its beauty to provide joy, peace, and love to you all.

Thanks to Christine Keleny of CKBooks Publishing, New Glarus, for her steady hand and wisdom while publishing this series.

And, finally, thank you to my beloved, treasured inner circle: my husband and our dear Pomeranian, Mocha (who waits for us at the Rainbow Bridge.) ♥ Love you always and forever.

xx,

K.

One —

There's crashing a party—and then there's crashing through a gate on a cold November morning.

One gig is way more fun than the other.

I, Mel Tower, raked leaves in my backyard. Inga Honeythorne, the manager of my craft mall, burst through my fence like an out-of-control John Deere, breaking my gate. I hadn't seen her coming.

"Mel—something t-terrible has happened!"

I dropped the rake. "Slow down, Inga." The poor woman appeared shocked. She wasn't wearing a coat and wobbled like an inflatable lawn decoration. "Are you hurt? What's wrong?"

"I c-can't believe this, Mel."

She gestured wildly toward my craft mall. The Bell, Book & Anvil was up the hill from where we stood.

My friend gasped. I feared the seventy-year-old would go down. "Don't fall, Inga. Take a breath."

"I couldn't help h-her."

"Help who? What happened?"

Inga buried her head in her hands and sobbed. Tears spilled through her fingers, and dark spots dripped to her red blouse—they looked like blood. She shook like a Christmas ornament hanging on a wind-whipped tree, and I scanned her for cuts.

Had something happened to an artist? I looked toward my craft mall. The holiday season approached. Everybody had been acting stressed: The greeting card makers had writer's block. The silversmiths were bent out of shape. The macramé artists were tied in knots.

A distinct waaahhhh rang out.

Police sirens at eight o'clock in the morning? Sirens hardly ever pealed in Cinnamon, Wisconsin; someone had alerted the gendarmes. I recalled our village police force—young fellows, part-timers. They'd probably been sipping coffee at the Tool & Rye bakery, discussing traffic control for the holiday parade and upcoming parties.

Typical stuff for our touristy village.

Back to Inga: She staggered over the leaves like a zombie. I removed my coat and placed it over her shoulders. She patted my arm, then collapsed into me; we almost fell onto the gate's nails and boards.

The wind ginned up, gusting down the alley, swirling like a zephyr. My long hair twirled to the sky, then—whoosh!—slapped my face. My mug was cold anyway—the weather in Wisconsin is a difficult bridesmaid—and the lashing stung.

Decomposing leaves rose like a brown tornado. In an instant, Inga and I were pelted by flying mulch.

I hugged my friend while hearing police sirens get louder. The wails came closer.

I didn't wonder for whom the alarm bells tolled.

I knew they were meant for me.

Two —

The artisans of my mall installed a gate in my fence six months ago. They'd claimed I needed easier access from my home's backyard to the business.

I preferred my world the way it was—controlled and quiet, with few visitors popping over and telling me to fix my fixer-upper or how to run the mall.

Since I'd retired from fashion modeling, I'd been operating the business for four, no five years. That darn gate ruined everything. If my fence didn't have one, Inga couldn't have crashed it. Then maybe Kat Gold would still be okay.

Faulty logic.

I'm aware, thanks.

But the horror of hearing that Kat—bright-eyed, talented, one of my newest artists—had been killed under a barn door, messed with my critical-thinking skills.

I looked at my building, held back from entering by a fluttering yellow ribbon that taunted me like an insouciant yellow bird.

My friend Steven Delavan stood next to me. He knew what I

was thinking. "Melanie Tower, do not touch the police tape. We cannot go beyond it."

Law enforcement officers scurried across the loading dock, disappearing inside, then reappearing again.

The wind blew on my neck, and I shivered. It felt like I had a stalker behind me. "It's my building, Steven. I should be able to go in. One of my artists is hurt."

He put his arm around my shoulders. "I'm sorry, Mel. To put it delicately, Kat Gold is more than hurt. She's gone on to the great craft mall in the sky."

It had been an hour since Inga catapulted onto my grass with the shocking news. She sat in a police cruiser.

"Steven, you were inside?" I asked. "What did you see?"

"I made my morning drop-off, as usual. Lots of packages today cuz of the holiday kick-off week comin' up. Inga had just arrived. She was hysterical because she found Kat pinned under that door."

"The big one you delivered a few days ago?"

"Yeah, that vintage thing. Weighs a ton."

How Kat got into the storage room off the loading dock was a mystery. Kat did not have the entry codes. Only a few people did, and she wasn't one of them. "Why was Kat inside so early? Who let her in?"

"Mel, I drive a delivery van six days a week. I'm not a detective."

Not true.

Steven traveled the countryside of our county delivering packages. He brought medicine to the ill, gifts to children, and boxes to mom-and-pop businesses. Because of his time on the road, he assisted at car accidents, rushed people to the ER, and rescued stray pets.

Steven regularly witnessed unusual circumstances. I suspected he knew more secrets about our citizens than the village's newspaper editor, and that fellow knew a lot.

Steven asked, "Kat was teaching a social media class this week, right? I delivered materials to her."

"She'd booked the mall's workshop space...."

"And?"

"Her regulars were attending. Not many others."

"Kat had her detractors, didn't she?"

I stomped my boots on the pavement. "She hadn't made friends yet, that's all. Some crafters appreciated her new ideas; others didn't."

"Know of anyone who'd want to hurt her?"

"No."

Yes. Maybe.

Kat ruffled feathers when she joined the Bell, Book & Anvil family a year ago. She was a horse fly in the frozen custard, as we say in the Dairy State.

She'd been polarizing from the start, wanting to "transform the craft-marketing space." She claimed to be a social media star. I gave her a chance because I like to help people.

But Kat offered unsolicited advice to artisans who didn't need her marketing ideas. Their sales were word-of-mouth, and it worked great for them.

Further, Kat offended Inga; I witnessed that set-to.

Inga is a calligrapher. With amazingly strong hands, she penned invitations and announcements, a hospitality trend that was coming back, according to her. Inga claimed that when the world ran out of money, civility toward one another was all humanity would have left.

About a week ago, outside my office, Kat pestered Inga one too many times about starting a social media page. "Think of all the likes and shares you'd get—you'd go viral!"

Inga was as docile as a Brown Swiss grazing in a field of buttercups. But she uttered an "Uff da!" like a Norwegian sailor and clog-stomped down the hall so loud I thought the beams of the mall would cave in.

I shuddered. "I can't believe this is happening, Steven. It must have been a terrible accident. How awful for Kat."

Steven sighed, puffing out his cheeks. His breath floated on the wind and shape-shifted into little gray hobgoblins. "The door couldn't have fallen on its own, Mel."

"But—"

"Someone pushed it."

I was afraid he was going to say that.

Bah humbug.

I used that phrase a lot in New York City as a model. The fashion industry lacked good cheer at times.

Since I'd moved back to my hometown, I hadn't used the phrase. But today? Just before the holiday season, when a woman was found deceased in my building?

Bahhist of humbugs.

In my kitchen, Steven sipped a mug of Wiscocoa—hot chocolate, Wisconsin-style. Tasted like our state in a cup. Notes of dark chocolate, rich cream, cinnamon, campfire, and brandy. A vendor in my mall made it. Delicious.

Steven glanced around. "Too bad you don't know any artists, Mel. You could display some of their pieces on those bare walls."

My friend was part delivery driver, part smart aleck. "I've only been home a few years, Steven. Decorating takes time."

My vendors have offered photographs and art for the walls of my humble abode. But I told them to sell their wares, not doom them to obscurity in a fixer-upper house with a curmudgeon for an inhabitant.

I poured a mug, then sat across from Steven. He stared at me. "I told the police you'll help solve the case, Mel."

"You did not."

"You're a master at body language; that's what modeling is about, you say. Who better to spot a 'poser' than someone who worked as one?"

I studied his face. Steven was thirty-four, ten years younger than I was. He had sparkling green eyes and curly hair that tumbled over his forehead. He reminded me of a labradoodle at times, given his goofy energy. "You should solve it, Steven. Who better to find a faker than someone who knows bad addresses?"

"Don't be a grinch. There are no bad addresses in Cinnamon."

"What did the police tell you?"

"That they're too young and inexperienced to figure this out."

"What does that mean?"

"You know the part-timers who work in the village. Nice guys, but one of them still believes in the Great Pumpkin. The other one couldn't find a pumpkin patch if his life depended on it."

"Maybe there's not much to figure out. Kat was pinned by a door that fell over." I cringed at the gruesomeness. The word pinned will forever have a different meaning; there's the social media term—and now a deadly one. "It had to be an accident."

"My guess is they'll bring in an outsider to investigate. I wouldn't leave the future of my business in an outsider's hands."

"You watch too much TV."

"Today is Wednesday. The holiday season starts Friday, two days away. It's your vendors' biggest weekend of the year. But the cops said they're shutting down the mall because it's a crime scene. No idea when you'll get it back."

Wisps of steam drifted from my mug and floated over Steven's head. I imagined it spelled the phrase, "You're doomed."

Sorry, I make things up sometimes. It's from twenty-five years of being a mannequin.

What else did I have to do while being pinned, poked, and photographed? No one wants a model's opinion. I learned to observe people and their body language. To quote baseball's Yogi Berra: "You can learn a lot by watching."

Steven scowled at me over the top of his cup. Usually, the guy was happy-go-lucky and embraced the bright side of a situation—but not now.

I got the message.

Three —

From my kitchen window, I watched the officer walk through my backyard.

He stepped over the destroyed gate, taking no notice of the broken boards. The young fellow acted like the mess was landscaping. It appeared the dastardly deed had occurred at that spot, not in my mall.

I'm not a detective, though.

Neither was the cherubic-looking officer who landed at my kitchen table. I knew the guy. I'd seen him at village board meetings. Linus was half of the part-time duo (the other fellow was Luce; hence, the *Peanuts* references) who patrolled the sidewalks of Cinnamon, population 2,500.

Linus sipped Wiscocoa, then asked for another cookie. "Snickerdoodles are my favorite." He scanned the bare counters of my kitchen. "You make 'em, Ms. Tower?"

Just as my home's walls are empty, the kitchen follows. I dislike clutter. "My cousin Louella Jingle made the cookies. But about Kat Gold—"

"Yeah, too bad."

"What do you know so far, officer?"

"I ask the questions. Here's one: Did you do it?"

"Excuse me?"

"Did you tip that heavy door onto Ms. Gold?"

"Of course not! What are you implying, officer?"

"Just kiddin'. I'll be a detective someday. Gotta practice. But the whole thing is weird."

"What happened?"

"Nope. I ask the questions."

He chewed a bite of doodle, then snickered.

I think he did it on purpose. Was the young man playing mind games with me? "Officer, I'm concerned. A person dying in my building is horrible. Is there a killer loose in Cinnamon?"

He frowned. "You tell me. Where were you when Kat Gold was murdered?"

I felt shocked to be questioned like a suspect. After the officer left, I dialed Steven.

"What did you tell him?" he asked.

"I defended myself. I wasn't near the mall. I'd been raking leaves, then Inga showed up hysterical. You and she are the only two people with access—"

"Think for a sec, Mel."

"But neither of you would—"

"Hold on. Gotta stop."

I heard the van's engine shut off, then a door slam. I stood in my living room, watching out its French doors. Battleship-colored clouds formed in the sky, and they rolled over the village, advancing toward my yard like roly-poly phantoms.

It looked like Cinnamon was under attack by giant, gray marshmallows.

Steven returned. "Snowstorm on the way. Could be a lot."

"Tell me what you're thinking."

"Mel, I don't want to scare you, but the police will solve this the quickest way possible. It's like how I make deliveries. I go to the easiest places first. Then, I travel farther out."

"What does that mean?"

"The police will investigate from the inside out, like a dough-nut, no pun intended. They'll look at the people who found her—Inga, then me—and those around her, which includes you. Pro-cess of elimination. Do they have any reason to suspect you?"

"Kat and I got along fine."

"Ever hear the rumors about her?"

"What rumors?"

He sighed. "I never said anything to you, but I was going to. Stories were going around that she wanted to be like you, have a business like yours—"

"Kat wanted to be a recluse with an absent boyfriend and manage a barely profitable art business? Can't imagine why I hadn't heard that."

"Yeah, no offense, but it doesn't make sense. That's why I wasn't worried. But if Officer Linus got weird with questions, you should know the rumor. Someone told him."

I wish Steven would have said something earlier, like when Kat Gold was among the living.

Competition did not scare me.

I'd worked in fashion. Those folks eat Competitor-Os for breakfast. It's like the round-O cereal, but the nuggets are lacquer black and insanely expensive. It's the breakfast of runway champions.

Had I known about Kat's ambition, I would have handed her the keys to the mall. Let her have a trial run at the business.

She could manage a diverse group of artists, collect rents, pay the taxes, trap the mice. (The mall building was one hundred years old; the mice came with it.) She also could communicate with Fern Bubble, of Bubbles & Fiber Public Relations, about promoting the place.

Kat would find out if she was management material. Given what I knew about her, I had doubts. Seeking social media popularity was one thing. Leading people was another.

Nothing I could do about it now.

What was done was done.

My phone pinged with text messages. I turned it off, imagining the scene at the Tool & Rye, the village hangout. The place is half hardware store, half bakery. A pot-bellied stove divides the two stores.

Locals would have gathered around the fire to gossip, the word about Kat Gold spreading like salt on snowy roads. Discussing her demise with the masses was an experience I'd avoid for now. I needed to speak with someone I trusted, so I hopped into my Saab. The car's clock read noon, but it could have been half past the Age of Aquarius. It felt like I was having an out-of-body experience.

Cruising High Street, I saw a line of vehicles parked in front of the T&R. The street's vintage lamps and cheerful red bows comforted my soul. I drove past my mall. The place had been a blacksmith shop, three stories of cream city brick and thick wooden timbers. I'd remodeled it, adding windows and craft booths on each floor.

The mall was dark, locked like a prison cell. A squad car idled out front. I should have been in my office, prepping for shoppers and talking with artists and crafters about the hectic holiday weekend ahead.

How had my world changed so fast?

I pressed the gas, hustling out of town, stopping at a stop sign after about a mile. I had three choices: A left turn took me to farms and fields. Straight ahead was the dense forest of the Kettle Moraine. A right turn meandered out to Lake Cinnamon, a sparkling blue gem during summer, a boiling tureen of white caps and dangerous waves in November.

I hooked a left, speeding toward open countryside.

When I first returned to Cinnamon from New York, I'd driven the same road, amazed at the long views and the homestead farms dotting the hills. Yes, I'd grown up with it. But after many years away, the sight had been stunning.

Still was, even on a day like this, with low clouds that skimmed the silos. It felt like I was driving under a mattress.

Fern Bubble, my mall's PR person, resided on an old dairy farm. I turned into her place's gravel drive, winding along a fenced pasture. Horses lifted their heads at the sound of my car. I saw Tulip, the rescue mare I sponsored.

Tulip wasn't really a horse; she was more like an aircraft carrier. That was why I could pick her out among the other equines in the herd, all of which were rescues. Tulip was a draft, which seemed to be a cross between a dump truck and a sofa.

I didn't know anything about horses, just that their noses were soft, and they smelled exactly like they should: a mix of fresh air, green grass, and the best garden dirt money can buy.

I selected Tulip to sponsor because she reminded me of me— long hair that knots in the wind, quiet-natured, and taller than her friends. We also had big hooves. (My feet are like flippers, by the way.)

We've both stayed single all our lives. Rumor was Tulip

needed to have a serious talk with her on-again, off-again fellow, but that could apply to me and not the horse.

I pay the big gal's rent and her monthly unlimited carrot plan, the equine version of a cell phone bill.

I parked in front of the barn, emerging from the car to inhale the cold air. Glorious. Nothing like rural Wisconsin oxygen to invigorate the blood.

Fern had converted the milk house into her firm's headquarters. I stepped inside. "Fern, got a minute?"

"Mel, I've been trying to reach you. Terrible news about Kat Gold."

"Shocking, to say the least."

"Let's walk."

Fern believes in moving meetings, not sedentary conversations. She says it inspires C&C, creativity and clarity. I grabbed a wool barn jacket from the closet and slipped on tall rubber boots marked with my initials.

She provides garb for her clients because, well, it's a farm. Animals and the gifts they deposit are part of the experience.

We strolled through the barn. Fern had replaced the cow stanchions with horse stalls long ago. Each box was clean and freshly bedded, with hay piled in a corner. "May I move in, Fern? I could live here with the animals and be happy."

"Do not wish for an easy life, my friend. Pray to be a stronger person."

"Foghorn Leghorn?"

"Close. John F. Kennedy."

She knew what had happened in my mall, of course. Fern's job was to know. She monitors the social media party line like a switchboard operator of days past. Also, she has a Dixie cup with a long string that travels from the farm to the ear of the newspaper editor, Wooly Gallagher.

I do not have an online presence.

My previous career was showy enough, thanks.

Fern's company, Bubbles & Fiber, PR, runs the mall's social media. She does a fabulous job with it, bless her soul.

She slid open the barn's end door, and we stepped into the corral.

I sank about five inches into muck. The sludge nearly sucked off my boots. I felt like I was going down in smelly quicksand.

Yeah, that summed it up.

Four —

We squish-stepped to the pasture.

Fern offered carrots to the horses. They indulged, and I noticed their summer hair had grown into fluffy fur. The animals followed us like puppies, except for Tulip; she plodded behind us, too, but it was like being tailed by a Buick station wagon.

"Give me your insight about what happened to Kat," Fern said.

"This morning, about seven o'clock, Inga opened the business like usual. She found Kat in the storage area off the loading dock, pinned under a door, deceased. Steven showed up right after to make his morning delivery and called the police."

"How did Kat get in? No one has access except you, Inga, and Steven, right?"

"And you."

My friend stopped, looking down at the ground as though searching for a lost horseshoe. The wind tousled her salt-and-pepper curls and reddened her cheeks. "You don't have cameras?"

"No, that's why I limit access to a few people."

"What would Kat be doing there so early?"

"No idea. She'd booked the workroom to teach a social media class. But it was tomorrow, not today."

"Hmm."

"Did you hear about Kat wanting to open an art business?"

Fern looked up. "Like yours? Really?"

"Steven told me."

"I had no idea, but I'm not surprised he knew something I didn't. Delivery people get major scoops these days. They're everywhere. See everything."

She offered the horses the last of the carrots. "Do you think Kat was asking your vendors to join her? Could she have been poaching artists away from you?"

"What do you think?"

"Yes, absolutely. I've seen too much in my career to be shocked by anything."

I watched Tulip chew an orange stem, thinking about what I'd learned while running the Bell, Book & Anvil. Owning a business isn't all fun and games. All fringe and glue, if you will.

Designs get stolen. "Handmade" can be mass-produced junk. Semi-precious stones are fakes sometimes.

As the proprietor, it's my job to protect against that nonsense.

I've offended a few folks by asking them to leave. I had to do the dirty work; the buck in managing the place starts and stops with me.

"Yikes, let's step back, Mel."

Fern towed me away from the horses. The carrots must have kicked in because the animals began acting like they had a snootful. One of them danced on his hind legs. The others squealed and jumped like they'd just gotten out of horse jail. A couple of them backfired, even.

Tulip stepped protectively toward Fern and me. It was like a tank moving into position, shielding us from the mischief-makers.

Fern patted the mare's monstrous neck. It sounded like thumping a boulder. "The authorities have cordoned off your building?"

"It's a crime scene, so it's wrapped in police tape like a Christmas present. An officer is watching the place. No idea when I can reopen."

"I'll post a notice to your social media accounts and send emails to the vendors. I'll keep them updated."

"Can you do something else?"

I told her what I wanted.

We hiked back to her office.

Fern stared at her computer. "I don't see anything suspicious."

"Isn't all social media suspicious?"

"Drink your sarsaparilla."

Fern has heard my complaints about the internet before. She soothed me with root beer. I sipped, then asked, "What was Kat posting? Check out her ex-husband, too."

"She doesn't have much on here for someone who claimed to be a social media expert. I'll print out what I can before her accounts go dark."

"Thanks."

"Here's something: Kat's Pinwheel account is her biggest. Lots of followers."

"Followers? Was she some kind of apostle?"

Fern ignored me. As I said, she's familiar with my grumpy troll schtick. "Kat probably bought followers to appear like she had a larger audience."

"Bought them?" I asked. "Like my cookie jar guy? He collects vintage jars, then buys mountains of cookies to put in them. It's genius. Sells like crazy."

Fern swiveled from the computer to jot a note in her daybook. I never saw her without the red tome; she claimed it held her public relations powers.

But it also was her downfall.

She claimed she'd lose her PR magic, like Superman encountering kryptonite, if it were misplaced. "Mel, when Kat applied to be a vendor, what did her application say? What was she selling?"

"Bracelets. She shared a booth with the Broadways."

"And you let her?"

"I probably shouldn't have. I wanted to give her a chance."

"So she sold bracelets supposedly 'handmade' by the Broadways and taught social media classes that no one took?"

"Not all the bracelets were bad. When I confronted Char and Crystal Broadway, they removed the fake stones and the dupes. And a few vendors liked Kat's classes."

"Who were they?"

"The Broadways ... and a couple others."

"Could Kat and the Broadways have had a falling out?"

"Everyone argues with Char and Crystal eventually. They're professionals at it."

"But you get along with them. How do you avoid fighting with those two?"

I placed my mug on a side table, then extended a hand to Fern. "Hi, Ms. Bubble. My name is Mel Tower. I once worked in fashion."

Fern and I debated what had happened to Kat for a few more minutes. Fern offered a guess: "I say the Broadways did it in the Bell, Book & Anvil storage room with a vintage door."

I nodded. "Two people could have tipped that cargo barge onto Kat Gold, no question. The door was heavy as a ship's anchor. A duo could manage it."

"Why, though?"

"Excellent question."

I pondered what I knew about Char and Crystal Broadway. The mother-daughter duo lived on Lake Cinnamon, and Char had always been a handful, zipping around in a fancy car and showing off her latest handbag.

Not that I cared; it was her life. Char could live as she pleased.

I liked Crystal. When she was decanted from mum, when you got the young woman away from her "momager," Crystal was delightful. She was twenty-two, with a bright smile and a passion for books.

"I can't believe either woman could be a killer," I said. "Or that one lurks in Cinnamon. I love this area. It's too crazy to comprehend."

Fern agreed. After a few more minutes of chatting, she walked me to my Saab.

Snow drifted from the clouds. The fat flakes looked like white confetti. The fluff alighted on the decorations draped on the barn, making the place look like Mrs. Claus's Animal Rescue.

"Whatcha thinkin' about, Mel?" Fern asked.

"How many murder cases have you worked on?"

"Exactly none. Murderers don't need publicity."

"I might need your help."

"Okay, sure. And I might need yours."

I heard a snort. I wanted to blame the horses for the heehaw, but the noise came from me. I knew what was coming.

"Mel, when was the last time you spoke with Rand?"

"Who?"

"The pilot you've dated for seven years."

"Yesterday ... last week."

"I know a fellow you should meet."

"Another one?"

"He's great, I promise."

"Is he a draft? Would he and Tulip get along?"

"He's human, Mel. Two-legged."

"I prefer four."

"He lives up north, five hours away."

"I'll meet him, then. Next summer when the roads are clear."

"He's coming to town."

Sort of like Santa.

I didn't say that, of course. Fern meant well. She always did when introducing me to one of her guy friends. Before I left, I agreed to meet him.

Fern didn't know what she was proposing, though. No man would get involved with a suspect in a murder investigation.

I parked in the Cinna-Bowl's parking lot, guessing at a space because the snow camouflaged the lines. Footprints led to the front door.

A good sign.

It meant editor Wooly Gallagher had stuck to his schedule.

The local news bugle, *The Cinnamon Roll*, gets "put to bed" Wednesday. So Wooly gets the afternoon off. With the holiday weekend, plus a murder in our quaint burg, I wasn't sure if he'd be at his usual lane, practicing his technique.

Two giant bowling pins flanked the entrance. They were decorated like penguins and pierced me with black eyes. I felt intimidated.

I dashed past and entered. A bowling ball Christmas tree had been built in a corner. It was a feat of engineering but a questionable decorating decision.

I envisioned a kid bowler "borrowing" a ball from the tree. The pile would collapse and smash the front window, rumbling down High Street like a round-ball river.

No one would stop sixteen-pound cement spheres with a head start.

Overall, the Cinna-Bowl felt hazardous to the health.

I spotted Wooly at the top of a lane, drying his hand on a towel. "Mel, great to see you. I was hoping you'd show up."

You'd think murders happened every day in our town. Nothing phases Wooly.

I greeted him, and he responded by picking up his custom-made globe, then posing like a raptor at the top of the lane.

Wooly eyed the pins with the intensity of a hawk hunting mice. He stepped forward and snaked his arm behind him. Then, with his body coiled, he launched a rocket toward the pins.

They exploded—boom! The crash shook the walls of the building.

Wooly wasn't a large guy; I was taller. But his bowling form was perfect. His wrists were iron ropes—his body pure torque.

He made knocking things over look easy.

Five —

f I were to write a news article about the Cinna-Bowl, its head-line would read: "Local Lanes Turn into Tunnels of Terror."
Wooly's intense demeanor, combined with thunderclaps of smashing pins, gave me a headache.

The newspaper editor finally stopped the carnage after twenty minutes.

We took a table a fairway away from the ball tree, but the Bowler de Sade, who'd decorated the place, chose to hang more balls from the ceiling.

They could have been plastic. Probably were because the joists would have collapsed. But it was like having lead balloons over our heads.

I kept waiting for a ball to drop on our skulls.

Wooly ordered fried cheese curds, golden deliciousness. He savored one, then said, "Mel, have you checked out Kat Gold's ex-husband?"

"Are you on the Mel-should-investigate bandwagon, too? Was I deputized at some point?"

Wooly frowned. "The county sheriff just retired due to health issues. The village doesn't have full-time law enforcement to lead this investigation. Cinnamon's last homicide was ten years ago. They'll bring in outsiders—"

"But have I been charged with a crime?"

"Everyone who knew Kat is considered a suspect. You were around her frequently. She was at your mall a lot."

Wooly knew this because his wife, Cozette, was one of my vendors. She hunted the countryside for vintage thermoses—thermosi?—and resold them for a profit.

Quite a lucrative venture.

Cozette was not a fan of Ms. Gold, FYI.

I chomped a fried curd. Ouch. Grease seared my tongue. I gulped water to soothe the pain. "The authorities have closed ... my b-business," I hacked.

"I noticed. And we're headed into the holiday kickoff. With the parade and the week of events, this week's paper is double its normal size because of it. But the police have to examine every inch of your building. It's three floors; it'll take a while."

A bowler hit a strike. He must have been named Godzilla because the walls quaked, and the decor above us shook like a rollercoaster had rumbled overhead.

"Are the police watching the mall?" Wooly asked.

"Yes. I don't recognize the officer."

"Must have been sent from another department. I'll try to find out who's running the investigation. Can law enforcement see your house?"

"The guy guarding the loading dock can see my place perfectly. Direct line of sight across the backyard."

"Hate to say this, Mel, but they're watching you, too."

I sipped water, wishing it were something more potent. "What's your paper doing, Wool? Is a reporter investigating?"

"We'll file open records requests, but information will be

withheld. I've got a lean staff; we don't have talent to spare. I'll pass along intel, though."

"Thanks, I guess."

"Be your own advocate, Mel. Don't let this thing get out of hand."

Funny statement from a bowler who manipulated a ball in his hand with the finesse of a surgeon.

I did not laugh, however.

The convo with Wooly had me seeing red. Was I really a suspect in a murder?

I sat in my car, watching the snow drift from the sky. It was nearly six o'clock. My phone buzzed all day, but I'd ignored it.

I looked at text messages. My cousin, Louella Jingle, volunteer extraordinaire and baker for the masses, had been trying to reach me. I called her. "Hi, Lou—"

"Mel, what the heck happened at your mall? Ya gotta come out to the ranch."

"Kat Gold—"

"Never mind, I heard the whole story at the Tool & Rye. Everybody's been lookin' for ya."

"Everybody but a police detective, I hope."

"You had nothin' to do with it! The bettin' pool says the killer is her mystery boyfriend. Money's on him."

"What about her ex-husband?"

"Tim Gold is on the list of suspects. But let's talk when you get here. Got a pot of chili on the stove. We have to talk about the mall's parade float. It's in the barn. You gotta see it."

I should have known something was up; I swear the streetlamps flickered, and a rooster crowed three times while she talked.

I agreed to her demands and cruised out of town.

This time, at the red sign at the end of High Street, I drove straight ahead into the forest of the Kettle Moraine.

Cousin Lou and her husband, Jason, resided on forty acres of woods north of Cinnamon. Took about twenty minutes to get there, thirty on snowy roads.

They had a log house and an old barn that Jason fixed up. It was his workshop and Lou's torture chamber.

Did I say torture?

I meant party room.

Lou loved entertaining. The barn had plank floors and rafters big as tree trunks. It was one of those picturesque interiors that got tons of likes on social media. My vendors constantly used the place for photo shoots. Lou sent them home with enough cookies and baked treats to fill their freezers for a year.

When I'd spoken with her on the phone, she'd ordered me straight to the barn. "Ya gotta see the float. Jason just finished it," she'd said.

I parked in front of the barn, hopped out of the car, and rolled open the barn's giant door.

"Surprise!"

Yowza—those saying I should investigate Kat Gold's murder should note: I'm a dope. I fell for Lou's surprise birthday trap like a goose landing among decoys.

Not the best look for someone who should be investigating liars—or killers.

"Happy Birthday, Mel!" Lou cried. "Gotcha!"

"Wow, you sure did."

I looked around and saw Jason, her husband, and a gaggle of my vendors. Crepe streamers drifted from timbers, lights twinkled like fireflies, and a giant poster screamed, "45 never looked better!"

A luscious, frosted cake sat on a sideboard. Propped around it were photos from my modeling days—cringe. Steven, the deliveryman, stepped toward me with champagne. He kissed me on the cheek. "Happy Birthday, my dear."

"But it was last week."

"And we didn't celebrate."

"Because I hid from you guys."

"We're gonna pull ya outa your shell whether ya like it or not!" Lou exclaimed.

To Whom It May Concern: Do not under any circumstances reveal your birthdate to my cousin, Lou. She will broadcast it via the network that begins at the Tool & Rye. She will refuse "No" for an answer.

Further, be advised that she will attempt to change one's spots. Lou prefers sequins and animal print, so buyer beware. She is a cowgirl who lopes to the beat of her own horse.

She hugged me, then pointed at the walls. "Do ya like those modelin' pictures, Mel? Ya look like you're seein' ghosts."

I stared at the giant posters on the walls. There I was with big hair, high-waisted jeans, and frosted eye shadow.

Yes, I saw a few ghosts.

Wooly and Cozette Gallagher strolled in about thirty minutes later.

I stood in a corner next to a cardboard John Wayne, who wore a birthday hat. I shook my head. "Wool, you should have warned me."

"And miss this? Never."

"You couldn't get Lou to cancel after what happened today?"

He didn't answer. We both knew that getting Louella Jingle to cancel a party was like telling a thoroughbred not to run. Or a collie not to be friendly. The Rock of Gibraltar would erode to a sand dune before Lou changed her plans.

The Thompson twins, octogenarian cross-stitch queens, popped over with birthday greetings. "It's not the number of years in your life that count—" Edna began.

"It's the life in your years," Ellie finished.

The ladies speak in cross-stitch. They'd had a booth in my mall since I opened.

"No one is a failure when she has friends," I replied.

Oliver Roberts, the village librarian, approached with a tray. "There's nothing better than a friend unless it's a friend with cake. How about a slice for the birthday girl and her beautiful younger sisters?"

The twins giggled. "Always be a rainbow in someone's cloud," they cooed.

"All's well that ends well," Oliver replied.

He spoke in Shakespeare and resembled The Bard with his pointy chin and dark eyes. He had been at the library for a year. "Mel, I selected the lemon curd for you."

"Super."

Oliver made me feel odd; he knew so much about me. I checked out a gardening book, and he knew what I was planting. I got a cookbook for Lou—I just got one about baking with lemons—and he offered lemon cake.

Lou saw us and quick-stepped over, the fringe of her blouse swinging with her strides. "So nice seein' you two kids together. You're both so tall. Ollie, did ya know Mel likes books?"

She beamed. Wooly, Cozette, and the twins drifted away. Even John Wayne looked in the other direction. No one interferes when Lou Matchmaker casts a spell.

Oliver looked at me. "A Wisconsinite by any other name would never smell as sweet. Mel is delightful."

I pointed at the float. "What's delightful is that parade float. Excuse me, but I need a closer look."

I stepped past the food and drink tables to enter the workshop. The float occupied most of the space and was a testament to DIY craftsmanship.

Jason, Lou's better half, was an excavator. He moved earth as a job, but the guy could build anything.

He'd built an outstanding replica of the mall on a flatbed trailer, matching its cream-city brick exterior and wavy glass windows. A "Bell, Book & Anvil Art Mall" sign hung over the front door.

Lou added touches, too. Fake snow on the building's roof glittered under the warm lights of the barn. Icicles shone like long diamonds. Presents were wrapped in cheetah-print paper.

I felt a shove. Lou asked, "Whaddya think?"

"It looks fantastic."

"Turned out great. I got cowgirls for your candy throwers. An outrider on a paint horse will hand out leaflets—no, that's the dude ranch's entry." She grabbed a clipboard from the float and flipped through notes. "Rats, your candy thrower was Kat Gold. She volunteered for it. Don't worry; I'll find someone else."

"Thanks."

"Nobody's been pesterin' ya about what happened, I hope. Told 'em not to at your birthday shindig."

"Not at all."

"Good—so what happened?"

I shook my head. "I thought you learned everything at the Tool & Rye."

"Yah, but sometimes ya gotta hear it from the horse's mouth."

"What do you know about Tim Gold, her ex?"

"The bettin' pool has him in 'Place.' 'Show' is you."

"What?"

"Just kiddin'. Third spot is 'Disgruntled Business Partner.'"

"That's Char Broadway."

"Calamity Char, I know. Watch your back, Mel. What happened to Kat was gawdawful; may she rest in peace. But there's a bad seed in Cinnamon."

Steven entered the workshop holding beverages. "I have a delivery of sparkling waters, ladies. Louella, the parade float is stunning. Better than last year, even."

"Thanks. We wanted to surprise Mel."

"And you did. She loves surprises."

He winked at me.

I'll get even with you, Steven.

Lou said, "This is nothin'. Wait 'til you see what's comin' next."

Six —

ou sent me back to cardboard John Wayne and ordered me to close my eyes.

Steven accompanied me to the corner. "Don't peek."

I feared their game.

Bad things come in threes, people. First, there was Kat's terrible accident. After that, I was tricked into attending this party. (I dislike surprises. The last one I experienced, about twenty-five years ago, is why my emotions resemble John Wayne. Flat and cardboard-like.)

But let's not go into that now.

It is my birthday party.

Anyway, I stood in the corner like a stiff, listening to guests talk and shuffle while my eyes were shut. Three dozen Wisconsinites populated the barn, and Dairylanders are not a quiet breed.

The room's noise level was between a herd of Holsteins and a Cummins diesel.

Suddenly, the place hushed. Not a creature stirred—not even the loud pipes of Louella Jingle.

The stillness heightened my senses. I smelled the old barn, which held aromas of hay bales and livestock in its walls. Notes of sugar hit my nostrils. The sweets table was only a few steps away and loaded with cake, fudge, and chocolate chip cookies.

The air felt electric. I heard a squeak. What was that?

The pip sent me back several years. My late collie had a favorite toy, a rubber depiction of Illinois. Where Lou found it, I'll never know. I retired the toy after it had been chewed beyond recognition, but I knew its squeal.

I opened my eyes. What in the world?

Scrambling across the planks toward me was a mass of fur. I saw white paws, furry ears, and a happy canine face. The animal strained against a leash held by Fern Bubble. She grinned maniacally, like someone who'd kept a secret and finally could reveal it.

The dog was grinning, too, probably due to the toy in its mouth. Yes, it was the one I remember. This one was new with no teeth marks embedded in it.

I suspected the dog received it from his Aunt Lou. I looked at her. She stood near the sweets, leaning on Jason's shoulder, dabbing her eyes with a chamois.

Steven pulled me toward him. "Mel, meet Max. He's a border collie mix about five years old. He can't wait to be your fella."

I bent down, and Max buried his head in my chest. He smelled like sunshine and horses.

Fern must have been keeping him at her place. "Max is perfect for you, Mel," she said. "You're going to love him."

I hugged the bundle of fur.

Yes, I was in love.

✴

I looked in the rearview mirror of the Saab and spoke to the smartie in the back. "Max, from now on, you answer any invitations we receive. And you're my stand-in at surprise parties."

He woofed in agreement.

Turns out that partners-in-crime Fern Bubble and Lou Jingle had been fostering the dog for about a month. Behind my back, they discovered Max was a supreme ball chaser and unbothered by loud noises. He also showed no beef with delivery people.

Good news for Uncle Steven.

Max loved the vendors at the mall. He'd been snuck in to visit several times and was a hit with everybody.

He desperately needed a person who now was yours truly.

Turns out the party was for him. He got oodles of presents, which filled the car's trunk. Max received a new bed, homemade treats, and tennis balls. He also got a leash, bags of his favorite food, and note cards inscribed with an "M" from Aunt Inga Honeythorne.

She hadn't attended the party. Given what had happened in the mall, her absence was understandable, but I needed to talk with her.

Headlights flashed behind me. Steven followed us in his van to ensure our safe travel through the Kettle Moraine Forest. The snow fell in buckets. After about forty minutes, we landed at my place.

Steven helped unpack the car. Then he kissed Max and patted me on the head—yes, you read that correctly—and went on his way.

"Max, you're home," I said. "Let me show you the place."

Together, we walked in the front door.

"Who does our new bundle of joy resemble, you or me?"

"I'm not sure. What do you look like again?"

The phone line fizzled, cutting off Captain Rand Cunningham's response. I heard few words: "—sorry we haven't seen—birthday flowers on the way—"

"How's Newark?" I asked.

"Gorgeous—honeymoon here—someday."

We hung up because the connection was so bad. Rand, my longtime fella, had been in the cockpit, stuck on a runway due to bad weather. He'd call later, he said.

I walked across the living room to gaze out the French doors. The sky was orange-pink, the sun just below the horizon. A squad idled behind my building, puffing exhaust. I'd been told the officer was monitoring for trespassers who may want to look inside.

Was the officer watching me, too?

I heard Max step beside me, his nails clicking on the floor. Mornings are my favorite time of day, and Max appeared to be an early riser, too.

It felt different—in a good way—to have a pooch trailing after me. It had been a while. My collie succumbed to old age last year. She'd been a rescue, and we'd had a short, excellent life together.

I looked at Max. "I'm glad you're here. I hope you like me."

The dog's eyes were intense. He wanted to answer, it seemed.

"Max, let's go for a walk. Perfect time for it."

I bundled him in his gift jacket, and then he and I stepped outside. I kept Max on his leash because the gate still was a mess. We avoided that area while he did his business.

The air felt warm for November. Humid, even. Fog rolled in, obscuring the view from my yard. While Max sniffed around, I watched the police squad until I could see only its red taillights.

I decided to pack up some birthday party treats and walk over for a visit.

✳

Life is mostly froth and bubble, but two things stand like stone: trust few people and solve things on your own.

At this juncture, I was not confident in the law enforcement assigned to the Kat Gold case.

Max and I walked to the mall. Marshmallow snow covered the ground, I took hot coffee and goodies to the officer guarding the loading dock. I stood about ten feet from the police vehicle and waved. He powered down the window.

"Officer, good morning. I'm Mel Tower. I own this place."

"Morning, ma'am."

"I brought coffee and cake. Want some?"

"No, thank you. I'm on duty."

I set the basket on a stoop and held up my ID. "Here's my driver's license. My dog's name is Max. He doesn't drive, so, ah, he doesn't have a license."

"He should have a tag from the village."

"I'll apply for it today. I just got him last night."

"Don't step toward the vehicle, ma'am."

"Mind if I ask a few questions?"

"I'm sorry, but I can't reveal anything at this juncture."

"Where are you from? You're not one of our village officers."

"My position is with another county."

"Are you the only one watching the place? What happened to the squad car that was watching the front?"

"I am the only officer here at this juncture."

"What if someone tries to enter the front?"

"The building is secure at this juncture."

"Do you know the detective assigned to this case? Have you heard—"

"I can't reveal anything at this—"

"Juncture, yeah."

"Get those dog tags, ma'am. Have a nice walk."

I picked up the goodies. Then, Max and I walked the long way to my place. The dog didn't wag his tail at the guy, I noticed.

I was shoveling my sidewalk when thirty feet of metal with a giant red blade attached rumbled up. Fern Bubble rolled down the window of her truck. "Need a plow?"

"Sure."

She U-turned and cleared my driveway in seconds. It would have taken me an hour. Then we both cleared the sidewalk and clomped inside, leaving our snow pants and boots in the garage.

Max was delighted to see Aunt Fern. The dog leaned against her legs, grinning with a toothy smile. She patted him. "Found him up north, near Minocqua. He's smart, doesn't like a lot of fuss. Like you." She handed me a gift bag. "I brought you something."

I pulled out a framed photo and darn near cried.

It was a picture of Max and Tulip.

They were in the pasture. The old horse grazed along the crest of a hill, the sun rising behind her. Tulip's coat glowed, and the big horse looked stunning, even elegant. Max lay in the grass, watching the horse. Like a good collie, he appeared watchful. He was keeping an eye on his charge, doing his job. The pose captured the animals' spirits, their inner beauty. It was like the Mona Lisa but set on a hillside in Wisconsin.

Fern asked, "Now, will you put a picture up in this place?"

"Yeah … this should be … somewhere." I dabbed my eyes. "But where—how?"

She smiled. "How about the fireplace mantle?"

I handed her the picture. "That'd be nice. Go ahead—"

"Mel, you put it up there."

"Huh?"

"Do it yourself."

I stomped from the kitchen into the living area, only about four steps. (My house is an old, tiny, federal-style box. Like a horse stall but with a second story.) The living room mantle always intimidated me. I frequently built a fire in the hearth underneath it, but the mantle, the place of honor in a home, sat empty. It was like I had no life.

Or no connection to my life, anyway.

I looked at Fern, the photo, and the mantle. Slowly, I placed the picture on the wood, propping it against the brick—oops, someone forgot to dust this week.

"It looks great, Mel," Fern said.

"Thanks. It means a lot."

Fern and I sat in the living room, admiring the new picture like museum curators. Max had arrived last night, and now I had a photo on the mantle.

My world was changing fast.

Fern sipped coffee. "What was modeling in New York like? You never talk about it."

"I was eighteen; I needed to work. My parents were dead. I had no siblings to rely on." I posed in the chair. "All I had was my height and an ability to be still. Modeling in a big city—and lots of it—was my only skill."

"You say that, but no one believes you."

"I am tall, almost six feet."

"You have more skills than just standing still."

I looked at the mantle. "I'm getting to be a darn good decorator."

She smiled. "We'll get you there."

I pushed a platter of cake toward her. "Eat more, Fern. Otherwise, you'll be plowing food out of my kitchen. I was supposed to share the leftovers with my vendors today. That plan is out the window."

"It's terrible for them. Their inventory is just sitting in their booths." She glanced through the French doors at my building. "How's Inga?"

"I don't know. I'll try to reach her today."

"Did she and Kat ever have words?"

I shook my head. "Inga wouldn't hurt anybody. She's salt of the earth, like all my artists and crafters."

"You do a lot for them. More than other managers of art malls, I imagine."

I savored a bite of cake before answering. "I want them to be happy. Creating art, then selling it, use opposites sides of the brain."

"Is that why you let Kat into the vendor group? So she could teach your artists to sell?"

"Partly, yes. She joined the Broadways' booth. They've always been on the margin in terms of behavior with their 'dupes.'"

"The knock-offs, you mean?"

"Yes, they tried candles like a popular New York brand, but I stopped that. Then they duplicated a vendor's purse. The vendor had created the design and sold them at the mall as fast as she could make them. The Broadways found a mass-market bag like it and tried to undercut her sales."

"What about the fake bracelets?"

"Susan Victory fixed that problem. She gave them advice about making their own. She's helpful like that."

Susan was my top jewelry designer. She'd been at it for years and had a fantastic customer base. She'd built her brand before online marketing strategies existed.

I said, "Kat Gold learned from Susan, too. Kat tried to reciprocate by teaching Susan about social media, but it didn't resonate."

"Did Kat and Susan get along? Any bad blood there?"

"Not that I know of, but I keep gossip among vendors at a minimum. Whisper campaigns and negative chatter are toxic to a place."

Fern sipped her coffee, then observed, "That's a perspective every mall owner should keep in mind."

"I'm not sure I was successful at it, though."

"What do you mean?"

I stared out the window at my mall. "Kat Gold and Char Broadway could have had a falling out. Or, if Kat was stealing my vendors to open a new place, what if someone got angry?"

"That person could have done something awful."

"I hate to consider it, but yes, that's what could have happened."

Seven —

t. Bruce DuWayne showed up unannounced at my door.

The element of surprise is police work 101, but the shock was on the detective. By the end of our conversation, he'd clearly developed a crush on Fern.

Cute, but I became even more worried about discovering who killed Kat Gold.

DuWayne entered my kitchen, and Fern stuck around. I'll never need a defense attorney as long as she's on my team. She could work as a lawyer if she weren't a public relations expert. Or a ravishing, sixty-five-year-old Bond girl.

We sat at the table. Within minutes, DuWayne appeared enamored with her. He was around her age. Fern served refreshments, moving lithely around the kitchen. She's the only woman I know who can make Carhartt overalls look like a catsuit.

The detective inquired about her business. "Bubbles and Fiber is the name of your public relations company, Ms. Bubble? How charming."

"Call me Fern," she purred, voice smooth as a panther. "May I call you Bruce?"

He ate cake while she spoke, the fork in his hand wobbling as though he'd been struck by a personal earthquake. "It would be my pleasure, Fern."

"More coffee?"

She asked the question with flared nostrils, the whole bit.

He croaked, "Yes, please," and sputtered another question about her agency.

I thought DuWayne was here to grill me, so I was surprised by the detour into Fern's world. Not that I'm complaining. I'll play the third wheel any time. I used to book modeling jobs on the premise. As I aged, younger gals displaced me in photo shoots. They were the ones featured in the forward plane of fashion images, and I was pushed to the back, the Uecker seats of a photo.

Fine by me. The job still paid the bills.

But back to Fern, who held the lieutenant in the palm of her hand. Or, in the live well of her boat, as we say in the state of muskie fishing. She poured coffee. "I've been in this business a long time."

"Not so long, surely. We appear to be of similar vintage."

"At our age, we have the benefit of hindsight. Life is composed of work and fun. One must be diligent about both, keeping things in balance. It's never all one or the other."

"Ah, yes, sunshine and clouds. Exercise and rest."

"More cake?"

"Please."

Fern slid into the chair next to him. "Clients want everything these days, immediate results. Especially with social media. But I tell them that building a brand or a business takes time."

"You are wise beyond your years."

He dug into his second slice of vanilla-strawberry cake while

I said as little as possible. That's what one does in this situation. Well, I've never been queried in a murder investigation, but I've been to casting auditions.

Similar experiences, I believe.

When attending castings, the less said the better, especially when one has a nasally Wis-CAHN-sin accent. Better to have casting directors suspect oddness than open one's mouth and confirm it.

Fern discussed her latest podcast, "How to be less social with media," while DuWayne consumed his cake. Finally, he dragged his gaze to me. "Ms. Tower, I must ask a few questions."

"Shoot."

Horrible response. See what I mean about keeping my mouth shut? Fern should have been preparing her client for this interview rather than flirting.

DuWayne asked, "How was your relationship with Ms. Gold?"

"Fine."

"She taught social media classes for you?"

Fern jumped in. "No, Kat Gold was a vendor in the mall, like everyone else. She taught marketing classes for them, not Mel. Kat was never Mel's employee."

"I see. How long had you known Kat Gold, Ms. Tower?"

Fern, again: "Kat had been in the mall for about twelve months. She and the Broadways were co-vendors."

"The Broadways? Are they a person?"

"They are a mother-daughter social media team. They sell bracelets."

"Is that correct, Ms. Tower?"

"Yes," I said.

"How did Ms. Gold get into your business yesterday morning? Did she have a key?"

"No."

"Do you have cameras in the building?"

"No."

"Do you know who would harm her?"

Fern: "Bruce, have you questioned Tim Gold, Kat's ex-husband?"

"I have many people on my list."

Fern dug out her red notebook. "Do you have his contact information? He's also in public relations. Mr. Gold has a firm in Chicago, I believe. I have his private number."

That was news to me.

I watched as Fern shared the contact with the detective. Given her occupation, she probably had everyone's private info in her phone, which was way more intel than I'd want about my neighbors.

I listened while Fern and DuWayne chatted. It was like I'd hired a lawyer. But Fern answered honestly, as far as I was concerned.

The detective departed after getting her phone number. She promised to pass along information to him—a spokesperson for me and a resource for him during the investigation.

He seemed delighted; she seemed confident.

Why didn't Fern tell me she knew Tim Gold?

Fern hugged Max, then climbed into her truck. Before driving off, she shared Tim Gold's phone number with me. "You want to talk to him."

"I do?"

"Don't leave your future in anyone else's hands, Mel. The detective is sharp. Be your own advocate."

Where had I heard that before?

Wooly Gallagher, editor of *The Cinnamon Roll.*

The weekly paper had been delivered while Fern and I were shoveling. I returned to the house, checking the time on the stove; it was almost mid-afternoon on Thursday. I looked out the kitchen window to see the police vehicle still idling behind my building.

Temps were around forty degrees, but the sun angle was low; it cast an amber glow over the village. Sunset was only an hour away.

I read the paper while standing at the sink. There was a short article about Kat's death, and it included a picture of my mall, snapped at a high angle.

I studied the image. I saw the shops on High Street: the Tool & Rye, the flower shop, the candy store. Cinnamon is a tourist town, and its stores range from candles to cheese, from leather to lotions. In the photo, I saw Hank Leigel's attorney's office and the vacant place next to his, which should be a bookstore, in my opinion.

I spied the library, too, at the end of the main drag, about a four-block walk from my place.

I flipped through the rest of the paper. It was fat, featuring advertisements, an interview with one of my artists, Susan Victory, and a schedule of upcoming events.

Cinnamon's holiday shopping season began this Saturday. The week of festivities started with the Cheese Ball. The high school gym would be transformed into a heavenly dairyland. The ball was like a prom for cheesemakers.

I attended each year to support the local dairy farmers. Steven may have joked a few hundred times that "wallflower" was my favorite cheese.

I set aside the paper and began running hot water in the sink. Agatha Christie said the best time to plot a novel is while washing dishes.

It was also a perfect time to ponder what happened to Kat Gold.

✳

After finishing the dishes, I walked to the library. The place was locked tight, surprisingly. But Oliver Roberts saw me through the glass front door and dragged my carcass inside like he'd netted a stray cat. "Mel, come in. Make yourself comfortable."

"I'm returning these books—"

"Don't bother. After what happened in your mall, they're yours."

"But—"

"You must feel terrible. Shall we search for a book about grief? You may keep that one, too."

"Why is the library closed?"

"I gave the staff the afternoon off. The holiday kickoff week will be hectic. My devoted underlings deserve it."

"I'll be going, then."

"Nonsense! You trudged across town to get here. Rest for a moment, lest you catch your death of cold."

He took my book bag and guided me by the elbow through the lobby. The library was an old opera house, a marvelous stone building remodeled with wooden bookshelves and cozy seating.

Oliver steered me past the checkout desk to his office. "How about a hot toddy for what ails you?" he asked.

"When did the library add a bar?"

"Libraries should never be drab, my dear. Even librarians need libations."

We stepped into his atelier. I was impressed; it was like we'd entered a fashion designer advertisement. Or the private quarters of a country house. I saw polished wood furniture, brass lamps, and books. The room smelled like leather.

An antique cupboard was open to reveal a coffee bar containing much more than coffee. I sat in one of the chairs and tapped a quick text to Steven without my cheaters.

Oliver poured hot water into mugs, adding honey, lemon, and apple brandy. He swirled a cinnamon stick into mine, then handed me the potion. "Enjoy."

"Thanks."

"Now, Melanie, what can I do for you?"

"I just wanted to return the books."

"Nonplus, my fair lady. They're yours."

I sipped my toddy. Strong. "Well, as long as I'm here, Oliver, do you mind if I ask questions?"

"Most certainly!"

He raced to the chair next to me like a cartoon character. I swear I heard a zip and a pop as he landed on the leather seat.

I began, "Kat Gold—"

"Lovely creature. I can't believe she's gone."

"She taught social media classes at my mall. But also here, in the library's conference space, right?"

"She did, the poor thing."

"What did you know about her?"

He sighed dramatically, like he was playing to the back row. "Kat was … a troubled soul. To my eyes, she was Ophelia with an iPhone. Beautiful and tragic."

Weird. I saw her as ambitious and confident. "What inspires you to say that, Oliver?"

"I recited this same tale to Lt. Bruce DuWayne. He was here earlier. Have you met the fellow? Sherlock Holmes meets Fred Flintstone."

"I've met him."

"Wonderful, it's reassuring to know Cinnamon's Inspector Clouseau is on the case. I revealed that Kat Gold spent time in this office, in the very chair you're in, Melanie. However, I must say she was nigh as lovely as you."

"Thanks, but—"

"Kat revealed personal misery along with deep regret."

"About what?"

"Many things. To quote Shakespeare: 'When sorrows come, they come not as single spies, but in battalions.' Kat told me she regretted her divorce, the difficulty of building a new career, and the struggle with the monster that is social media."

"She did?"

"In my estimation, Kat confused online popularity with true friendship. To paraphrase the doctor in Macbeth: the patient could not minister to herself."

"What are you saying, Oliver?"

"I suspect Kat's inner demons got the best of her. I presented this observation to Lt. DuWayne. Has anyone considered that she pulled that door onto herself?"

Huh.

Interesting, my dear Watson, er, Roberts.

Interesting, indeed.

After finishing the toddies, we moved to the library's media room.

I inquired about the controls for the village's security cameras, remembering that the library and my mall had been remodeled at the same time.

Oliver said, "Village administrators placed the cameras' controls within the library because it was the most recently updated facility. There are two on downtown buildings." He gestured toward a black metal box. "But Melanie, someone erased the recordings from Wednesday evening, the night Kat met her demise. Unusual, but not suspicious."

"I think it's incredibly suspicious, Oliver."

"This space is unlocked because it's used for storage. And it's adjacent to the kitchen—heavy foot traffic in both locales. Volunteers abound with the 'Midwinter's Night at the Library' event next week. Anyone could have pressed a button thinking it was connected to an audio-visual display. It's happened before, sadly."

"Who are your volunteers? Anyone I know?"

"I'm the head of the committee, of course. But the team includes Char Broadway, Inga Honeythorne, and your cousin, Louella. Kat Gold, as well. Her ex-husband stopped by and expressed a desire to take her place. I told him yes, absolutely."

I pointed at the controls. "Has Tim Gold been in here?"

"Not to my knowledge, but he may have. As you can see, the doors are open."

"No offense, but this is a casual approach to security."

Oliver shook his head. "Not to belabor the point, but I believe Ms. Gold was her own Ophelia; she was the hand in her undoing." He changed the subject. "I hope you'll attend the Midwinter party here on Tuesday evening. I have a role for you to play."

I shook my head. "I'm not an actor."

"Do not deny your talent, Melanie. You are a modern Katharine Hepburn—earthy and strong, with a Midwestern wholesomeness. Ms. Louella suggested you for a role, and I agreed."

I'm no Hepburn, but Lou gives me heartburn, that's for sure.

Oliver explained, "It's Reader's Theater. You'll read from a script. No memorization is necessary. It's Pyramus and Thisbe from *A Midsummer Night's Dream*. Are you familiar with the production? Delightfully absurd. Let me get you the materials."

He raced to his office for a script. Within seconds, he materialized in front of me with my book bag. "The script is in your bag, Melanie. Please call on me. I foresee difficulties for you. Beware the Ides of Cinnamon. I am here as your humble servant and protector."

"Thank you, Oliver. I'll remember that."

"Anon, my dear," he said. "Anon."

"What does drinking at the library mean?" Steven shouted. Around us, bowling pins crashed like thunder.

"I was at the library, having a drink. Why didn't you respond?"

"I thought it was a typo. No one drinks at the library!"

"Take a break after your next frame!"

It was Thursday night league. I was at the Cinna-Bowl, seated on my usual barstool, watching Steven's team, the Bowling Wilburys.

I had a monstrous headache, probably due to the contrast between the quiet library and the percussion effect of the bowling alley. It was like traveling from a meditation garden to a volcano.

Steven finished his turn. Then we hiked through the bar to a side room, the Eleventh Frame, a party space that groups could rent. Praise to the bowling gods; it had doors to shut out the noise.

Cousin Lou, captain of the Rollin' Rebels, was exiting. "Where do you two rascals think you're goin'? This spot is off-limits."

"We need a quiet place to talk," I said.

"Gotta blindfold ya. No one can see what's in here. It's the games for next week's VIP Bowling Night. Can't see what we got planned. Don't want ya to cheat."

"I'm not playing the games, Lou," I said.

"Ya never know."

Cut to Steven and I standing just inside the glass doors with red bandanas over our eyes and Lou peering at us through the glass.

Or, I imagined she was; I was blindfolded.

It smelled like paint and glue. Volunteers must have been drawing signs for the games. "Steven, I need your help. You and I are breaking into my mall."

"But the Wilbury's are winning—"

"Not now. Later tonight."

"Why?"

"I need to check it out."

"That may be criminal trespassing. Not sure."

"We won't go all the way inside. Remember a few months ago when the keypad wouldn't work? You went up the fire escape and used the window on the second-floor landing."

"I shouldn't have told you about that."

"I want to check if that window is locked. Maybe Kat got in that way." Something brushed up against me. "What was that?"

"Sorry, my balance isn't good when I'm blindfolded."

"Come to my place after bowling, okay?"

"I guess."

We gave the bandanas back to Lou. Then I followed Steven through the bar to the alleys. He wasn't enthusiastic about my plan, but I needed a trusted sidekick to investigate. Steven is my best friend. Plus, he has the door codes or keys to every place in the county.

My only other option for a sidekick was Lou.

That would be a disaster. Her approach to solving problems wasn't bull in a china shop; it was bull in a big box warehouse. It would be like working with a rattlesnake that wears rhinestone boots and carries a fringed handbag.

I looked at Steven. He stood at the top of the alley, shaking his head like a puppy, waiting his turn. Remind me never to blindfold the guy; it apparently affected his equilibrium.

I had doubts while I watched him.

To investigate Kat Gold's death, I needed help, but Steven may not have been it.

I read Captain Rand's text when I got home. He wrote that he'd flown to Frankfurt and sent a picture of his dinner: sauerkraut piled on top of a brat.

I smiled because it reminded me of our first meal.

He and I met in New York on a rainy October morning seven years ago; we were hailing the same cab. He was in uniform. I was walking to my apartment after a modeling job. I deferred the car to him because he had a plane to catch, I figured.

He refused, saying I should take it.

We both recognized "Midwest Nice" when we saw it. "There's a green-and-gold pub around the corner," he'd said. "How about an early lunch?"

I'd asked to see his pilot credentials. (It had been close to Halloween; the guy could have been in costume.) He showed his badge. It turned out he did not have a flight to catch. He'd landed at LaGuardia and stopped on the way to his hotel to buy a birthday card for his mom.

It was our first date. Not many people would indulge in a garlicky bratwurst smothered in onions, mustard, and sauerkraut for a first meeting, but this Wisconsin girl did.

Rand and I dated long-distance ever since.

He was based in Chicago. Our relationship had its ups and downs. For example, after the Kat Gold disaster in my mall, I probably should have talked with my significant other about the problem, right?

Our communication is better described as a missed connection.

Cousin Lou says Rand is like a seven-layer salad. "Guy is busy, full of flavor, and been around the world seven times seven. Hates to be in one spot. You're plain cheese dip, Mel. Great, but stuck in your ways."

As I was replying to Rand, another text came in. Steven sent a message saying that Lou's bandana made him dizzy; he was going home. "Talk tmrw," he wrote.

I couldn't blame the guy. Asking him to check the window was a solo mission I should do myself. Steven was a trusted resource. Not just in the village, but the whole county, including the lake folks, who relied on him to find the gravel paths leading to remote cottages. He knew every hidden entrance and secret doorway to those old places.

He had intel on everybody. Steven hadn't revealed all the shenanigans he'd witnessed. He even stopped a burglar once. I shouldn't put him at risk by crossing a police barrier. "Drive carefully," I wrote and added a van emoji.

I looked at Max, who rested at my feet in the living room. "Looks like it's you and me, Max. Let's take a walk."

Another thing about Steven: he'd been absent for the last couple of months, like he'd disappeared from socializing.

He and I used to walk to the Tool & Rye about twice a week for a grilled turkey sandwich on Kimmel rye—salted, caraway-flavored manna from heaven. I'd never seen anyone happier than when he was eating his favorite meal. He was like a Labrador on a bass boat or a golden retriever curled by a fireplace. Content, enjoying the moment.

Lately, when I ran into him around town, he seemed distracted, like something was on his mind. But he had always been a bit of a doofus. At ten years younger than me, he's like my little brother. (If I had one. No sibs for me.)

I figured Steven's mood was due to the holiday season. Deliveries were insane, and his job had gotten busier.

He enjoyed the career; I knew that much.

Like me, he'd had no chance for college. Out of high school, he needed work and jumped into the delivery driver position. Seventeen years later, he was a local hero who'd succeeded by buying his own home and taking care of himself.

I moved to the hall closet. "We need to chat with Uncle Steven, don't we, Max?"

The dog looked up at me, his eyes sparkling. I pulled on a black hat and gloves, then a dark jacket. With his black fur, Max already wore his stealth colors. I clipped a leash to my furry friend's collar, and we slipped out into the night.

Like silent sentinels, Max and I followed the trees that bordered my property. Clouds obscured the moon, and the wind sighed gently. An owl hooted, the bird's moody song carrying across the town. If I didn't know it was mid-November, I'd think it was Halloween.

We turned onto a path, taking the long way to the mall. It's the route I took before the cursed gate was installed in my fence. It was a five-minute meander through a park, a tiny forest along the main drag. It ended about twenty yards from the front of the Bell, Book & Anvil.

There was only one car watching my place. It was behind it at the loading dock. The building's front was unguarded.

It was Thursday night, and the Green Bay Packers were playing the Chicago Bears. My guess was the officer was listening to the game on the radio. I prayed for a high-scoring match that drew law enforcement eyeballs to the squawk box, not my building.

Max and I wound to High Street. The tricky part would be to step invisibly down the sidewalk. I needed to get to the side of my place where the fire escape clung to the wall.

That side of my building was hidden from the village cameras because of tall pine trees.

The night's inky mist worked in my favor. The fog obscured the streetlamps, making the village look dreary. I half-expected Charles Dickens to scurry past on one of his midnight walks.

But speaking of writers, John Muir was about ten feet away. Not the actual naturalist but a statue dedicated to him within a stand of arborvitae, a perfect shield for a woman and her dog to sneak behind. "C'mon, Max—shhh."

We tiptoed to the memorial, Max shadowing my staccato steps. Quick inhale to get my bearings: Street still empty. Mall to my right. A few cha-cha moves, and I would be at its fire escape.

We scurried and arrived at the building. I grabbed the fire escape steps and pulled. The platform silently slid toward me. "Thank you," I whispered to Sunny Days Restoration, the maintenance company I paid to look after the place. Guys showed up regularly to make sure my ancient ruin ran smoothly. Geniuses with hammers and oil cans.

Max and I moved upward like cats, as though our joints were liquid and our feet padded slippers.

I crawled onto the landing, then reached for the window. I'd installed new ones when I'd remodeled. No screens, and all had safety locks. On occasion, I opened this one for fresh air; it was on the landing of the steps that led to the second floor. There wasn't a risk of a patron falling out because of the fire escape.

I pushed upward on it. No go, locked tight.

I tried again.

Yep, the window was locked.

Eight —

My favorite delivery man showed up at seven o'clock with breakfast from the Tool & Rye.

I was surprised to see Steven. As I mentioned, he'd been absent lately.

He confessed to feeling guilty about ghosting yours truly after bowling. He made up for it by bringing wedges of lumberjack ham-and-cheese pie, a specialty of the T&R. Fills the stomach for a week. Add one of the T&R's cinnamon rolls, and you're a Midwest Superman, able to jump barns and leap lakes in a single bound.

Did I say lake?

The word gave me an idea.

We filled plates and settled at the table. Steven asked, "Three people have the passcode for the loading dock's keypad, right?"

"Four: Inga Honeythorne, Fern Bubble, you, and me," I said. "And Max. He knows it now, just in case something happens to me."

The dog heard his name and trotted over. Uncle Steven

offered him a nibble of ham. "Could Kat have hidden in the mall all night?"

"No. I closed up and checked the place. It was empty. And the fire door between the mall and storage area was locked. Kat couldn't have exited from the mall to where she was found."

While I talked, Steven glanced at his watch. I asked where he was delivering. "Fridays are busy," he replied. "Got a bunch. Going here, there, and everywhere."

"Lake Cinnamon area, too?"

"Yep."

"Mind if Max and I tag along?"

He nodded. I knew he couldn't say no because he felt terrible about letting me risk life and limb to climb the fire escape alone.

We finished breakfast, and then the three of us headed out on Steven's appointed rounds.

Lake Cinnamon, or "Lake Cinn" as it was known, unnerved me. It always had been dark and choppy. I saw it as a giant puddle with anger issues. In summer, its temperature "warmed" from icebox to teeth chatter, and its waves calmed—slightly.

But that was like saying an alligator wouldn't attack because he'd just had lunch. He was still a carnivorous reptile, and you still were potential lunch, no matter the conditions.

We'd driven to the yacht club and stopped in its parking lot. Steven needed to organize packages for delivery.

"People live on this lake yearround?" I asked.

"Some do."

"Do they get hazard pay?"

He ignored me and stepped to the back of the vehicle. From the passenger seat, I watched the water boil like soup in a witch's cauldron. The sight reminded me of New York City, a churning sea by another name. I'd lived in the same fourth-floor walk-up for years because it was cheap.

I never knew when my modeling gig would end. I was a B-list "working girl," never a top model. Catalogs, brochures—who printed those anymore?—and body parts.

When I got old and aged out of fashion advertising (my late twenties), fit modeling was the best-paying job I could get. I stood for hours while patternmakers pinned and snipped sample garments on me, a human mannequin.

I'd fled Cinnamon and moved to the Big Apple before cell phones and Google Maps existed. I'd used a pay phone in a donut shop to call my agency and navigated with a map clutched in my hands.

I used to stare out my apartment window and pray to see hayfields. But my view was buildings and a sliver of sky that usually was dark, light, or mud puddle gray.

Steven climbed back into the driver's seat.

I asked, "Anything in this van for Tim Gold?"

"You'll find out." He fired the engine. "We'll do the big lake first, then head to the pond."

Lily's Pond was a smaller lake connected to Lake Cinn via a channel. One of my mall artists, Susan Victory, lived in a cottage along its shores.

We left the club, driving on the lake access road. Sure enough, Gold's place was one of the first stops. His house was a brick tri-level. He probably tore down the original cottage and built the larger home in its place. It had a black-lacquered front door that appeared freshly painted.

The entrance looked familiar.

The porch was decorated but with a mash-up of holiday props. Past-their-prime pumpkins sat next to mini-Christmas trees. A fall wreath hung on the door, and witch's brooms were piled on the concrete.

Steven hopped out, grabbed several boxes, and trotted down the driveway. He knocked on the door, then waited. A man finally opened it. The guy was in his forties, medium height. Big-headed, with thick, blondish hair. Reminded me of an East Coaster. A tanned Long Islander who nodded and smiled, showing gleaming white teeth.

Steven handed over the goods. The homeowner signed for them. They must have been certified or verified—whatever they call "don't just leave the box and hope for the best."

I studied Tim Gold, if that's who he was. He kept smiling—but the guy had just lost his ex-wife.

Seemed happy about it to me.

Steven kept his eyes on the road while he spoke. It was twisty as a goat trail; careful driving was imperative. "Tim Gold grins while he talks. He's in sales; those guys do that. He's been a good customer."

"What did you deliver to him today?"

"Box of books. Probably about how to get away with a crime."

"Huh?"

"I'm kidding. But my customers deserve privacy. I don't know what it was."

We drove in silence. The gray sky drooped over us like an old bathrobe, and the snow had turned slushy. The road appeared to have been wiped with a dirty mop.

We were on the big-house side of the lake. The homes faced west and captured sunset views over the water. We approached a concrete and glass place that looked like a big-city dentist's office. It looked to be designed by an architect with experience in road construction, someone who bought cement by the mile.

Abruptly, Steven steered off the road into a lay-by. He parked behind a tree, out of sight of the dentist's office place. "Does Max need to go out?"

"Sure, he can take a break."

I clipped on the dog's leash, and we stepped outside. My jacket whipped open. The wind rocketed off the water, nearly blowing me over. "This lake has always had something against me!"

"You're not dressed for this. I'll take him."

I handed over Max's leash and hopped back into the van. I watched while Steven and the dog trotted down the gravel road. A sign said it was a cross-country ski area. Maybe for abominable snowmen. The wind rocked the van, and I was glad when Steven and the dog returned.

He fired the engine. "I need to tell you about Kat Gold. It's the same stuff I told the detective. You should know, too."

"You spoke with Bruce DuWayne?"

"Yeah, I'm not sure about that guy. Told you they'd send in an outsider."

"Where's he from? I forgot to ask."

He thumped the steering wheel. "Mel, he's from Madison. You gotta ask these things."

"I'm sorry."

"I'm in a tough spot, revealing stuff about Kat. My customers trust me."

"I won't say anything. Your delivery stories are safe with me. Max, too. He won't reveal a word."

Steven ignored my joke. "Kat was living with Tim Gold. She got packages, and her car was always there."

"But they were divorced, right?"

Steven nodded. "Yeah, Tim told me that months ago. Said his ex-wife was staying. He was helping her start a business."

"But wasn't she involved with a mystery boyfriend?"

"I heard that, too. It gives me a weird vibe. There's more:

Tim told me that Kat was opening her own place. It would be 'an upscale art and craft store like the Bell, Book & Anvil, but better.'"

I frowned. "Was Kat's murder a crime of passion? Tim was helping her, housing her, advising her about a business, but she was seeing someone else. Could that have made him angry?"

A gust rocked the vehicle. I imagined a tornado sucking us to the sky à la *The Wizard of Oz*, transporting us to a different, freaky existence.

"Tim just told me there's a memorial for Kat at the yacht club. It's next week." Steven put the van in drive and gassed it. "Plan to go. Never know what you could find out."

"Do you have your seatbelt on?" Steven asked.

"Yes, of course."

"Max?"

The dog didn't answer. He was harnessed into the seat behind the driver. "He's good," I said.

We drove to the dentist's office. I spied a familiar red SUV in the drive. Its license plate read, "CHARBRL."

Charbroil, a.k.a. Char Broadway.

I should have known.

Before Steven could unbuckle, the garage door lifted. Char stomped out like a rhino charging a lorry. She wore fuzzy slippers, sweats, and a tiger-print robe that billowed around her. She yelled, "I told you to back in here, Steve—you're gonna demolish my mailbox one day."

Steven powered down the glass. "But your SUV's in the way, Char. I can't see around it."

"Got my stuff?"

I looked into her garage. Boxes were piled to the ceiling. There wasn't room for a car.

She saw me. "Mel, what are you doin' here? What's the news about Kat? They find out who did it?"

"They're working on it."

"When does the mall reopen? I need to sell—big week comin' up."

"You're getting updates about the mall's status via email—"

"Don't read those. Why don't you tell—"

Steven interrupted, "I'll get your packages, Char."

"Wait—did you tell Mel about the store Kat and me were opening?" Char didn't wait for his response. "Top-end stuff. Did you know about it, Mel?"

"I focus on my own business, Char."

"I told that detective you heard about our plan. Maybe you didn't like competition and shoved that door onto Kat."

"That's out of line, Char," Steven said.

She pushed her face inside the vehicle. "Mel, I've always liked you, but I had to tell the cops what I thought. My business partner is dead. I'm upset."

I saw a vein bulging on her temple.

I've had a soft spot for Char because I like Crystal, her daughter. And, from what I've heard, Char has had significant pain in her life. There's been illness, a couple of husbands, and money woes.

But none of that precluded me from defending myself. "I did not kill Kat Gold."

Char said, "I'm still opening a place that's going to compete, even if Kat's gone."

Steven opened the van door, forcing her backward. He pointed toward the house and said things I didn't hear.

She marched into the garage while Steven retrieved purchases from the van.

Two things, Char: First, you don't need any more crap. Your garage is a disaster. You couldn't stash a pair of rubber gloves in there, much less more boxes. Second, be my guest. Open a competing business.

I will never be afraid of you.

We had a couple more stops on Lake Cinnamon.

Delightful ones, thankfully, that tempered the misadventure with Char Broadway and the odd vibe of Tim Gold.

We cruised eastward, and the road dipped toward the water. We entered a grove of pines where the houses were modest. Steven pulled into the drive of a pristine one-story. Not a pine-cone in the yard and front porch flagstones that shined like they were polished.

"You're gonna love these two," he said. "Bring Max."

Before we got to the door, it opened. "Steven, good to see you. And you've brought guests!" an elderly man said. "Who is this handsome canine?"

That was all Max needed to hear; dogs know dog people. Max sniffed the man's hand, then placed his head under the guy's palm. "Shirley, we have visitors!" the man cried. "Bring one of your biscuits."

A woman bounded around a corner. She wore an apron and a huge smile, the gal's blue eyes lighting up. "I just pulled banana bread out of the oven. How about a slice, Steven? Who are your friends?"

"Mr. and Mrs. Weaver, I'd like you to meet Mel and Max, her better half."

Steven dropped off vitamins for the couple and a new foot-rest for Mr. Weaver's wheelchair, which we helped attach.

Then, Mrs. W. sent us on our merry way with a loaf of bread, a bundle of bratwurst, and homemade biscuits for Max.

"They're why I love my job," Steven said. "Their place is my favorite stop on the lake."

There were a few more, with Steven leaving goodies with cheerful homeowners or placing deliveries in designated safe spots. He also entered garages to drop off boxes, tapping a code on a pad or using a hidden key.

I'd never done a ride-along with him before. Like I said, Steven is a hero. He works for an independent delivery business, not the "prime" one.

His employer had been in the area for decades. The company began as a milk-delivery business, and its founders kept it alive by adapting to the market.

I think Steven was his own manager at this point. He plans his route and schedule, answering to himself. He could be promoted, he was said, but preferred to be in the van, delivering packages like a year-round Santa, working among customers who had become friends.

Most of them, anyway.

Could have been a stretch to claim Char Broadway as a buddy.

We stopped at another lay-by. This one was a gravel parking area near the bog, a swampy spot between Lake Cinn and Lily's Pond. Pine boughs hung over us like Spanish moss, and the snow hadn't melted.

I remembered the low spot hardly got daylight, even in the summer.

Steven checked the back of the van for missed deliveries. Finding none, he said, "Time to head over to the pond. I've got a box for Susan Victory. She'll be glad to see you, Mel."

Nope, she wasn't.

Turns out, my dear friend Susan may have gotten herself into awful trouble.

✳

"Mel, have a Bloody Mary with me?" Susan asked.

"No, thanks."

"But you're not driving. Steven, I'll make you an espresso."

Susan Victory made two quart-sized Bloodies. She served Steven an espresso that dilated his pupils to quarters.

We moved to her back porch, Steven carrying the tray.

She sipped her drink, looking at Max. "He's so expressive; I adore him! He's perfect for the Christmas photo shoot we're doing here next week."

Susan inherited her cottage from her parents. I called it "The Little Cottage That Could." Editors of home decor magazines use the home for social media photos. With its water view and vintage-chic vibe, the cottage is a dream location.

A fire crackled in the potbellied stove, and tiny evergreens decorated a table. The cozy spot had a gorgeous view of the pond, the clear water reflecting clouds like a mirror. The peacefulness was a world away from volcanic Lake Cinn.

Susan gestured, almost tipping the tray with drinks. "Did they catch the person who hurt Kat? I hope so."

"Whoa, don't spill, Susan," I said. "Are you okay?"

"Yes, I'm just, hic, excited to see you guys. I've got jewelry to sell. When does the mall reopen?"

Steven asked, "Were you expecting someone, Susan?"

"Like Hank, you mean?"

"Yeah, got a box for him in the van."

"He's not stopping today."

"I'll drop it at his office, then."

Hank Leigel was Susan's significant other, a real estate attorney. Had an office on High Street, about a block from the mall. He and Susan were long-term, like the pilot and me. But they were functional and lived in the same county, not states or countries apart.

"How is Hank?" I asked.

Susan rolled her eyes. "He's busy helping the mayor with that boat race at the yacht club. They're, hic, like kids about it."

"Got your boat name picked out?" Steven asked.

She wobbled her head back and forth. "I am not playing."

The Mayor's Race was part of the holiday festivities. Rubber ducks got dumped in a creek. Betting ensued. The wagered cash flowed to the lake preservation charity fund.

Fun was had by all.

Except Susan, it appeared.

Strange. Her duckie stable historically had performed well. I believe one stand-out prospect captured the winner's trophy in the past. "Susan, will you be selling your jewelry there again this year?"

"I can't afford to miss it. It's a great event. But I wish I didn't have to go."

"Susan, do you know Tim Gold?" Steven asked. "He's a club member."

"I know the family. They were my parents' generation, been on the lake for eons. Most of them are gone—like we will be someday." She sipped. "Mel, you never answered my question. Have they found who killed Kat?"

"Nothing yet, but—"

"So there's a monster loose in Cinnamon?" She gulped the last of her drink. "Kat and I weren't friends. She once backed into my station wagon at the club. It was her fault. Everyone agrees the accident was her fault. I can't believe I had to pay to fix my own car."

"I'm sure Kat felt bad, Susan."

"Kat was a narcissist. My ex was like that. You know what I

say about those people: There are narcissists in the world, and then there's everybody else. Kat was unable to feel remorse."

Steven began, "I think—"

"I don't want to hear it."

Yikes, who replaced my friend Susan with Cruella de Vil?

Susan and I were the same age. She was lovely, with delicate features and olive skin. But half-moon circles hung under her eyes, and her mouth pursed in distress. Susan had always been temperamental, but she was an artist, a creative type. Think I haven't encountered that personality in my career?

I adored her. Susan Victory was one of my first artists in the mall, and we'd been wonderful friends. Lots of shared moments together. A few drinks, too. I'd never seen her like this.

Steven finished his espresso, and then we showed ourselves out. Susan barely acknowledged our departure. She stared at the pond, sucking the ice in her drink.

Later, driving back to Cinnamon, Steven revealed a secret that could have explained her volatile mood. "I've noticed a strange car parked in Susan's driveway. I suspect she knows I've seen it."

"She has people at her place all the time. It probably was one of the magazine folks."

"At night? Staying over?"

Susan's place had two bedrooms—a master and a second smaller one used as her jewelry studio.

A sick feeling crept through my body.

Oh, Susan, I hope things are okay between you and Hank. I hope you didn't hurt Kat Gold.

I pray you didn't do something you'll regret.

We drove back to Cinnamon.

After the revelation about Susan, Steven didn't say much. As I mentioned, he'd been distant lately.

"Thanks for taking me on this trip," I said.

"No problem."

I wasn't sure if he meant it. Revealing intel about his clients wasn't his vibe.

We returned to High Street, where Steven dropped off a package at Hank Leigel's office, leaving it with his assistant. Then we putt-putted down the alley behind my mall.

At the alley's end, I saw the yellow tape. It contrasted with the cheerful vibe of the narrow lane.

Even the alley gets decorated in Cinnamon. Most shops had wreaths and twinkle lights on their back entry doors. And goofy signs for restricted parking marked parking stalls: "Reindeer parking only. All others will be disbarred." (Can you guess whose office? We were just there.)

The sign behind the Tool & Rye read, "Bakery parking only. All others will be toast." The one behind my mall said, "Delivery vans only. Otherwise, expect your package to go missing."

That one was Steven's idea.

An officer still sat in a police cruiser at my dock. Steven stared at the vehicle as we rolled past. "I have deliveries for you, Mel. Want them at your house for now?"

"Yeah, sure."

"Hey, look—it's Wooly Gallagher. He's fixing your gate."

Straight ahead was my backyard and its fence. Wooly stood where the gate had hung, a toolbox at his feet. He wore a green jacket, and his green truck was parked nearby, new boards sticking out its bed. It was like a leprechaun handyman had arrived to solve my problems.

"Drop us off here, please, Steven."

He braked, saying he'd stash the boxes in my garage. Max and I got out. "Wool, thanks, but you don't have to do this."

"I installed this thing once. I can do it again."

I knew it. He'd just confirmed my suspicions about how the portal got there in the first place. My artisans had been the instigators, but a victim had to do the dirty work. Wool just copped to it.

"What's new?" he asked, "Find out anything?"

"You go first."

He reached for a thermos stashed in the toolbox, then poured himself a cup of coffee. Steam floated in the air as he sipped. He eyed the police cruiser before speaking. The vehicle was about fifty yards from where we stood. Its windows up, engine idling. "We filed an open records request with the county sheriff's department. But they haven't responded. It's standard protocol. They have to withhold info at this stage."

"Has your reporter gotten leads? Any anonymous tips from concerned citizens?"

"Nothing we can use."

"Are you searching social media for videos of the area from Wednesday night? Did you check the village cameras? I did. They've been erased—"

"You're good at this, Mel. Want a side gig as an investigative reporter?"

"No, I'm busy keeping myself out of jail. Did you hear about the village cameras? The recordings from Wednesday night are gone."

"Yes, I spoke with Oliver Roberts. Interesting development."

"Has that ever happened before?"

He nodded. "I'm surprised the cameras operate regularly. If it weren't for Oliver Roberts maintaining them, they wouldn't." Wooly sipped again. "As you're aware, Mel, our 'mayor' is an honorary position; he's paid only a stipend. We have a town clerk and a committee of volunteers who run things. Cinnamon is basically a medieval village where nothing changes, and not much happens. Tourists descend on the weekends and one holiday week a year. Otherwise, this place is a land that time forgot."

"That's why we live here."

"Exactly."

He took another sip of coffee. Then, as if we had the same instinct, we swiveled our heads toward a sedan parking next to the police cruiser. Even Max got in on it, standing up and staring at the new arrival.

A man emerged from the car. My dog stepped forward, straining his leash, nearly pulling it from my hand.

He woofed.

Lieutenant Detective Bruce DuWayne walked toward us. He had an intense look on his face.

Oh, no.

DuWayne introduced himself to Wooly. "Sir, I'm Lt. Bruce DuWayne."

"Wooly Gallagher."

He turned to me. "Melanie, is there a place we could chat?"

I glanced around. A few shoppers walked High Street, but they were a football field away. Besides the gal in the police cruiser, the alley and my yard were deserted. "Is here okay?"

"Surely, you would prefer privacy?"

"No, this is fine."

DuWayne studied us, the breeze ruffling his salt-and-pepper hair. He wore a trench coat and galoshes over his wingtips. His gray eyes twinkled even under the cloudy sky. If he hadn't been out to ruin my life, I probably would have liked him.

He took a notepad out of his breast pocket. It appeared new.

That intimidated me because it showed he meant business. Like he'd made an early New Year's resolution to accomplish a goal, to solve a problem. (Which involved yours truly, unfortunately.)

"Melanie, I'm following up on the talk we had two days ago."

"Sure, shoot." I've got to stop saying that. "Go ahead, I mean."

"You claimed to be at home at the time of Ms. Gold's accident."

"I was."

"Will you provide details, please?"

"I closed up the mall at nine o'clock. I worked in my office for a half-hour, then walked home."

"Were you alone? Did you speak with anyone?"

"I called Rand at about eleven."

"Captain Rand Cunningham, the pilot?"

"Yes."

"And he will confirm this conversation?"

"I, ah, left a message on his phone that night. He was flying. Or, just landed, I think."

"Where? I'm a travel enthusiast. A fascinating life, the captain must have."

"Frankfurt, maybe? No, Brussels."

DuWayne jotted notes. "How long have you been dating? Feel free to answer in time or miles."

He smiled, and I looked at Wooly, who hadn't said a word. Probably the wiser choice. I should have declined to talk. I was halfway into the convo with the lieutenant. As mountain climbers say, never jump a crevasse in two bounds. "About seven years," I replied.

"You called the captain from your home or the mall?"

"I was home. I just told you that."

"Did you do anything else? Make another telephone call?"

"I went to bed."

He looked toward my house. "Can you see the mall from your upstairs bedroom? Did you notice activity?"

"No, the pine trees block the view."

"And the next morning—what happened?"

"I got up at seven, had breakfast. Started raking leaves. Then, Inga Honeythorne crashed this gate, and my world changed."

"I've spoken with Ms. Honeythorne. She's a delight."

"Yes, she is."

"I appreciate your candor, Ms. Tower." He returned the notebook to the breast pocket. "You are not under arrest. But, please do not leave the county until the murder of Kat Gold is solved."

Nine —

"Maybe Kat had a stalker," Fern Bubble said. "That person could have followed her to the mall and committed the murder."

"I'm going to commit one if I don't see a waiter."

Fern had rescued me after the convo with Lt. Bruce Du-Wayne. She showed up, then dragged me to a restaurant.

She took me to the Fish Inn, the place where locals go for Friday night fish.

Fern knew the owners and requested a table far from civilization. Thus, we sat at a two-top in a corner, away from the hustle and bustle. The table was hidden from prying eyes, but I feared our waiter had forgotten about us.

"How are you feeling?" Fern asked.

"Hungry. And claustrophobic."

"Nonsense, we're next to a window looking over Lily's Pond. Take a deep breath."

I glanced at the busy side of the room. "I'm not used to encountering so many people."

"You once lived in a major city, Mel."

"I know, but I'd do my work and go home. Sometimes, I wouldn't talk to anyone until my next job or an entire weekend. Same thing I used to do here in Cinnamon until two days ago. Oh, look, the server is coming. What are you having?"

Fern ordered the walleye. I had the cod. Dinners come with a relish tray, coleslaw, potato pancakes, warm German potato salad, and rye bread. It's all homemade. Desserts are, too.

The Fish Inn—fishin', get it?—didn't take reservations; if you're not from the area, don't bother trying to get a table.

Sorry. I'm hungry and stressed.

I bit into a carrot. It was ruffle cut and reminded me of my childhood; the memory hurt. Fern asked, "You took a ride-along with Steven today. What did you learn?"

"That he's a saint on wheels. And he knows everybody's secrets. I mean, he's delivering customers' personal items day and night. He's seen plenty of strange things. If I didn't know better, I'd think Steven was the target. Someone could have been after him, not Kat."

Fern stopped mid-bite. "What did you say?"

"If I didn't know better, I'd suspect Steven was supposed to be under the door."

"But he could have been the target."

"What do you mean?"

"We've all assumed this is about Kat. But maybe she was at the wrong place at the wrong time. It could be about Steven. He delivers to your place every morning."

"I literally set my alarm by him."

"I do, too. He comes to my farm every day, almost. Even the horses know when to expect him."

"Steven stops all over the county. Why hurt him at my place?"

She pointed at me with a radish. "That answer is easy, Mel—to frame you."

The idea seemed so crazy I ordered a brandy old-fashioned sweet. I don't drink those, so it came to our table as a shot of whiskey.

I gulped it like apple juice, and the hooch burned my gullet like liquid flames. I ordered another. Fern was the designated driver tonight, so I could indulge.

"Has Steven seemed weird to you lately?" I asked.

"It's Steven—yes, he's weird."

"More than usual?"

Fern blinked before answering. "Not that I've noticed."

"What about Inga Honeythorne?"

"Do you think she wanted to hurt Steven? And got Kat instead?"

"No, what if the murderer was after Inga? Her schedule at the mall is regular, too."

Fern shook her head. "Steven is the one who sees peoples' private business. He's more likely the target."

The food and my second shot arrived. I ignored my fish and sipped the flames. Fern tasted her walleye, which glistened in a robe of crushed saltines, flour, and garlic. I smelled the bacon-y aroma of the German potato salad, with its onion, vinegar, and dash of sugar first tossed in hot bacon grease, then dressed over the warm potatoes.

Also on our table was a stack of Kimmel rye from the T&R and butter churned from the liquid gold of local cows. Add potato pancakes and coleslaw, and the meal is a feast for royalty.

The restaurant is standing room only for a reason.

"What about the detective?" I asked. "Do you think he suspects that Steven was the target?"

"No idea, but I'll put it in Bruce's ear tomorrow."

"Bruce? Is he your friend now?"

"I'm in public relations. It's my job to be everyone's friend."

"Did you notice that he resembles a thermos? Narrow head, wide shoulders. Tall, thin body. Doesn't bend when he moves."

Fern laughed, nearly choking on her fish when I said that. "Bruce doesn't look like a bottle, Mel."

"It's not bad. I've got a dealer who collects thermoses. She's one of my most popular vendors. Put DuWayne on a shelf, tell him to stand straight and smile, and he'd sell. Lots of ladies would take him home, especially if he wore a plaid shirt."

"You spoke with Bruce this afternoon? He asked you not to leave the county for now?"

"Yes, and your place is on the county line. I shouldn't visit Tulip, but I'm going to. No one tells me I can't give carrots to my favorite horse. Would you like another drink?"

"Eat your fish."

"Look, there's Char Broadway."

Char had walked in, and it was impossible not to notice. The woman has the subtlety of a monster truck. She hung on the arm of a guy whose back was to us.

Char wore an orange, red, and black caftan that billowed around her; she looked like a cold-weather sunrise. Her hair curled around her head, and on her feet were heels with little wings. I recognized the brand, one of my favorites, actually.

"She's with Tim Gold," Fern said.

"No way."

"Yes, look."

Sure enough. The guy turned around. Even though we were in the bleacher seats, I could see it was the smiley homeowner from earlier today. His shirt collar was "popped," or up, and he wore a sweater over his shoulders, very Camelot.

He and Char were among a group of people. A few hugged him, looking concerned. Gold grinned, appearing to acknowledge their compassion.

I asked, "Fern, I have a silly idea. Do people kill for money these days? Do you think Tim had a life insurance policy on Kat?"

She watched him. "Good question."

The problem with brainstorming a murder is that it frightens waiters.

Fern and I debated killer scenarios: A stalker lurked in Cinnamon. A delivery customer was after Steven and purposely ruining my life and business. Mistress Greed seduced Tim Gold into doing something awful to his ex-wife.

Further, after observing Char and Tim Gold, Fern speculated that Ms. Broadway could have been the perpetrator. "If she and Kat were business partners, they could have fallen out. As a result, Char did something terrible."

My head spun during the conversation. The ideas were wild.

When our server approached, Fern and I didn't talk murder. We clammed up and looked guilty, like we were plotting a bank heist.

He probably thought he was serving Thelma and Louise.

After the candle on our table flicked wildly, and an unusual November thunderstorm rolled in, the poor guy threw the tab on the table and fled.

A lightning bolt crashed to the ground, lighting up the room. "That was close!" Fern cried. "Let's talk about something else; it's giving me the creeps. We both have to go home to empty houses."

"Not for you, Fern. After this, you may have a tall hot water bottle named Bruce warming that farmstead of yours."

"Mel, you've had too much whiskey."

"I know, and I shouldn't joke about a guy trying to put me in jail." I gulped water. "Seriously, though, speaking of death, I'm updating my will. Let's do it right now, Fern. Write what I say in that notebook of yours, and I'll sign it."

"Mel—"

"My assets go to the Tulip and Max animal rescue foundation. My vintage clothing collection gets split between you and Cousin Lou; she'll want anything with a sequin. Not much of that, so expect to get the bulk of it. Wooly gets custody of my modeling pictures. He has them already, anyway."

Fern rolled her eyes, but what I said was true. My estate was going to animal rescue groups. And Wooly did have images of my career in a file at the newspaper office.

My parents passed when I was eighteen, pre-internet. There was no one else to compile my pictures except for Lou, who'd been busy with her own life. Wooly had taken it upon himself to be my personal librarian over the years. It was where the images had been pulled for the blow-ups for my birthday party, I was sure.

Fern said, "Okay, but before you pass on, you must meet that guy I mentioned."

"What do you mean? I met Max. I love him."

"Max is great, but he's not the guy. He's a human being."

"No, you meant Max, Fern."

She gave up.

Fern knew better than to argue with a fool who had a few; she was in public relations. Knowing when to quit and fight the battle another day was part of the job.

We split the bill, leaving a huge tip for the waiter who'd

probably jumped in a rowboat to escape and was halfway across Lake Michigan.

On the way home, we chased the thunderstorm. It was eerie watching the sky light up with white daggers. I felt like I was watching the future, and it wasn't good.

I said a silent prayer, asking the Man Above for protection.

Fern dropped me off. "Take an aspirin before going to bed. Drink water."

"Text me when you arrive at the farm, please."

I dashed inside, and Max greeted me. I urged him to step out for his evening constitutional, but the dog refused, heading upstairs instead.

I was tucked under the covers, and Max was snoring when my phone pinged. Fern wrote: "Home safe. I'll call you tomorrow."

I closed my eyes. But to quote Dickens, I slept little and thought much. For the first time since moving in five years prior, I tensed at hearing the nocturnal creaks of my old house.

I thought I heard footsteps in the hall.

I'm sure it was a dream. Most likely from the booze.

That's what I get for talking about murder and death before going to bed.

Ten —

I awoke on Saturday morning feeling better than I deserved.

I got up, dressed, and took Max for a walk.

Friday night's storm brought in mild air; it felt like spring. The forecast called for sun, no wind, and pleasant weather.

That's where the good news ended.

For the weekend, two events were on the docket. Tonight was the Cheese Ball, a gala unlike any other, a cotillion dedicated to the art of fermenting milk.

The high school gym was reborn into a cheddar wonderland. A king, queen, and court were named, and the royals presided over the parties to follow, beginning with the holiday parade on Sunday. Floats glided down High Street in a parade of Christmas scenes, including the Bell, Book & Anvil's entry.

I ate breakfast over the kitchen sink, observing my new gate at the back of the yard. Wooly found a rotted post, he said.

My phone beeped. "Wool, hello. I was thinking about you."

"How's the gate?"

"Great, except for the hinges. Should be a solid fence."

"We're gonna pull you out of your shell, you know."

"Just what I want. Great."

"A source says your place will be released soon. Either later today or tomorrow."

I squinted to see the squad car that idled at the dock. "But how will the police surveil me if they're not sitting behind my building?"

"Maybe they don't need to keep an eye on you anymore. Or, they'll tail you wherever you go."

"Perhaps an arrest is imminent."

"I'll let you know if I hear anything."

We hung up. I meant to ask him something, but another call came in. My building maintenance guy was on the line. "Hi, Kevin. I was going to phone you."

"Yah, I'm at the Tool & Rye havin' coffee. Heard your place is reopening. Want me to come by with my repair truck?"

"That would be great."

"See ya in five."

Kevin Sunny stood in my kitchen holding a Tool & Rye mug. He wore a Carhartt jacket with "Sunny Days Restorations" inscribed on it.

His firm rescued my building from ruin five years ago. They maintain it, too. Kevin's crew were artists—geniuses with lumber, nails, tile, grout, and HVAC.

"Talked to your insurance company yet?" he asked. "Betcha the site cleanup is coming out of your pocket, Mel."

"Yes, and yes."

"What do you want me to do?"

"Clean the storage area, then repaint. I don't want people

imagining what happened to Kat, thinking that's what she was about; it's unfair to her."

"I can get it done quick. Like as soon as you get permission to go back in."

"Your painter knows the color scheme, so I trust whatever he picks. And add some shelves, too. Change it a bit."

"No problem-o. My guys can build shelves where there ain't even a wall."

He clomped out, and my phone rang. "Mel, what are ya wearin' to the ball tonight? I got a cowgirl dress without a body— the thing needs yours."

"Lou, you're in charge of the volunteers for the evening, right?"

"Yep, like always."

"Steven is a waiter tonight, correct?"

"Yep."

"Do you have an extra uniform?"

"Yeah, but it's just a white jacket and slacks. No glitz."

"I'll be a volunteer server, too."

"But you're my show pony—"

"I want to help."

"Well, if you wanna be behind the scenes, go ahead. Hey, I hear your place is gonna reopen."

"Were you at the Tool & Rye this morning?"

"Nope. I delivered cheese danishes to the newspaper office. Got to chattin' with the receptionist."

"Any change in the pool for Kat's killer?"

"Yeah, Char Broadway has pulled ahead; she's in the 'Win' spot. Might take the prize."

"Being charged with murder is not a prize, Lou. Why do people suspect her?"

"Don't know yet, but I'll snoop around and find out."

"Let me know, okay?"

"You betcha. I'll drop off the uniform this mornin'. Are you sure you don't want the dress—"

"I'm sure, Lou."

"See ya soon."

"Thanks."

Steven's last name is Delavan. Thus, his distinctive yellow delivery truck is nicknamed the "Dela-van," with emphasis on the "van."

While driving to Inga Honeythorne's place on Saturday morning, I spied the vehicle. It idled next to a car at the lay-by between Lake Cinn and Lily's Pond.

Shocked was this murder suspect (me, falsely accused) to see Crystal Broadway's red BMW near Steven's truck. I pressed the Saab's accelerator, zipping away, winding down the road that circled the pond.

Why would Steven be meeting with Crystal?

I liked the young woman but steered clear of her due to her mom. Char dominated conversations when the two of them were together. Steven always had done the same—in the past, at least.

I turned onto a road leading into the Kettle Moraine Forest, away from the water. The woods gave a witchy aura, especially this time of year. Skeleton trees soared overhead, their leaves looking like dried snakeskin.

The piles obscured the road's edge, making it seem even more narrow. The summer birds, the woodpeckers, the warblers, and the finches were gone. I saw vulture-sized crows perched on branches, the trees' limbs hanging over the roadway, looking like twisted arms.

Inga's stone cottage was at the end of a long driveway. She and her late husband built the place years ago. Many times she'd said, "We put it up with our bare hands, rock by rock. Couldn't do my calligraphy for a year—fingers were too cramped."

Max and I were bringing Inga a care package. The week had been crazy. Can you imagine being the person to find a dead woman pinned under a door? What a shock that must have been!

In a basket, I'd packed local honey, herbal tea, and a bag of dog treats for her Pomeranian, Mocha—a dog that rivals Max in charm and good looks.

When I arrived, Inga wrapped me in a hug like I was a pilgrim who'd traveled the ocean. "How are you, Mel?"

"I should be asking you that question, Inga."

"I'm fine; are you okay?"

"Y-yes."

I don't cry much, only in front of certain people.

Inga was one of them.

Inga made tea for us. I sipped and tasted mint. Honey, too.

We were in a glassed-in porch that overlooked her backyard. The grassy space was cleared of trees, so the afternoon sun blazed over the spot. It was like Inga's home and yard was a terrarium in the forest.

"Twenty minutes of sunshine and a cup of herb tea makes us all feel better," Inga declared.

I dabbed my cheeks. "You've always cheered me up."

"Never had much cheering to do. You've taken care of yourself for a long time. I'm so proud of you, Melanie."

"I'm going to cry again."

"Let it out. You were the only young lady in high school who didn't weep at *Cats* when we took a bus trip to see it in Chicago."

"I'm too practical to understand musicals."

"I'll make more tea."

She returned to the kitchen, and I heard water splashing into a kettle. Inga was Cinnamon's retired high school librarian. She was responsible for my career, actually. No, she would say I was responsible for my career. That was Inga—redirecting a woman to recognize her own success.

When I was in high school, she'd handed me a fashion magazine, pointed to an advertisement, and said, "You could do this, Melanie."

Then, when I was a senior, and my parents were killed in a car crash, Mrs. Honeythorne became adamant: "You need to do it. I'll make phone calls for you."

After a month, she'd found an agency. "We need to take what they call digital snapshots."

I'd worn jeans and a black T-shirt. She took Polaroid photos, then directed me to the post office to mail them. (It was pre-internet, remember.) The agency called Inga back in a week. "Send her out here," the New Faces director said.

In the meantime, I'd buried my parents. I was numb. They'd left me enough money for a hot meal and a few months' rent somewhere. That was it.

Inga bought my bus ticket as a going-away present. "Mel, phone your agency when you arrive in New York. Then, call me. I want to know you're safe."

The rest, as they say, is history. I'd made it work, saving almost every penny I earned. Retired when I was too old to make a living in such an expensive place.

Something was missing in my life, though, and I didn't know how to fix it.

Inga returned to the sunroom with tea and cookies. Inga's shortbreads were legendary. If she hadn't been a calligrapher, she could have established a cookie empire.

Inga changes the sugar color according to the season: pink for Easter, orange for fall, red for Christmas. Everyone swoons for her shortbreads, as they do the bounty from her fruit trees and garden during the summer. Sour cherries, pears, and apples, all harvested by Inga.

She settled into a chaise across from me. "That detective was here yesterday. He asked if I killed Kat Gold."

"I know you didn't."

"Of course not! I'd kill her with kindness, nothing else. I would never hurt another human being in a million years!"

Max and Mocha raced around Inga's backyard. The two dogs were different in size but similar in abilities. It was like watching a black race car chased by a gold wasp.

"I adopted Mocha through Fern Bubble," Inga said. "She knows when an animal is perfect for a person; she's magical in that sense."

We strolled a path where flagstones met the forest. Inga pointed out her favorite plants. "All of these hostas came from one I planted thirty years ago. I kept splitting them; now they line the whole yard. They're dormant for the winter. But during the summer, they're delightful."

"Yes, they are, Inga."

"That detective and I took this stroll, too. I don't know if he believed me, to be honest."

"What did you tell him?"

"That I did not do it, of course."

"Inga, I don't want to bring up a terrible memory, but I'd like to know what you saw."

We walked several steps before she responded. "Do you remember the movie *The Wizard of Oz*? When the witch's shoes were under that house? Finding Kat was like that. Wednesday morning, I opened up the mall, like always. I unlocked the storage area and walked toward the big garage doors...."

She grabbed my wrist; I was amazed at the strength of her hands. "Mel, I was shocked to see a pair of red boots sticking out from under that gigantic door!"

I couldn't imagine it. How horrible.

Inga continued, "I saw a hand with polished nails. I saw blood, then started ... crying." She gasped. "I ran back into the mall—Steven showed up—he c-called the authorities."

I let her catch her breath, then asked, "The heavy door was secured to the wall with safety straps. Someone had to loosen them. Did you notice that or see anything out of place?"

"I ran in the opposite direction. Everything was a blur."

"I understand, Inga."

"Did you know the police suspect the person who finds the body? I wasn't aware until I spoke with Hank Leigel. I called him even though he's a real estate attorney." She shook her gray curls. "He said I didn't have to speak to the police. But that's not helpful. They need to know what happened."

The dogs stopped chasing and flopped down in the middle of the yard, panting and looking exhausted.

I felt the same.

I did not ask Inga about the set-to with Kat a few days before the accident—the time they'd loudly argued. I feared someone else might have. If anyone—Char Broadway—knew about the hostile conversation, Lt. Bruce DuWayne did, too.

It would look like Inga was withholding information.

I felt someone's gaze. I was being driven to the Cheese Ball by Oliver Roberts. He stared at me in the rearview mirror. "You appear deep in thought, Melanie. What's on your mind?"

"Nothing, as usual, Oliver."

"Do not sell your intellect short. But if an idea troubles you, remember Hamlet's advice: There is nothing good or bad, just thinking makes it so."

"Hamlet was nuts."

He laughed. "Aren't we all to a degree?"

Oliver had picked me up in the library's van, a vintage ice cream truck retrofitted as a mobile book shop. The vehicle was recommissioned as an Uber during the holiday week for those working at events.

"Melanie, when I heard you were volunteering, I jumped at the chance to escort you. I hope you don't mind riding in the 'Cheese Whiz.'" He patted the bus's dash. "That is my nickname for our chariot on this night devoted to dairy. The van and I will whiz passengers to their destinations."

He was driving the long way to the high school, I noticed.

After touring High Street, he veered in the opposite direction of the school, steering up a hill that led to a row of historic homes at its top. "The view from up here is astounding. It reminds me of Galena, Illinois. Have you ever been there, Melanie?"

"No."

Not true. My high school ski club used to bus it to Chestnut Mountain, Galena's ski hill. But I didn't want to discuss those visits with Oliver. The guy made me shut down. But most people do that, so perhaps it wasn't his fault.

I looked out the window. "The view is stunning, Oliver."

"Sunset is the best time of day, is it not?"

"I prefer sunrise."

"Look at the lights of the village. It looks like a fairyland. There's your mall, Melanie, and home and backyard. There's your fence and gate, too."

I looked down at my place. It looked vulnerable, like a dollhouse. With the leaves gone from the trees, I saw more of my house than I thought possible. The pines shielded part of the yard, but much of my home was open to prying eyes.

I wondered if the police had been up here, watching me. "Let's go, Oliver. I don't want to be late."

Cheese Ball volunteers, the "curds and whey," as Cousin Lou calls us, were instructed to enter at the rear of the building. "Don't bother with the main entrance," she'd told me. "It's a rodeo. Takes forever to get inside."

Oliver drove past the cars idling in the valet line. Cinnamon rolled out the red carpet for the Cheese Ball and added cow-costumed greeters. Cheddar-headed carolers strolled about. It had the vibe of a movie premiere.

I glimpsed the school lobby, which had been transformed into a cheese-themed Christmas wonderland. I spied a sleigh and foam cheese workshop outlined in twinkle lights.

We cruised to the back. Oliver parked the bus, then escorted me to the service doors leading to the kitchen.

"This isn't necessary," I protested. "You must have other people to pick up."

"I insist, Melanie. A gentleman never stops being gentle."

He opened the door, and I stepped into the hallway, startled to see a tall, thermos-shaped shadow inside.

"Good evening, Ms. Tower. You seem surprised. I had to speak with someone—"

Oliver said, "Lieutenant, this is a public event. Surely, there's a better place to question individuals."

DuWayne cleared his throat. "Ms. Tower, I will release your building tomorrow. I'll have the police tape removed in the morning."

"Good to know, detective. Thanks."

"Enjoy the ball."

He brushed past us, slipping out the doors into the night.

Oliver observed him, then said, "Melanie, if that man attempts to disrupt your life, please call me. As I said, I believe Kat Gold's demise was at her own hand. I'm willing to prove that outcome." He took my elbow, guiding me toward the light of the kitchen. "Further, if you need assistance reopening your facility, reach out. Neither snow, rain, nor demanding library patrons shall keep me from my appointed round of protecting you."

"Thank you, Oliver," I said.

Eleven —

I stood in the kitchen, staring at my reflection in a stainless-steel refrigerator. A foam cheese bowtie wasn't the gear of an undercover agent.

Steven's well-being was on my mind. If someone was out to get my friend because he knew a code or delivered a suspect parcel, I'd protect him.

Cousin Lou had a different motivation. "Sequins are better, Mel, especially for what's gonna happen tonight, but you clean up, okay."

"What's going to—"

"There's Steve-O. C'mon, I gotta give instructions."

She pulled me toward Steven, who'd entered the kitchen wearing similar garb: white jacket, black slacks, foam cheese bowtie.

Lou studied his face. "Stevie, how's the other guy? Left him standin', I hope."

He rubbed his eyes. "I didn't get much sleep this week."

"Bar fight is a better story."

I said, "Lou, no one is going to believe Steven was in a bar fight."

"Good point. Everybody likes him too much."

The place bustled with volunteers dressed in yellow T-shirts that said, "Havin' a Ball." Lou was in charge. She wore jeans, a gold blouse, a scarf with bells, and a sequined name tag that read, "Head Cheese."

She gave orders: "Stevie, you and Mel are my offensive line. Need ya in the lobby. It's the toughest room. People are hungry as hibernatin' bears, but we don't release 'em to the buffet for an hour. They'll attack the hors d'oeuvres. Watch out."

"Got it," he said.

She looked at our shoes. "Ya got sturdy shoes on, cool. That's gonna be good for later."

"What's going on later?" I asked.

She ignored me. "You guys are serving cheese bites, cheese wontons, and mini cheese pizzas. Come back to the kitchen to reload. Watch out for plate hogs, especially the lake crowd. They're always a hungry bunch." She extended her arms. "Huddle up. On three."

Steven and I put our hands on hers.

"One, two, three, cheddar!" Lou cried.

Lou wasn't kidding about hungry guests. I had to juke with the appetizer tray and quickstep to the kitchen for more.

I was speeding through the empty cafeteria when I heard my name. "Mel, can I talk to you?"

I turned to see Crystal Broadway. "Sure, but I'm busy—" Was she crying? "What is it, Crystal?"

"I did something dumb."

She grabbed my sleeve, towing me to a corner. She wore an

empire-waisted dress that reminded me of the Gunne Sax look from high school. Her hair was naturally curly, falling down her back in waves. Once again, I noticed how different her style was from her mother's.

"Crystal, are you hurt? Are you okay?"

She dabbed an eye. "I need your help."

"What is it?"

"I'm so upset, and I'm so sorry."

"What is it, Crystal?"

Steven came striding through the room, and I turned around to see if he noticed us. Within those seconds, Crystal vanished, fading out a side door.

I think, at least. I'm not positive she used the door; I didn't hear it open or close. She may have walked right through it like a spirit.

Steven kept walking toward the kitchen. The cafeteria was dark, and we were off to the side. My choices were to follow him to the kitchen or exit through the door to find Crystal.

I picked the door.

Definitely not a smart choice.

I found myself alone in a school hallway. It was dark as a dungeon, and my footsteps echoed. My only weapon for self-defense was a serving tray with a cow glued to it.

I turned and pressed on the door I'd just used.

Locked, of course. What a dope. Crystal had disappeared. If she'd intended to trap me, I'd fallen for the ruse.

I scanned the tunnel in both directions. Couldn't see anything. The school had been remodeled since I'd attended. I had no clue which way led back to civilization. In my head, I wrote a headline for Wooly's paper: "Business Owner's Demise Due to Her Own Stupidity."

A killer lurked in Cinnamon. How had I forgotten that?

Somebody was not who they seemed. I recalled a quote from a high school English essay: "One can smile and smile and still be a villain."

A door opened, then clanged shut. Footsteps tapped the tile floor. I pressed into the wall behind me, feeling the plastic tops of pushpins in my back.

Bulletin board. The steps came closer. Pins could be used as weapons. Mighty small, though.

"Melanie? My dear, is that you?"

"Oliver?"

"Why are you hiding in a hallway? Your light should never be under a bushel—"

"Which way back?"

I spied white choppers; Oliver's teeth were beacons. "Where do you desire to go?"

"Steven. Wherever he is."

"At once, m'lady. Take my arm."

I reached for his elbow.

Nope.

I touched a cold metal bar instead.

I'd grabbed a serving cart, turned out. Oliver had been pushing it down the hall. Its wheels were recently greased, he'd claimed. The thing was silent as an assassin.

We hooked right, then left. I suspected Oliver took me the long way, like he did in the library van.

No matter. He presented me like an hors d'oeuvres into

the lobby, actually offering to put me on the cart and push me through the doors like a block of white cheddar.

I declined.

He winked. "Perhaps next time, Melanie. Enjoy the party."

The lobby was a cheesy, Christmasy wonderland. Christmas decor and Mrs. Claus (a.k.a. Fern Bubble) were in a booth selling raffle tickets, the funds providing mental health services for agriculture workers. I watched her speak energetically with a buyer. She'd scored a big sale, it seemed.

I scanned the room. Where was Steven?

My instinct told me to protect him. I didn't want him standing next to heavy vintage doors. Or anything else that could be a booby trap.

I stood next to a life-sized, cheddar orange nutcracker. A woman stepped around it, then charged toward me. "Mel Tower, did you make Crystal cry?"

"No, Char Broadway, did you?"

Her jaw dropped. I wanted to stick a big ol' chestnut in there to see if she could compete with the nutcracker but stopped myself. Char was not used to abruptness from yours truly.

Usually, I'm diplomatic when conversing with Mother Broadway. Words are red flags to her. The wrong combination triggers her anger. I did not have patience for Char's shenanigans. She'd threatened my business twenty-four hours ago—she deserved a red flag.

She wore a one-shouldered animal-print smock and a chunky white necklace. Her hair towered in a beehive. She looked like Wilma Flintstone, the Cheese Ball version.

Char sneered. "Crystal is sobbing, and it's your fault. You spoke to her last. What'd you say?"

Cousin Lou hustled over, thank goodness. Char and I stood chest-to-beehive, and the ball had the potential of turning into a wrestling match.

Lou shoved her serving tray between us. "Hey, Calamity Char, have a cheese bite. Settle down. You're lookin' like you wanna kill someone."

I agreed.

Lou's "boss mare" intimidation worked. She's the only person who forces Ms. Broadway into submission by glaring and squaring her shoulders.

Lou said, "We're openin' up the gym, Char. Food, drinks, and dancing. Giddyup on in there."

On cue, the doors opened, and the happy tinkles of a band playing "Jingle Bells" floated toward us. I saw the gym had transformed into a wonderland of holiday magic. Christmas trees glistened with ornaments, and oversized, sparkling snowflakes dangled from the ceiling. The space resembled the set of a romance movie.

Enamored, Char trotted off like a teenager pursuing a heart-throb.

I looked at Lou. "Where's Steven?"

She jerked her head toward the auditorium. "Practicing his polka steps, like you should be doin'. Still remember how? One, two, three. One, two—"

"Is he okay?"

She nodded. "As okay as Steven can be, I guess. Can you dance in those shoes?"

"Why?"

"Cuz."

"Lou—"

"Gimme that serving tray, Mel. Get yourself to the gym. Just for tonight, have a good time."

✳

What was Lou saying? I have a good time at public events. In my way, that is. I wear dark clothes and stand in a corner, then disappear after a polite length of time.

It worked in New York.

I funneled into the gym with the partiers. I recalled how my first modeling agency wanted me to schmooze with clients at parties. I knew few fashion so-FIS-tee-cats would relish small talk with a shy Midwesterner. I attended the soirees for a time, but then I departed that agency because its director and I rarely saw eye to eye.

(Sorry, model humor. The director was short; I was a skyscraper. Fashion jokes are rare, folks. One must take them where one can get them.)

Back to the Cheese Ball. Patrons frolicked toward the buffet like sheep in a meadow. I saw a band on the stage and holiday-decorated tables. There's nothing like a winter cotillion to energize a small town.

The mayor and his wife appeared thrilled with the turnout. He greeted the multitudes, shaking hands. His wife mingled with Susan Victory and artists from my mall. The group held champagne glasses in the air and appeared to be enjoying a toast.

Near the sweets buffet, Cozette Gallagher stood next to Wooly, her husband. The dessert tables were about a football field long and featured cookies, a chocolate fountain, and a towering cake with king and queen foam cheese figures. Char Broadway held a drink and chatted with Oliver Roberts.

I felt a hand on my elbow. "Would you care to dance?"

"Steven, where the heck have you been?"

"Where have you been, Melanie? Last I saw, you were in the kitchen. Then you disappeared."

"Don't play games."

"Can we? Just for tonight?"

I looked at Steven's face. In his eyes, just for a second, I saw a glimpse of my old friend, the guy who used to be carefree and enjoyed a good laugh.

"Sure," I said, playing along. "You lead."

The shocked look on my face appeared on the newspaper's website Sunday morning. The photographer captured my wide-eyed expression while I was standing on stage.

Horrible timing.

I'm getting ahead of events. The first half of the Cheese Ball, when attendees were invited into the auditorium, and the band struck up its first tune, was superior to the second. Similar to a sporting event where the home team scores in the initial minutes but then blows its lead.

Upon review of the evening, I should have withdrawn to the safety of my home and its fenced backyard after an exhilarating Chicken Dance. It was Oscar Wilde, I believe, who said, "Leave audiences wanting more." Also, "No good deed goes unpunished."

To clarify, Mr. Wilde uttered only the quote about punishment, which is how I felt: tired, punished, and still pondering who committed the dastardly deed of murdering Kat Gold.

Steven and I had toured the gym to admire the splendid decor. The volunteers had outdone themselves. We also frivoled for an hour around the dance floor like professionals to the "Y.M.C.A.," the "Hokey Pokey," and the "Cha-Cha Slide."

Steven even led Susan Victory and my mall artists in a high-energy "Twist and Shout."

It was delightful to see Susan and Steven get on as friends again. She pranced like a show horse, expertly balancing her champagne flute. Perhaps I'd imagined the tension between Susan and Steven during the Friday visit to her cottage.

Susan's better half, Hank Leigel, wasn't on her arm. But pilot Rand wasn't on mine, either. There was zero reason to hold Susan's singleton status against her.

Steven appeared transformed by the magical environment, the lively music, and the incredible food. I saw the spring return to his step, the gleam to his eye. He became jolly Steven again—a carefree elf who every day steered a chariot of cheer around the Wisconsin countryside.

It was after indulging in steaming plates of prime rib, when the polka band took over, that the evening veered off course. I'd gulped the last of my chocolate peppermint cupcake when I heard my name. Rather, our names. The band leader paged Steven and me to the stage.

The spotlight is not my cup of beer. But I went along with the gag because I was a self-appointed shadow for my friend. Determined was this amateur sleuth to keep Steven from harm during the evening.

He took my hand, and we weaved through the crowd toward the podium.

Remember what I mentioned about good deeds?

Nope, they do not go unpunished.

Uneasy rests the head that wears the crown. Steven and I stood among court royalty. I was crowned Princess Mild Brick; he was Prince Mild Brick.

Cousin Lou clapped maniacally when we accepted our regalia—a tiara for me, a sash for Steven. She had a hand in the game, clearly. Palace intrigue and behind-the-scenes machinations are her thing.

Steven accepted his title with grace. "Thank you, selection committee, and those who voted for us," he said into the band leader's mic. "Mel and I will serve our constituents with utmost honor—and on-time deliveries. I promise."

He curtsied, and the crowd cheered. Our royal peers included the Colbys, the Buttermilk Blues, and the Limburgers. Named as King and Queen Cheddar were elderly cheesemongers who'd been in the business for half a century.

The accordion-wearing maestro declared, "Folks, this is your court for Cinnamon's holiday extravaganza week. Tomorrow, they'll lead the parade. After that, they'll be at celebrations at the bowling alley, the yacht club, and the library. Aren't they grand? Give 'em a hand!"

I scanned the crowd, sidling behind Steven to search faces. I wanted to mentally record who was in attendance.

Remember, one can observe a lot by watching.

I pondered the benefit of being coronated: attending galas for seven days wasn't the worst way to search for suspects and clues. My gaze settled on Char Broadway and the people seated at her table. Crystal was absent, but I saw Tim Gold. Tan, brilliant smile, tousled locks. Next to him was a woman. Black hair, bowl cut. Round face. Red lipstick that I could see from the stage.

I gasped. I knew the woman! She was familiar to me—not in a good way.

I stared at Eden Hoff, model agency director, Gotham City. I felt myself frowning, a crease forming between my eyes.

Ironic.

The Eden Hoff I knew would order me to cease: "Mel, models never invite premature wrinkles. And please don't show emotion. The client doesn't need to know that you think."

Harsh, but those were the dictates of my era.

I became a model in the Dark Ages, before social media. A selfie didn't exist. I wouldn't dare promote myself with a photo not approved by my agency. Further, B-list models like me were seen but never heard. The last I knew, Eden had packed her passive-aggressive quips in her designer briefcase and retired.

She was from Chicago, I recalled.

What was she doing at the Cheese Ball?

The band leader tapped his music stand. I could be mistaken, but I think the band launched into the Shock-Faced Polka.

The photog snapped a picture for the paper.

Good thing Steven grabbed me.

I felt like I was going to faint.

Twelve —

ousin Lou phoned Sunday morning. "Picture isn't so bad. Ya look like ya got stuck with a cattle prod, Mel," she said. "But have ya seen social media? There's worse."

I heard paws clattering on a floor. She said, "Hold on, gotta let the dogs out." A door squeaked, then, "You were sayin' somethin' about Steven last night. What's going on?"

"Not sure."

"I'm not the sharpest spur in the tack room, Mel. Ya gotta say more than that."

"I don't want gossip about Steven on the Tool & Rye party line." I stepped into my living room "Lou, what did you learn at the ball? Anything I can use about Kat Gold's death?"

"Hold on, gotta let the dogs in." Door squeak, paws. Then, "Char Broadway is hiring Tim Gold's marketing agency to open her craft business. They wanna kick your—"

"Is Tim still hosting a memorial for Kat at the yacht club?"

"Yeah, that's weird, but the lake crowd floats on the wave of their own pontoon, I guess."

"When is the service?"

"I'll find out. Want me to volunteer as a bartender? Members love it when I show up at the club. I know how to mix a drink."

Not a bad idea.

But I had to be cautious with Lou. She proposes lots of ideas, most of them horrific. This one sounded legit. "Sure, let me know the date as soon as you can."

"I heard a ghost from your modelin' past showed up last night, that Eden Hoff woman. She sure isn't built like you, a racehorse. She's more like a bumblebee."

"Why was she with Char and Tim? What do you know?"

"I know she ate seconds of my prime rib but turned her nose up at Inga Honeythorne's shortbreads. Gal's got no taste."

I set my mug of tea on a side table. The view out the French doors toward the backyard was nil, still dark. But the fireplace blazed, and Max was curled in front of it.

I loved my home, my cocoon, but sensed it was threatened. I didn't like it.

"Mel, you still there? I gotta tell ya about the parade."

"Shoot."

"You, Steven, and the other royals will be leadin' the procession on the Big Cheese float. How does it feel to be a grand pooh-bah?"

"I thought the mayor was the grand pooh-bah."

"Yah, he is. You're a minor one. But you're the only one solvin' a murder. That makes you an undercover pooh-bah."

"What happens after the parade?"

"The royals have to be at VIP Bowlin' at five o'clock. Got cool games that'll knock everybody's rental shoes right off their feet."

"I don't have bowling shoes."

"Got it covered. I'm bringin' 'em for the court. Yours have sequins."

Super. She added that she'd drive the mall's float in the parade. "Gonna pull it with the dually. Got a couple of your artists throwin' candy. Don't worry. Everything's good."

We hung up. I suspected my cousin planned to hijack my float before I'd been crowned, as though she knew it was coming.

I looked outside. The sun peeked over the horizon, sending slivers of pink light through the yard.

Yes, Lou may have clues about the future.

But I sure didn't.

An undercover pooh-bah.

Despite my tense mood, the phrase made me smile.

Max and I sloshed across the backyard to the mall. The sun warmed the ground, melting the snow that was left. Temps were supposed to be near fifty degrees later, wonderfully warm for a holiday parade.

Kevin Sunny, contractor extraordinaire, met us at the loading dock. The police tape had been removed. Earlier, I'd received a message from Lt. DuWayne saying I could reenter my building.

"Hiya, Max," Kevin said. "I already looked inside, Mel. I've got ideas about adding shelves and reconfiguring the storage area."

I stared at the metal door leading into the space. I felt goosebumps at the thought of seeing where Kat met her demise. It was a relief to have Kevin and Max with me.

"Are you okay?" Kevin asked.

"Yeah."

"You sure?"

"What does it look like in there?"

He reached down to ruffle Max's fur. "I've been on a lot of these scenes. Accident cleanups, deaths. It's never easy. But it's not bad."

"I'm afraid my mall will never be the same; I love this place."

"It'll be okay. Contractor's promise."

I looked at him. "And then add twenty percent?"

He grinned. "That's about the usual amount."

"After you, Kevin."

I felt Kat's energy in the storage space.

There were no physical signs of her presence. The place looked the same as before the accident, minus the vintage door. Gray concrete floors, stone walls. Two giant garage doors opening to the dock. Vertical shelves to store large pieces that wouldn't fit into artists' booths.

Seasonal decorations for the building were in plastic tubs on high shelves.

I'd always been focused on the business, so I'd been lackadaisical about what was stored in the big room. Who overthinks a drafty mini warehouse?

The killer door had been impounded for evidence, according to Lt. DuWayne. But the place where the accident happened—Kevin guessed about the spot—appeared clean.

"The authorities did a nice job for you, Mel," he said softly. "Be grateful for that."

"It's awful what happened to Kat. I hate that her life ended here. It shouldn't have happened." Max clung to my side. I was certain the dog sensed the tension in the chilly space. "What can we do, Kevin?"

"I'll improve it, Mel. No one will be reminded of the accident."

"But I don't want to erase her. That doesn't seem right."

He hugged me. A surprise; we weren't that close. "Let me handle it. My guys and I will make this place new. No, better than new."

"I appreciate that, Kevin."

"You find out what happened to Kat and catch whoever did it."

Max and I entered the mall. It felt eerie in the space. Had the killer gotten inside? Would I find a clue?

Impossible to tell.

My place was an old blacksmith shop. One hundred years old, three floors high. Ten thousand square feet of history constructed with local granite and timber. Seventy vendors in booths selling candles, original art, jewelry, refurbished furniture, hand-painted signs, and vintage clothing. Also, books, felt animals, and hand-stitched purses.

A few of my artists were employed by Sunny Restoration, Kevin's company. A plumber created shelves from pipes and salvaged barn boards. An electrician made one-of-a-kind light fixtures from bottles.

Both fellows sold their wares like crazy.

I stepped into the first-floor corridor, a space with booths along each side. In all, it was too much inventory to mention.

How would I know if a ne'er-do-well skulked around and moved a paperweight? Or dropped a glove?

How does law enforcement dust for fingerprints in a place like this?

My office and a workroom were on my left, near the front entrance on High Street.

I recalled the stealth visit to the fire escape on Thursday night, two days ago. Would the window still be locked?

Time to check.

Max and I crossed the plank floor, his nails clicking the

wood. We ascended the stairs, stopping on the landing. I looked through the glass, seeing the small park and statue of John Muir.

Empty lawn chairs lined the street. Locals placed them in the early morning to hold spots to watch the parade. A few groups had set up tents and grills.

I grabbed the window's handles, then pulled. Locked. Just as it had been Thursday night.

No one entered via the landing—

Yikes!

Max lurched against his leash. The move jerked me over the staircase. I windmilled my arms like a drunk. Steps are not the place to lose one's balance. "Max—stop!"

He growled—border collies don't pretend. Someone was behind me.

"Who's there?"

"Mel? You okay?"

"Kevin?"

"Just wanted to say I'm leaving. I'll email the plans, then get the fellas here. Shouldn't take more than forty-eight hours."

"C-cool."

"You sure you're okay?"

I rubbed my wrist where it hit the railing. "Hold on a sec. I'm coming down."

Kevin explained what he'd do with the storage area, pointing to where horizontal shelves would be installed along with other improvements.

I okayed the job. "You'll paint, too?"

"Sure thing."

Max and I walked out to the alley with him. The storage space had a vibe that unnerved me, and I didn't want to be alone.

Before Kevin left, I asked, "How'd you get in earlier? When you checked out the place before Max and I walked over from my house."

"I ran into Fern and Inga at the Tool & Rye. Inga gave me the code." He shook his head. "No, maybe it was Fern. Can't remember." He stepped into his truck. "Cheer up, Mel. It's gonna be okay."

"Thanks, Kev."

I looked at Max. The dog waved his tail gently while watching the contractor depart. There was no sign of the tension he displayed earlier.

So why did he growl?

Thirteen —

The parade had been uneventful—a good thing. Steven and I rode with the court. No doors fell over, and no former bosses of mine showed up.

I'd been so busy I hadn't had time to question why Eden Hoff had been with Tim Gold.

Steven and I were in the bowling alley dressed in royal garb: a sash and crown for him, same for me.

He asked, "Did you purposely pelt Char Broadway with rock candy in the parade?"

"No."

"It looked like it."

"She was standing in a bad spot along the route. My arm slipped."

I rubbed it for emphasis. My wrist still ached from the episode on the stairs in the mall.

We'd been appointed to open the VIP Bowling Games of Chance.

It must not have been the organizer's intent to make the

games a medieval-style, win-or-die Olympics. But, heavens to the Marquis de Sade, they did. VIPs were escorted into the Tree of Balls reception area. I mentioned the "tree" when visiting Wooly on Wednesday afternoon. I glanced above my head, observing globes dangling on wires. Lord, I hoped they were fake. They reminded me of a ceiling of swords minus the pointy tips.

Cousin Lou approached, wearing a red sweater and a western hat with fur trim. "Glad to see you two."

I asked, "Do the royals have to stay the whole time?"

"Of course. I heard you beaned Char with Jolly Ranchers at the parade."

"That's unconfirmed."

"I did the same thing to that Eden Hoff gal. She was standin' right in front of your mall. Mighty cheeky, if ya ask me."

She watched Steven as he detoured to the lanes, chatting with volunteers dressed in costumes.

I saw Oliver Roberts in a billowy white poet's shirt and black pantaloons. He appeared to be William Shakespeare, the Bard Bowler. Wooly Gallagher was a Christmasy court jester in red and green stripes and a red clown nose. I also saw footballs, basketballs, and beach balls where bowling balls should be. At Oliver's alley, I saw ... wagon wheels?

Lou nudged me. "You and Steven ready to be our first victims?"

I wish my cousin wouldn't have phrased it that way.

Lou dragged me out to a courtyard. I'd wanted to remain inside to watch Steven.

"I'm running the bowling ball beer pong," she said. "Heave the ball toward the red cups. Smash as many—"

"Thanks, but I'll skip it."

"Pretend you're aimin' at Char."

"Okay, make it quick."

"This is a competition; gimme your scorecard. We got great prizes. Ya could win a trip up north to Copper Falls."

I handed over the sheet with my name on it. Copper Falls was a western-themed town in northern Wisconsin, but traveling there was not on my list of priorities. I did not want Steven out of my sight. He'd been starting the beach ball game when I'd stepped outside.

The area where Lou and I stood was lit by flaming torches that crackled and sent sparks into the black sky. I heard wolves howl, and a serpent hissed near my feet.

Yes, I'm kidding.

But it could have been true, given the bowling alley's dungeon decor. A bowling ball was on a stand about ten feet away from a triangle of cups. Most of the snow had melted, so the footing was dirty sand. I asked, "Just toss it toward the cups?"

"Ya gotta put on the costume first. Lemme help ya."

A leather duster was swung over my shoulders, and a plastic six-shooter buckled on my leg. A ten-gallon hat replaced the tiara. The look was Yosemite Sam meets back problems.

"Bend over, toss it from between your legs," Lou ordered.

I launched. Cups were crushed.

She recorded the score. "Ya got six."

"Great, I'm going in."

"Wait, I got a scoop. Kat's memorial service is on Friday. I'm workin' the bar."

"Cool. Gotta go." I took the costume off, then handed it over.

"Put your tiara back on, Mel. You're royal, ya know. But speaking of costumes, undercover boys are hangin' around."

"Who—what?"

"Undercover boys are in town, I heard. They might've been at the Cheese Ball. They for sure will be at Kat's memorial."

"Who are they? How do you know they're men?"

"They could be cowgirls. I just like sayin' 'boys' cuz it makes me sound like I'm on *Dragnet*."

"Anything else?"

"Char's spreadin' the rumor that you did it. But it's Char; nobody listens to her. She starts talkin', and everybody gets a gut twist."

"Thanks for having my back, Lou."

She handed me a clipboard. "Here's your scorecard. Ya got six points. Make sure ya keep track tonight."

I walked inside to see Steven wearing a pool floatie around his waist and tossing a beach ball toward blow-up pins.

Untraditional bowling form. I felt relieved he was safe.

The room had filled with VIPs, but who were we kidding? The event's title was tongue-in-cheek. There were no VIPs in Cinnamon. Ours was an egalitarian community that time, progress, and ego fortunately ignored.

I saw the mayor, his wife, and Susan Victory chatting at the bar. Other cheese "royals" and business owners mingled, several wearing period costumes. They looked like wandering minstrels.

Char Broadway stood among a few of my artists. The women played games while holding drinks and eating popcorn. I pulled out my phone and texted Fern Bubble, reminding her to update the vendors: "Please email the group saying that the mall reopens in two days," I wrote.

As I hit "send," a gloved hand reached for my phone. "M'lady, what is this device, this devil's magic, you possess? Are you a witch?"

I smelled leather. Must have been the gloves. "Good evening, Oliver."

"Lady Mel, you look ravishing." He removed his felt hat and bowed. "May I interest you in a game of chance?"

"Can I have my phone back if I play?"

"Your wish is my command, Melanie." He offered an elbow. "Please step into my lair."

"Welcome to the Merry Tires of Windsor," Oliver said.

His "lair" turned out to be Lane 6. Its pins were painted like medieval characters, and the ball was a small rubber-coated wagon wheel.

I picked it up. "I roll toward the pins? Fine, let's get to it."

"We mustn't rush. First, a bit of history. Are you aware of how the Bard got his start in writing?"

"By studying Ovid?"

"No, he composed tire-rotation manuals for medieval wagons. Further, and this is little known, he penned heartbreaking sonnets about round objects." He sighed. "Deeply moving."

I glanced at a silver chalice near Oliver's seat. Behind him, there were ice buckets with bottles of booze. I suspected he'd indulged in a few holy cocktails.

"Melanie, you are without a beverage. May I offer you a Taming of the Shrewdriver? Quite refreshing."

"No, thanks. Here's my scorecard."

"I shall record your success as though you are my queen and I'm your scribe. By the way, that tiara is stunning. Are the stones precious? Where was it acquired?"

"My guess would be the dime store of Windsor."

He laughed. "Being both funny and beautiful is rare, Melanie."

"Shall we get on with the game?"

"Of course. The rules are simple: Your ladyship is to roll the tire toward the pins. Stepping over the line is a disqualification. As is spitting in the gutter."

"Got it."

"One more thing: I must blindfold you."

An odd look flashed in his eyes. Like a magician, he slid a scarf from his sleeve. The fabric was stunning. Silky and elegant, with black horses printed on it.

"Hermès," he said. "I thought you'd appreciate it, Melanie. Please turn around."

Oliver marked my scorecard with a feather pen. "You demolished eight of ten pins, Lady Mel. That's outstanding. You're well under par."

"I've played this game before."

He smiled. "A modern renaissance woman. I should have known."

"May I have my phone?"

"Of course, m'lady." He returned my phone and clipboard. "Please stay for a glass of bubbles."

"No, thanks."

"I insist, my dear." His voice dropped. "I have pertinent information for your investigation."

I glanced at Steven, who was three lanes away. He'd finished Wooly's game but still wore its costume of a red clown nose and jester hat. He and Wool compared hands, appearing to discuss game strategy. It looked like it would be a long conversation.

"Okay, sure."

"Wonderful. Let's sit."

He gestured toward a row of plastic-molded seats behind the lane, then poured two glasses of champagne, handing one to me. Before speaking, he looked around, making sure no one was within listening distance. "I detest gossiping about my library patrons, but I am hearing whispers about a customer. She is a member of your vendor group."

"Char Broadway?"

He sputtered. "Heaven's no! Despite my encouragement, Lady Broadway has yet to apply for a library passport. That's what I call them. Are library cards not passports to knowledge?" He sipped. "Char has limited potential as a reader. Her daughter, however, is another story. Crystal is quite bright."

I gasped. "The intel is about Crystal?"

"It is not; however, the younger Broadway has tongues wagging, as well. The rumor is she's a modern Juliet, suffering romantic malaise. Crystal is in love, but the feeling is unrequited. Who her Romeo is, no one knows."

Oliver sure gossiped for not liking gossip.

"Back to the investigation—"

"Yes, forgive me for wasting time." He paused to drip more champs into his glass. Took forever. "Melanie, I adore speaking with you, even if it is about a tragic subject. Have you always been such a wonderful listener?"

"Not really. What did you want to say, Oliver?"

"While I believe Kat Gold caused her demise—"

"You told me that—what's new?"

He leaned toward my ear. "It's bad news about Susan Victory. She's a superb artist. I possess several of her bracelets. But she has questionable judgment."

I felt my heart pound. "What does that mean?"

"Hank Leigel is her longtime paramour, but the rumor is she's turned the man into a cuckold."

"Susan is cheating on Hank?"

"No one knows with whom." He placed a hand on my knee. "Melanie, I fear her lover could be Timothy Gold."

Oh, no.

"And that means she could have become jealous of Kat, who maintained a cordial relationship with Tim, her ex."

I looked toward the bar.

Susan was still there, drinking. It appeared she hadn't left the spot since arriving a few hours ago. She stood near Char Broadway, giggling about something.

Susan, my dear friend—what have you done?

I stood at Lane 3, "The Slow Roll." Its premise was to use the least force necessary to tip the pins. Points were awarded for style.

Wooly Gallagher was the game operator. He was a jester in stripes and a clown nose.

"I'm befuddled, Wool," I said. "Discombobulated, too. And tickle-brained."

"The game is simple, Mel. Just tap the ball. The slowest roll with the most knockdowns wins. I won't even make you wear the red nose."

"I'm confused about Susan Victory and Tim Gold," I whispered. "And Crystal Broadway and her mom, Char. Steven, too. Did you know undercover cops are in town?"

Wooly looked past me toward the crowd in the bar. Boot-scootin' music blared. The party definitely had started. He and I were among the few people left at the lanes.

"Come by the newspaper office tomorrow," he said. "I've got intel for you. Not a lot, but it may help."

I played his bowling game, knocking down a rack of pins. I was awarded bonus points for delivery. Before launching the ball, I did a slow-mo pantomime of Munch's *The Scream*.

It was how I felt.

Wooly was impressed with my acting skills. "Well done, Mel. I'll see you tomorrow. Be careful getting home."

Fourteen —

Surprisingly, I came in third place in VIP Bowling. Prince Colby took second. The mayor won top honors and promptly reminded everyone to attend the next party, the Mayor's Race, at the yacht club. "It's tomorrow night, folks. May the best rubber duckie win! Remember, monies wagered go to the lake preservation fund."

Cousin Lou handed me a prize voucher. "It's a week's stay in Copper Falls. Ya need time off—it's the perfect place for it."

I shook my head. "My boss is strict about vacation days. No idea when I can get away."

"I'll write ya a note. And if that doesn't do it, I'll get wranglers. We'll herd ya outta town like it's a cattle drive."

Point taken. Never argue with a cowgirl who knows which bowling ball swinging overhead is the real thing.

Lou insisted that Steven follow me home, which I appreciated. Putt-putting through town, I kept my gaze on the rearview mirror. It was about ten o'clock, and flurries fell gently. The roads were slippery. Steven's van swerved a few times, I noticed.

His driving seemed too erratic for a light snowfall.

Was Steven okay?

He pulled into my drive, and I got out. He slammed on the brakes—the van barely missed me! It veered sideways into the street. I slip-slid toward it, then yanked on the passenger door.

Locked.

I pounded on the window.

My friend was slumped over the wheel. "Steven? Steven!" I yelled. "Open the door!"

Steven woke up after I pounded several times.

I got him in the house. He refused to go to the ER. "I ate a bad curd, that's all. Got my stomach upset."

"Don't let Lou hear you say that."

He rose from the kitchen table. "I gotta sleep it off."

"Where are you going?"

"Home."

"You are not. My spare bedroom is made up and ready for a guest."

"I'm fine."

"Steven, why are you inviting danger? You're like a Midwestern dad who goes outside when the tornado siren goes off. Isn't it smarter to be safe? Stay here so I can keep an eye on you."

He didn't answer, just stared into the middle distance and kept a hand on his belly. After a few seconds, he raced to my powder room.

Poor guy. We've all been there.

Murphy's law states, "Anything that can go wrong will go wrong."

But Murph has a cousin, Helen. She's a sour puss. She gripes, "Things won't just go wrong; they'll go to 'Helen' in a handbasket."

I moved Steven's van from the street to my driveway and retrieved his gym bag. I sent him to bed with tummy medicine, clear soda, and a cold compress for his forehead.

I made a cup of tea. Max and I settled in the living room in front of the fire. Sleeping was futile. My internal radar was tuned to the ill guest upstairs.

My phone pinged with a text from Rand: "Mel, are you home?"

"Yes, are you?" I responded.

"I'm here."

"Where's that? Sort of a meaningless term when it comes to a pilot, LOL."

"There's a yellow delivery van in your driveway."

Rand could see that from thirty thousand feet?

I heard a knock on my front door.

It's a little-known English-language factoid: the collective noun for a group of pilots is called a "calm." Aviators are trained to maintain composure at all times. Even when a plane, or a relationship, is nosediving.

The conversation with Rand did not go well, in short. It wasn't just a missed connection; it was a canceled flight with a "No Refunds" enhancer.

In my defense, exhaustion had bumped first-class thinking from my mind. I was worried about Steven. And I was a reluctant draftee into the club of amateur sleuths, a position I had no skills for other than an ability to ask vapid questions and get steamrolled by Char Broadway.

Sorry, I may be exaggerating. I felt exhausted.

Anyway, enter Captain Rand Cunningham.

He wore his uniform, making our breakup even harder.

He looked delicious in his blue pilot duds. A trim, smart-looking Scandinavian hunk. If he stood at the front of the plane and announced he was taking off in a storm while wearing his grandmother's trifocals and filled the jet's tanks with bubble bath instead of plane fuel, you'd still go up with him.

Further, if our scene were broadcast on a romance TV show, the audience would vote for him, not the contestant wearing bowling shoes with glued-on sequins and a plastic tiara.

I took the crown off and set it on the table next to me.

"I got a message from a detective while I was overseas," Rand said. "Before I replied to him, I thought we should talk."

I yawned. "What time is it? It's late to be talking."

"What happened in your mall, Mel? A woman was killed?"

"I didn't tell you?"

He claimed I didn't.

Yeah, our lack of communication was a problem.

Never complain, never explain.

A royal mantra I should adopt. It works, given the insane number of happily married bluebloods around the globe, right?

I made more tea, but it got delayed because the burner on my stove experienced mechanical problems. (Not lying.) It didn't bother Rand because a) delays were his business, and b) he was in the living room trying to make friends with Max.

After a bit, I walked in with the warm drink and a plate of Inga's shortbreads. I found Rand seated by the fire, the dog ignoring him, sniffing Rand's suitcase instead.

"Max is taking an olfactory trip around the world," I said.

Rand pointed to the new animal portrait on the mantle. "I like what you've done with the place."

"Thanks. Me, too."

"Mel, before we talk about the phone call from the detective, I want to say I'm sorry for missing your birthday."

I didn't reply. Nor did I sarcastically add that birthdays were easy to overlook because he didn't walk by gift shops or anything.

I held my tongue. Petty comments weren't worth the deviation. Rand and I had been distant for a long time. We hadn't addressed the problem like adults who cared for one another—and it was his fault. He was the one who traveled all the time. (Yes, that's a childish reaction. See note about being tired. I felt cranky, too.)

Rand questioned why Steven was in residence and wondered how often the guy stayed overnight.

I countered by highlighting my outfit. No seductress would wear saddle shoes, jeans, and a T-shirt that said, "Will Bowl for Cheese."

Case closed.

"Why didn't you tell me about the death in your business, Mel?" he asked. "Why didn't you let me help?"

"I don't know."

Our gazes locked. We sat across from each other, the fire between us. The amber light flickered, and it seemed to act as a light bulb for our souls. At that moment, I think we realized something important: we'd been pleasant company for one another for seven years, but no more than that.

Our relationship had stalled like an engine choked for fuel.

"This isn't working anymore, Rand," I said.

I added shocking words. It was like I'd hit turbulence in my brain, but it had a reverse effect. The turmoil dropped ideas into place rather than jumbling them.

To my complete surprise, I added, "I need something more."

Fifteen —

need something more.

What does that mean?

After I said it, Rand ran like a passenger hearing a final boarding call. For years, my subconscious warned me about his reaction if I sought deeper commitment. But like a responsible dysfunctional adult, I pretended my love life was fine and ignored the problem.

I collected the teacups and placed them in the sink.

After he'd left, I'd passed out in the chair, my slumber haunted by freaky dreams brought on by exhaustion. Or confusion. I still couldn't process that a murder happened in my little burg, the quaint village that time forgot.

To make it worse, the suspects included my friends. What in the name of Agatha Christie was going on?

Max lapped water from his bowl. While I'd slept, Steven had gotten up and exercised the dog in the backyard. Before my favorite courier departed for his morning rounds, he'd scribbled a note and left it on the kitchen counter:

Dear Mel,
  Last night was hell.
  Feeling better now,
  Headed to Tool & Rye to eat half a cow.
  Thought I heard voices last night,
  A nightmare where you and Rand had a fight.
  Must have been a bad dream.
  Made coffee for you; FYI, you're out of cream.
                              ~S.

Steven Delavan, delivery driver-poet.

The guy keeps adding value to everybody's life in Cinnamon.

I fed Max and myself. I chewed a hard-boiled egg while watching my building from the kitchen window. Service trucks jammed the parking spots at the loading dock. The repair guys were updating the storage space.

I needed to shower and get over there. The mall reopened on Wednesday, two days from now; I had to prep for it.

And solve a murder, too.

Let's not forget that.

A clown popped out in front of me, and I nearly tipped cooktop over teakettle.

I mean it. I was in the mall inspecting a booth containing tea supplies. Max and I had been wandering the first floor. I searched for things out of place, murder on my mind. Then a guy with a red nose and striped hat leaped into my field of vision.

The body-snatcher was Wooly, and he apologized. "I didn't mean to scare you, Mel. I was walking to the Tool & Rye for lunch and saw you through the window. Thought everybody in the bakery would get a kick out of my costume from last night."

"Yeah, they might. Hand me that bottle of water."

"Sure, and here's a chair. Sit down for a sec."

"Thanks."

I gulped H2O. Wool stared, looking concerned. "Do you need a cookie or something with sugar, Mel? You look pale."

"I'm fine, just need to catch my breath."

We hung out among the vendor booths for a bit, waiting for my heart to stop leapfrogging. Then we moved into my office because Wooly had confidential info to share, he said.

I told him I'd listen if the intel didn't involve clowns.

"I have bad news and not-so-bad news," Wooly said. "Which would you like to hear first?"

I looked out the window of my office. It was noon, but the sky had darkened, and the clouds mounded like gray ice cream. "The weather report."

He shook his head. "The sheriff's department hasn't resolved its issues. They had a fellow from another county to organize paperwork, but that was it. Things are moving slowly."

"That doesn't sound like the weather."

"It's November. It's cold, and it may or may not snow."

I didn't reply. I think he figured out the get-up was kryptonite to me. The hat and nose got removed.

"The press hasn't received updates," he said. "It may be because there aren't developments. Or, there are, and they don't want to release sensitive info."

"Which door would you pick?"

He pondered. "I learned Lieutenant DuWayne came out of retirement to investigate the case. The rumor is he's like Detective Columbo. He won't talk until he's got a solid theory. Even then, it may be misinformation to flush out a suspect."

Great. "What's the not-so-bad news?"

"I hear the undercover folks are recruits. Everybody knows everybody here, so they'll stand out. If they show up, that is."

"Who should I look for, Scooby and Scrappy-Doo?"

He smiled. "Keep your sense of humor, Mel. Ultimately, murders are stories with layers. Lots of them. You excel at reading people. You'll figure it out."

Was he right? No idea, but I liked layer cake. Maybe that helped. "Thanks."

"By the way, sorry about that picture on the paper's website—the one from the Cheese Ball. I have an intern who's into the 'no filter' look."

I shook my head. "I've taken a lot of bad photos in my life. No harm, no foul."

Wooly withdrew after taking my pulse and respiration to ensure I was okay.

Kidding.

The shock of seeing Cujo the Clown had worn off. But Wooly didn't put on the hat, nose, and megalomaniac Richard the III expression until he was out the door.

From the window, I watched him stroll toward the Tool & Rye.

A question lurked in my mind: I'd forgotten to ask him something about my modeling photos.

Max growled again, but this time it was at Fern Bubble. The dog calmed as soon as he recognized his friend.

She stepped into my office wearing a bright scarf but a concerned expression. "Hi, Mel. I saw you through the window. Have time for a chat?"

"Sure, sit down."

"Sorry I wasn't at bowling last night. I had a colicky horse."

"Funny, I had a colicky Steven."

"What happened?"

"He thought he ate a bad cheese curd. Felt awful for a few hours but was fine this morning."

She paused, then said, "Do you still believe someone was after him and not Kat Gold?"

"No idea, but I've got new information. We should discuss it."

"The special today at the Tool & Rye is white chicken chili. Shall I get bowls for takeout and come back?"

"Sounds good. It's on me, by the way." I reached for my purse. "Pick up a box of sugar cubes for Tulip, too."

Fern smiled. "You betcha, Mel. She'll love them."

We ate in the workroom, a space used for classes and luncheons. Years ago, the place was a general store that sold all things related to blacksmithing. When I bought the building, I'd cleaned the room, salvaged what remained, and used the iron treasures for decor.

The restoration guys repurposed tools for shelf brackets, and anvils were the bases for the giant maple conference table.

Fern and I parked at the table, then devoured chili with slices of cornbread. Max enjoyed chicken with a side of plain yogurt.

Dessert was thick slices of frosted pumpkin-maple bars for the humans and a "puppuccino" Wisconsin-style for the canine. (A dollop of whipped cream with a sprinkle of cheese.)

"Delicious," Fern declared when we'd finished. She pointed to the leather aprons hanging on hooks by the sink. "Let's clean up the dishes. You wash; I'll dry."

"It's okay. I'll do them later."

"No, I insist."

Two broken plates and a shattered glass later, I asked her what was wrong.

"I have to confess something," Fern said. "I took a meeting with Tim Gold. He and Eden Hoff are starting an agency. They want me to do public relations for them."

We were on the mall's second floor, strolling among vendor booths. I'd asked Fern for a "walking meeting" like at the farm.

I shook my head. "Lots of people start agencies. They're like law firms. Anyone can do it."

"Mel, please don't get defensive. I'm only the messenger."

"I'm not defensive." I watched her examine coffee mugs. "Don't pick those up, Fern. You break it; you buy it. No offense."

She sighed. "I won't touch anything."

"Big deal. Tim Gold and Lady Macbeth are starting an agency in Chicago. Eden burned her bridges in New York and wants to do it again in a different city." I stopped at the stairs leading to the third floor. "Go for it, Fern. It's probably good money. You need to keep the horses in hay."

"Mel, the agency wouldn't be in a big city. It would be here."

I smiled. "Not here, in my mall. I'm 'Midwest Nice' but not that nice."

"No, here in town. Kat, Tim, and Char Broadway were planning on starting an agency of social media influencers that included artists and crafters, some from your mall."

"I don't hear Eden's name in that posse. She would remain in New York and fly in to pester them? She'd be their 'Great Gazoo.' She looks just like the little guy."

Fern grimaced. "Eden and Tim are old friends, I guess. She's part of the agency. She wants to recruit you, too."

I shook my head. "I'm like that famous French actress. I vant to be alone."

"I hope you have that choice, Mel."

We moved to the third floor.

Fern acted as an upbeat Yukon Cornelius to my Abominable Snowman. She offered encouraging suggestions about joining an agency.

I wasn't in that headspace. "I have no desire to join. What's the agency's name?"

"It doesn't have a name. At this point, the idea is conceptual."

"Tell the conspirators I'm content in my land of misfit toys."

"I will, Mel."

I drifted through small shops selling homemade soaps and candles. Fern wandered to the other side of the space. The wide-plank floors echoed her footsteps; otherwise, the place was eerily quiet.

Downstairs, in the storage area, workers constructed shelves, but the building's thick walls and fire door insulated the noise.

After a few minutes, I approached Fern. "I'm sorry. Stress brings out my spicy side. I get it from my dad. As my cousin Lou says, "The Lord made a stoic swede, then added a dash of habanero."

Fern chuckled. "I know. Your mom was sweet, but your dad had mustang in his blood." She hugged me. "It will be okay, Mel."

"You and I don't have an exclusive contract. If you need the income, do it."

"I'm fine for now. Busy enough, and my animals are thriving." She jigged a step. "The vendors can't wait to get back in here. I'll announce the reopening of the Bell, Book & Anvil."

"You're worth the investment, Fern. I'm glad you send the newsletter and do my social media. I'm not into it. My past life was ample exposure for me."

I cringed at the memory. Sure, I was a B-list model, but I did catalogs, magazine ads, and splashy editorials in swimsuits. A couple of weirdos sought me out a few times.

I didn't need more of that, thanks.

We returned to my office. Fern jotted notes in her red book about upcoming events. Before she left, I reminded her to take Tulip's sugar cubes, then wrote a check. "For vet bills. Not much, but it'll help."

"Thanks, Mel. I have one horse off his feed, so I won't be at the Mayor's Race tonight.

"Are you in contact with Bruce DuWayne?"

She shook her head. "Nothing since Friday. But if he calls, I'll keep you informed."

She winked. It felt good to have her on my side.

I didn't tell her about the breakup with Rand. No one needed to know about that development. One word to Fern, Inga, or Cousin Lou and the news would travel the planet faster than Rand's jet. He'd land in Venice and get questioned about it by a tourist in a gondola.

Neither he nor I needed that distraction.

Sixteen —

Cousin Lou loves roasts. But she says the only thing that beats her meat is a roast that skewers a politician.

Who doesn't love teasing a pooh-bah for a good cause?

Once a year the Lake Cinnamon Yacht Club doors are opened to roast the mayor. Food, drinks, and fun are guaranteed. The event's highlight is the rubber duck race in the creek behind the club.

His Honor puts his ego on the line while bettors name steeds after politicians' peculiarities. Race winners have been called "Term Limits," "Tax and Spend," and "Wind Bag."

Mayor Paul S. Fess encourages partygoers to enter multiple "horses." He reminds the crowd that all monies go to the Lake Cinnamon preservation fund.

I'd put the cash toward therapists for those living near the stew-like water. Lake Cinn lives up to its nickname. But I live in the village. My summers aren't spent on the bucking waves, fearing being tossed from my boat after eight seconds. This cowgirl's voice doesn't count.

I met Steven outside the club. Temps were in the forties, and the sky glittered with stars.

"Great night for the race," he said.

"How was your day? I texted several times. Anything strange happen?"

He looked at me with narrowed eyes, like he wondered about my rapid-fire questions. "Here's my microphone. I'll carry the ducks."

"How are you feeling?"

"Fine."

"Anything strange happen today?"

"Nope, but I'm emceeing a rubber duck race while wearing a sash as Prince Mild Brick, cheese royal. That's not typical. This is Wisconsin, though. Life is different here."

I slapped him on the back. "That's funny. You should write another poem. Loved the one this morning. I didn't know you were a writer."

He stared at me. "Are you all right?"

"Fine, other than being a suspect in a murder—and I'm not worried you're involved somehow."

"You're worried that I'm involved?"

"No. Maybe. What do you think?"

"I've gotta set up the DJ booth to call the duck race. We'll talk later, okay?"

"I'll be in the bar. I need a drink."

That made him smile, and I saw the old Steven for a second.

We walked into the club, and the party began.

The club's bar wasn't packed with bettors—yet.

Grateful was this murder suspect because mingling among the soused was a road to psychological ruin. I'd get an earful of what citizens really thought about me. Alcohol is truth serum. With Char Broadway saying I was guilty as a corrupt politician, I did not expect the night to go smoothly.

Further, I had to watch for undercover sleuths, a snag that distressed me.

Attorney Hank Leigel stood behind the bar. He wore a name tag that read "Political Crony."

"Evening, Hank," I said.

"It's a pleasure to see you, Mel. How are you?"

"I'm okay, thanks."

He leaned over the bar. "I'm sorry about Kat. Please let me know if you need assistance. My office is only a few steps away from your mall. Door's open."

"I appreciate that."

"What can I get you?"

"How much is sparkling water?"

"Everything is ten dollars. Two for twenty."

"Wow, top dollar. And not even a price break."

He winked. "Government math, ma'am. The money goes to a good cause."

"Highway robbery, if you ask me."

"That duck is entered in the race." He pointed at the leaderboard on the closed-circuit TV. "Oliver Roberts reserved the name. That, and 'Let's Kill All the Lawyers.'"

"I thought the roast-the-lawyers barbecue was the summer fundraiser."

"Good one, and not a terrible idea. I'll take it to the board at the next meeting."

Several couples walked in. The signature beverages for the evening were Tax and Spend and Palace Intrigue. The first one was a Cosmo, the second a brandy old-fashioned.

Hank poured the drinks, then overcharged them, saying they'd have to fill out paperwork in triplicate to get a refund.

They merrily paid in cash, teasing him about skimming money off the top. They departed for the gift shop, where the best artists in the area—most of them mine—had tables selling Christmas gifts and high-end baubles.

I sipped my water. "How's Susan? I haven't talked with her in ages."

White lie. But Hank's an attorney. Doesn't count.

He replied, "She's been busy creating her holiday inventory." He nodded toward the door. "She's in the gift shop selling jewelry."

I saw his jade-green eyes darken. Uh oh, another confirmation that the courtship of Susan and Hank was not up to par.

Too bad. I liked Hank.

He was sweet to Susan's spice, the square peg to her tendency to spin in circles. From his office on High Street, Hank handled real estate transactions, wills, and legal actions for the village. Gentlemanly stuff.

I thought he'd make an outstanding trial attorney. With his folksy demeanor he reminded me of Robert Young from *Father Knows Best*. Hank could go for the jugular in closing arguments, but the jury would think it heard a love poem.

I put cash on the bar. "I'd like to buy a duck."

"Certainly, Mel. I'll enter it into the computer. Then your steed will appear on the leaderboard.

I told him what I wanted.

He laughed. "Excellent choice. I'm sure that name is still available."

"Illegit no carbon? That's a dumb one," Char Broadway said. "Another drink, please."

Char entered the chat.

She came into the bar with an empty glass. The name I'd selected was "Illegitimi non carborundum." Latin for "Don't let the Chars of the world get you down."

Mother Broadway wore a caftan. I complimented her on it, playing nice for the evening. "That's a lovely gown, Char."

"Yeah, one of my new vendors is gonna make 'em for my shop. They're cheap to make, but we can sell 'em for a lot."

I looked at Hank. "I'll take one of those drinks."

"I was here first," Char said. "I need a Tax and Spend, and I want more ducks."

Hank obliged. She chugged, then purchased Vote Early and Vote Often.

Funny names from a person who wasn't.

Perhaps there was hope of finding common ground with the woman, a chance of discovering the pony in the pile of compost, if you will.

I wished to discuss Crystal and her well-being with Char. I've found that honey is better than vinegar when conversing with almost everyone, especially those who use a snowplow to solve life's problems when a whisk broom would do it.

But Ms. Broadway began arguing with Hank about better pole positions for her entries. She was distressed because my "horse" somehow had gained the first slot and was going off at three-to-two odds. Any rational-minded human would understand that pole positions in a duck race are fiction, an even greater fable than the federal budget. There are no poles nor odds when rubber toys are released into a creek, subject to the current, rocks, and curious crows that gather along the bank.

One is lucky if one's steed bobbles over the line and into the awaiting net unscathed. The winner is best guess. Sometimes there are multiple first placers. I suspect the judges select the winner based on the most creative name because the mayor wears the moniker for the following year's race.

Winners get T-shirts and bragging rights—that's it.

But Char wanted to triumph, gosh darn it.

Hank soothed her by offering a free drink. She accepted and upped the ante by demanding a free duck for her troubles. He agreed, and she named her new racer "Emperor No Clothes."

Not awful. The woman had a gift.

She turned to me, scanning my outfit. Aside from the sash and tiara, which were new, I wore a black cashmere dress purchased years ago in New York City. It was the same vintage frock I always wear to cotillions if Cousin Lou doesn't corral me, dart me with tranquilizers like a runaway burro, and straitjacket me into sequins or animal print.

Char drained her glass, smacking her lips. "So, Mel, are you comin' to the meeting?"

I followed Char to the meeting. She did not describe its purpose, and I vowed not to trail her through a door à la Crystal. Think about it: The club was on a lake. Stepping blindly through a portal could get me dumped straight into angry water.

Fool me once, Broadways, shame on you. Fool me twice, shame on me.

We marched through the lobby. Char steamed past the crowd with the caftan billowing like a sail. Then she swooped down a narrow hallway, leading me away from the partiers. Confound it if the middle-aged trickster didn't disappear through a door, then slam it in my face.

Five seconds, Char. Then I'm going back—

The door opened. "Hello, Mel. It's lovely to see you again."

I nearly fainted.

It was Eden Hoff. I couldn't have been more surprised if the hall had filled with smoke and a genie appeared.

I gasped, which made me cough like an asthmatic. She stared with concern. Or, I assumed she did. My eyes were screwed shut so they didn't pop from my head.

On second thought, Eden probably tapped her foot while I heaved. Time was money to New Yorkers. They detested it if you wasted their precious minutes by dying.

I heard the door squeak, then slam again. "Are you all right, Ms. Tower?"

Tim Gold.

I wondered who else would pop out, praying it wasn't a clown car situation where editors from my past would dribble forth one at a time. My lungs couldn't take it.

Char yanked open the portal and stuck her head into the hall. "Who the heck is making all the noise out here?"

Good Lord. Someone get me a cough drop.

Char pushed into the corridor. The four of us crowded in the passage, clogging it like a hairball in a pipe.

Tim Gold wasted no time stating his purpose, selling his agency like a timeshare investment. "Ms. Tower, now is the time to get involved in our vision. The cost will go up—"

"Why'd you make my daughter cry, Mel?" Char interrupted. "She's gonna need therapy."

Eden cooed, "Melanie, we should have a drink together. You were delightful at photo shoots. You always made me chuckle."

Nonsense. Fashion people don't laugh. They frown upwards.

"Ms. Tower," Tim continued, "our idea is to dominate the craft-talent space by expanding beyond a traditional agency. With your history in the modeling industry, plus experience in the art mall business—"

A metallic rattle drowned out Gold's pitch. Oliver Roberts to the rescue. He pushed a book-laden trolley toward us. "Greetings, ladies and gentlemen," he announced. "I beg your pardon, but I'm going to the gift shop. Please disperse, or I shall run you over. Except for Lady Melanie, of course. As she is royalty, I must defer to her."

"I was just leaving, Oliver," I said.

"Wait, m'lady—I have a rare volume for you." He extended a hand toward Eden. "Fashion editor Hoff, I presume?"

"Please call me 'Agent Hoff.' I'm no longer an editor. I'm exploring other options in the talent industry."

"Agent Hoff, may I interest you in a library card application? I highly recommend our business books."

Char said, "We're openin' a business, and Mel needs to get on board. Even if some folks think she had something to do with Kat's death."

Oliver's eyebrows shot up. Once again, I was reminded about how he resembled Shakespeare. He wore the same Bard costume from the bowling party.

He said, "Charlene Broadway, may I suggest a volume on personal growth? We have an excellent audio series. No reading required."

Tim Gold patted Oliver on the back. "I have a great investment for you. It's ground floor—"

"Mr. Gold, are you conducting business during the mayor's charity event? Surely there's a better place. The library has a community meeting space. I'll reserve it for you."

"Well, ah—"

Oliver pulled a calendar and pen off the cart. "What day is best?"

✳

Oliver's comment about reserving the library's community room gave me an idea. But then Susan Victory had a meltdown, and I forgot about it.

Char Broadway, who'd had a few drinks, and Susan, who'd had more, bickered over a diary of sonnets on Oliver's sales table. Char didn't appear to want the booklet. (Her reading list was short, I suspected.)

Instead, Char acted irritated at the attention Susan received from the librarian.

I stood near the booths, "Desperate Hardware" and "Charlie's Antique Angels," watching the women. Oliver was between them, head ping-ponging.

I glanced down at his mini bookshop and spied a pamphlet of quotes by Mark Twain. I recalled the writer's advice about sparring with dimwits: "Never argue with a fool. Char Broadway will drag you down, then beat you with her experience."

I'm paraphrasing.

The quote is similar, though.

Oliver presided, and it was like watching a magistrate negotiate a settlement between Sir Falstaff and a grumpy Juliet. He de-escalated the situation by offering books and sympathetic hugs to the parties involved.

The women dispersed. I said, "You handled that well, Oliver."

"Thank you, Lady Mel. Librarians must be diplomats. At my previous place of employ, I had to peace keep between two geriatric collectors. Each sought rare editions of poetry." He smiled. "It's promising to see an interest in literature from Char Broadway."

"How well do you know Crystal?"

"She meets with the library's writer's group each week. She possesses a more mild temperament than her mother."

"Have you noticed anything different about her?"

He tipped his head toward me. "Are we suspecting Crystal is connected to Kat Gold's demise?"

"No clue."

"I see." In a low voice, he added, "After the race, let us chat. I may have insight for you."

Wooly "No Comment" Gallagher saved me a seat in the dining room.

The outdoor deck was standing room only. Patrons lined up to view the creek. Floodlights lit up the water. Those of us at tables watched on the closed-circuit TVs.

The mayor and Steven stood on a platform. Steven announced, "Ladies and gentlemen, welcome to the Mayor's Race. Mr. Mayor, you've had a less than stellar term, so I'm announcing your future opponents: 'Term Limits' and 'Dark Horse Candidate.' Please stand up, challengers!"

Mayor Fess laughed. "I'll be reviewing your memberships in the club. I'm commodore this year, you know."

"What's your name for the race, Mr. Mayor?" Steven asked.

"'Not Guilty,' I'm pleased to say."

"If my boat wins, you're guilty as sin!" someone yelled.

Fess waved. "Thanks for making this a great event, folks. We have many activities for the holiday kick-off week, but this is my favorite. Just when I think you've called me every name, you think of more. May the best name win!"

Steven took back the mic. "I hope you've placed obscenely large bets. It's for charity. These racers have been prepping since last year, lifting weights and swimming laps. As we know, it's impossible to predict a winner; there's no strategy. 'Illegitimi non carborundum' is in the pole position at 3–2. 'Believes His Press' is in second. 'Get a Real Job' will break third."

"My money is on 'Best Seller'!" the mayor's wife called out.

"I'm sorry, ma'am, the community art and literature awards are Thursday evening, hosted by Wooly Gallagher. You need to enter your boat at that event."

Wooly stood up. "Please support your local writers on that night, folks. Let's get this race started!"

Steven waved a checkered flag. "As you know, there are no prizes for this thing except T-shirts. So, I'm throwing in a week of free deliveries, starting tomorrow, for the winning duck."

The net dropped; the crowd erupted.

"It's a sloowww bobble toward the bridge," Steven called. "The course is rough this year, probably because 'Fix My Pothole' didn't do his job. 'Nepotism' takes the lead, followed by 'Fake It 'Til You Make It.' Those two are breaking from the field."

"Oh, no, 'Budget Crisis' and 'Pension Scandal' are caught in a riptide. 'Raw Sewage' is being boarded by 'Environmental Wacko.' Down the stretch they come—we've got a race!"

On TV, I saw ducks swirling in the water, bumping rocks, and tangling in cattails.

"It's 'Fake It' and 'Nepotism'!" Steven yelled. "They're beak to beak. Oh, no! Down goes 'Neppy.' Did a fish bite her? Looks like it. It's gonna be wire to wire. 'Fake It 'Til You Make It' wins! Whose boat is that?"

Turns out "Fake It" was none other than Tim Gold.

He collected his T-shirt. "Those free deliveries will be excellent for my new agency. Drop the orders at my place on the lake, Steven. You know the address?"

Steven played dumb. "It's the house near the water, right?"

Hee, haw. Tim and Eden took off.

Steven didn't stick around, either. He'd emerged from

his shell for the Master of Ceremonies gig but withdrew into himself when it ended. He told me the ducks were drying in a net in the club's basement, and he didn't need help carrying things to his van.

"Talk tomorrow?" I asked.

"Yeah, sure."

In the bar, I removed my tiara while looking out the front window. I watched Steven drive off into the darkness, wondering if he was going straight home or if he had stops to make.

"Lady Mel, may I interest you in a nightcap? They're serving High Crimes and Misdemeanors, also known as decaf."

"Sure, Oliver."

He retrieved steaming cups and two mint brownies from the bartender, a club member who'd replaced Hank Leigel.

Hank had driven Susan home, thank goodness.

Oliver and I sat at a table in the bar. I scanned the faces. "Did you notice strangers here tonight?"

"Are you implying there are interlopers among us?" He paused, studying the sailboat wallpaper. "No, I did not."

"You didn't see the guy in the duster coat? Looked like he rode in on a horse. He bought a duck, 'Land of the Free.' Stayed for a half-hour, then left."

"Heavens to Hamlet's ghost, you are observant, Melanie."

"I spent a lot of years watching people."

"Were you a golf pro in your past? They are trained to gaze into the middle distance. Or perhaps you were a Navy midshipman. They are experts, as well."

"Aye, aye, captain."

He chuckled and sampled the brownies. "Your cousin Louella created these. Like biting into velvet, then tasting the minty, fresh Irish coast. A chocolate sea breeze on a plate."

I sampled, too. Delicious. "Lou corralled the baking genes in the family."

He smiled. "You sound like they were running like wild stallions." He leaned forward. "I wish to share information about Kat Gold."

"Is this related to Susan? You mentioned her previously."

"No, it is not. But Susan is struggling, as evidenced by her behavior this evening. I hope she and Mr. Leigel repair their relationship, no matter if there were les liaisons dangereuses."

Oliver's syntax took getting used to. But he was a forty-ish guy who ran around in Shakespeare costumes. The clothes revealeth the man's speech pattern.

He continued, "I wanted to speak about Kat's ex, Timothy Gold. I have intelligence about the man. My sources, if you do not mind, shall remain confidential."

I nodded. "That's fine."

"Kat feared Timothy would dominate the business she created. Nor did she want Eden Hoff involved for a similar reason."

"What about Char Broadway?"

"Kat considered Char an ally. A person on her side if a battle for control were to occur. But my perception is that Kat was not aware Char's allegiance would depend upon the day; she would flip without remorse."

"Could Tim Gold have a life insurance policy on his ex? Could greed have played a factor?"

Oliver sighed. "'A fool thinks he's wise. But a wise man understands his own ability to be a fool.' Timothy Gold strikes me as neither brilliant nor dumb. But he easily could wear the mantle of greed. That is the most infamous of the seven deadly sins."

I thought it was pride but didn't correct him.

I savored my brownie, then continued. "A few days ago at the library, you said Kat was depressed and may have killed herself. Did she have a mystery man in her life who caused her depression? A difficult breakup, maybe?"

Oliver blushed. "I would not know nor venture a guess."

Puzzled, I looked up at the leaderboard on the TV. The names of boats still flashed on a scroll. I saw Eden Hoff's entry roll by "One Day You're In, the Next Day You're Out."

I shook my head. She had it wrong.

It should have been, One Day You're In, the Next Day You're Dead.

I used the powder room and then returned to the bar. A flat, book-shaped gift wrapped in red tissue was on the table in front of my chair.

"I bet you can't guess what it is," Oliver said.

"A wagon wheel?"

He laughed. "Open it, Melanie."

"You don't need to give me anything, Oliver."

"I'm aware, m'lady. But I collect books and enjoy sharing special volumes with special people."

I tore the tissue. Oliver explained, "*Tigers in the Cellar*, a first edition from 1963."

"How did you know?"

"You checked it from my library more than once. A grown woman does not peruse a child's book without reason."

I opened the cover, smelling old paper—what a memory! "My mother read it to me, and it's how I learned to read." I blinked, feeling tears. "It's one of the first books I remember."

"It's a fantastical story. A girl dreams that tigers live in her family's basement. One night, the animals emerge. She makes friends with the creatures, and they have exciting adventures." He leaned over my shoulder, looking at the pages. "Yet, the girl's mother, nay the reader, never knows if it's real. It's a young lady's Calvin and Hobbes but with a smidgen of danger."

I held it tightly. "I appreciate this. Thank you, Oliver."

"Your mother has departed, Melanie? You have my sympathies."

"She and my dad are in heaven. At this hour, they're playing Scrabble. She's ahead, but he has a few power tiles on his rack."

He smiled. "I will pray for a tie to preserve the family harmony."

"I should be going."

"Allow me to escort you to your car."

While walking through the lobby, I noticed Kat's memorial on the Upcoming Events board. Oliver saw it, too. "Make note, m'lady, that undercover law enforcement will be in attendance at Kat's finale. Perpetrators often appear at their victim's services. Authorities will watch for suspicious behavior among the guests."

"A guilty conscience needs to confess."

"Exactly, especially to strangers."

We stepped outside, and the wind blowing off the surf nearly slammed me into a concrete pillar. Good Lord, even Moby Dick would petition for a job transfer from Lake Cinn. No wonder Tim Gold and Char Broadway were murder suspects. Their best defense, if accused, would be that Lake Cinn made them do it.

Before I drove off, I asked a final question, raising my voice because of the wind. "Have you heard of anyone being upset with Steven Delavan?"

"I beg your pardon?"

"Steven delivers to my building every day. Maybe Kat was in the wrong place at the wrong time, and Steven was the real target."

Even in the dark, I saw Oliver's eyes light up. "I had not considered it. That would put an intriguing twist on this mystery!"

Seventeen —

I had dèjá vu Tuesday morning. At eight o'clock, I stood near my backyard gate pondering the mild November temperature and leaves at my feet.

For a moment, it was as if Inga Honeythorne had never crashed into the yard almost a week ago, shrieking that she'd found a body.

I enjoyed a few minutes of peace.

But then Lou called. The holiday kick-off week, and the mystery of who killed Kat Gold, continued.

"Hiya Mel, I heard you and Oliver Roberts liked my brownies."

"Everybody in the county does, Lou."

"That's true. I'm entering 'em in the baking contest on Wednesday. Oops, you're not supposed to know cuz you're a judge. Forget I said that."

"What do you need, Lou?"

"How'd you like my boat names last night? 'Sciatica Problem' and 'Pinched Nerve.' Kinda off-brand for the race, but

I named 'em after Char Broadway and Susan Victory. I heard they got into it—"

"Lou, my mall opens soon. I need to help Inga."

"You're goin' to the Midwinter's Night at the Library party tonight, right? Ya gotta because it's your royal duty."

"I'm aware, thanks."

"You're in the reader's theater play production. I told Oliver you'd do it. Steven, too."

"But—"

"I won't be there. Makin' my entries for the bake-off at the church. Oops. Contestants are anonymous. You didn't hear that."

"I'm not—"

"Don't be a stranger, Mel. Come out to the ranch soon, okay? You and Max can have a mini vacation. And you and I will paint the guest room. It needs it. Have fun tonight."

She hung up.

I watched Max sniff the air and trot in circles around the yard. He held his tail straight out, his body tense, as though he felt energy he didn't like.

My dog was stressed.

I was, too.

A vacation wasn't a bad idea.

I entered my office and saw the coupon for a week's stay in Copper Falls on my desk.

I'm not a person who takes time off, but the idea of a secluded cabin, a mystery novel, and Max snoozing at my feet sounded appealing.

Lou had hung up before I could inquire about the Tool & Rye betting pool; I'd assumed Char Broadway still held the lead.

Speaking of Mother Broadway, she'd shown up at the mall

and bullied past Inga. From behind, I watched Char huff and puff up the steps carrying bracelets to sell in her booth.

As the Bell, Book & Anvil owner, the buck stopped with me when handling difficult vendors. And, okay, speculating that Char was the favorite in the pool was unfair. But she was a kook. And irrational.

If hell needed an art mall manager, Char should apply for the job.

Inga and I followed her upstairs. Before she could arrange pieces in her booth, I told her to remove her items and leave. She counter-argued that she should be allowed to remain, that she was still a vendor in good standing. "I haven't done anything wrong," Char protested. "This is the best week to sell stuff."

"Char, you're opening a competing business and taking vendors with you. You don't think that disqualifies you from being in my mall?"

"Yeah, but I haven't done it yet. The plan is still in the works."

"You also accused me of having something to do with Kat's death."

"That was just talk. You're not arrested or anything." She pointed at Inga. "Maybe she did it."

"You have to leave Char. Vacate your booth before the other vendors arrive. You're in violation of the contract you signed."

"But—"

"Now, Char. I'll mail a refund for this month's rent."

"You'll hear from my attorney."

"Have that person contact Hank Leigel. He handles the mall's legal issues."

I gave her boxes and bubble wrap. Inga even helped her pack rather than bop her in the nose for the false accusation.

Char hustled out through the storage area with her wares. She offered a parting shot at me: "You weren't a very good model, Mel. Some of your old pictures are pretty funny lookin'."

I smiled. "To look on one's past with mirth is a gift, not a sin."

"Huh? What does that mean?"

"I wish you well in your future endeavors, Char."

She loaded her SUV, its CHARBRL license plate rattling as she dumped in boxes. Then Ms. Broadway hopped in, slammed the driver's door, and gave a one-finger salute.

"Drive carefully," I called out. "There are tourists in town."

She fired the engine. The SUV sped off, weaving down the alley, looking like a wobbly toaster on wheels.

I watched the vehicle tip as it zipped around a corner.

Glad she used plenty of bubble wrap.

Kevin Sunny showed off the new storage area. He and his craftspeople had transformed it into mini warehouse heaven.

The room had pipe-bracket shelving. Magnificent. A sienna-colored finish coated the floor, complementing the stone walls. The painters also used a blue accent color that sent out positive vibes. Perhaps if Char had paused to appreciate the new room instead of storming through it, she would have departed on a less vicious note.

"It's wonderful, Kevin. It's almost too beautiful to be a storage room. It's a party space. Artistic shelving is the new black."

He smiled. "Glad you like it, Mel. How you use it is up to you. We're just happy to have the business."

I sniffed the air. "It smells like a floral shop. How'd you do that?"

He walked toward the fire door, work boots echoing. On a sideboard that hadn't been there before was a bouquet of roses. "These are for you. Or, Kat, actually. Somethin' from me and the guys."

"That's very kind, Kevin."

"Want 'em in your office? I'll carry 'em inside."

I stared at the beautiful flowers. "No, they're perfect right there. It's a nice tribute. Everyone who walks in from the loading dock will see them."

"Yeah, gotcha."

"You'll email the invoice?"

"Sure thing."

"Please tell everyone I said thanks. The place is fantastic, and the flowers are really thoughtful."

Max wandered while Kevin and I talked. Before leaving, the contractor called the dog over and patted him, ruffling his black fur.

Max leaned into Kevin's legs, panting gaily, showing no signs of distress or fear toward the man.

I felt relieved.

I loved hearing voices in the building again. I'd missed my artists more than I expected. I was making connections, it seemed. Something I hadn't done while working in New York. *Socrates said to examine one's spiritual, personal, and moral connections to God, friends, and animals.*

I'm reminded of this philosophy daily because of the mall's sign maker artist. He has a booth on the third floor, across from the elevator. The fellow carves inspirational quotes onto breadboards.

Every ride up there provides fresh insight. (The artist also caters to Wisconsinites and our allegiance to a green-and-gold football team. The guy embraces sales philosophies about knowing one's audience, too.)

Socrates, the wise ancient, recommends studying one's

universe or life isn't worth bupkis. I've existed closer to the neglectful end of his counsel. But after this week, I felt released from my emotional jail. The revelation began with the outburst to Rand two days ago. Declaring, "I need something more," to another human amounted to a personal sermon on the mount.

Blessed are those who gain self-knowledge later in life, I say.

Do not reveal any of this progress to Cousin Lou. She gets wind of it—via her network at the Tool & Rye, no doubt—and she'll throw another shindig in the barn to celebrate. Then I'll be back in the corner with the cardboard John Wayne, wishing I could trade places with him.

We'd be back where we began.

I sat in my office, catching up on emails, the door open. Max trotted the mall, earning his new title of official greeter. The Thompson twins—remember the needlepoint sisters from the birthday party?—stopped to offer encouragement in their needle verse.

Ellie said, "You must never fear life's storms, Melanie. Rather, learn to sail one's ship."

"We're delighted to be back. There's no place like home," Edna added.

Ellie: "The roses for Kat are a lovely idea. We put one of our framed prints near it: 'Flowers are sunshine, food, and medicine for the soul.'"

I smiled at them. "Stop in the workroom and fill a plate. There are goodies from the Tool & Rye for all the vendors."

"Wisconsinites shall not live on bread alone," they sing-sanged.

I smiled. For once, I agreed with a statement about not being alone.

Fern texted, saying she couldn't come in for the mall's reopening. Another horse with a problem.

"How's it going?" she wrote.

"The place is packed. Max promoted to vice president in charge of happy shoppers."

"Was Susan Victory there?" Fern wondered.

"No, didn't show."

"I'll give her a call to find out what's going on."

"THX. The vendors say thanks for keeping them updated about reopening, etc. I need to talk to you about doing something for Kat Gold. Maybe a scholarship at the high school in her name? Let's meet later this week."

"Ok. Law enforcement fella left town, BTW."

That was an excellent development. It meant Lt. DuWayne was off my back for a few days. I replied, "Good. Keep me posted on his whereabouts."

She ended our text chain with a smiley emoji and a heart.

I replied with a row of skulls and crossbones, tiny danger symbols.

Little did I know how accurate they were.

Eighteen —

Holy smokes! Who—what is that?

I'd entered my garage and opened the door without flipping the light. A figure lurked against the wall. It was cloaked—a cloak? What the—?

Max growled.

I saw a dark form that moved. No, it didn't move. It glistened. Light from the streetlamp reflected its fibers.

I held leftover croissants from the mall. I pelted the thing with bread. "Stop right there!"

I looked for a weapon and saw a bucket of salt. An aluminum shovel. Max scrambled forward, rushing the ghoul.

Light—turn on the light, dimbulb!

I flipped the switch.

Sweet Jesus.

Who—what—why?

Why was a Vegas showgirl outfit haunting my garage?

Cousin Lou.

Need I say more?

She sent a text while I stood in the kitchen, hyperventilating, staring at the costume.

She texted: "Did you get the costume I dropped off? It's hanging in the garage. Didn't have time to put it in the house. It's for the reader's theater thingy tonight—have fun! Don't do anything I wouldn't do!"

I studied the outfit I had to wear as dictated by the event committee from the O.K. Corral. For my role in the Midwinter's Night at the Library, I would wear a black velvet cloak, a sequin bustier, red leggings, and patent leather cowboy boots.

I looked like Little Red Riding Hood on her way to the medieval disco.

What was I to do?

In past years, I'd mailed a donation for the party, then gone to bed early with a good book.

But as a cheese royal, I was mandated to attend.

Steven sent a text along with a photo. He wore similar garb, but his cloak was green with bright gold trim. He wrote: "I look like a Bay City Roller on the way to a football game."

"Or a player for the Green Bay Draculas," I replied.

"LOL."

I secured the house, hopped in the Saab, then putt-putted toward the library, reminding myself that attending holiday parties wasn't the worst way to solve a mystery.

The library was rockin', so citizens came-a knockin'.

One night a year, the building devoted to books and silence gets loud. Tonight was the perfect evening for it, too. I parked and got out, walking across the jam-packed lot toward the building. Silver-drop snowflakes whirled gently from the clouds, and spotlights crisscrossed the sky.

The place had a movie premiere quality to it. A lighted marquee flashed the program for the evening, including cocktails, hors d'oeuvres, and music in outside tents. Games for children and a reader's theater production inside the building. A craft and book sale in the community meeting room. "Thou Shalt Support Your Local Library!" the sign announced.

A red carpet and step and repeat photo backdrop captured attendees as they arrived. Crystal Broadway snapped pictures. I attempted to detour, but a woman wearing a crown, sash, and velvet robe was obvious.

Crystal displayed none of her previous vulnerability; she was all business. "Pose, Mel," she demanded. "It's for the paper."

Oh, no. Been there, seen that.

Just then, a children's choir wandered onto the carpet. Dressed as lambs, the tiny sweethearts were the perfect foil. I posed among them, looking down at their adorable faces. A photo was snapped, and this former model knew viewers would focus on the children, not her.

My royal duties for the evening were simple: I would mingle in the tents, then participate in reader's theater as Thisbe, one of the star-crossed lovers in *Pyramus and Thisbe*, a lamentable comedy.

I also had a self-determined role as a sleuth, but that intel is on a need-to-know basis. The tents beckoned, and like Dante in the Divine Comedy, I entered the flapping canvas portal, not knowing what to expect on the other side.

I did not expect to find Tim Gold behind the bar. Nor did

I allow for a guy at my shoulder wearing a Nick Bottom get-up, donkey head and all.

Tim made me the night's signature drink, a Puck's Fizz, and then pointed his phone at donkey-guy and me. "Mind if I take a photo of you two? It's for the 'gram."

I agreed, knowing that all eyes would be on the character from A Midsummer Night's Dream instead of yours truly.

I bought Mr. Ed a Carrotini, a vodka and carrot-ginger orange juice, shaken, not stirred. He trotted off, and Tim Gold said, "It's great to see you, Mel. I'd love a face-to-face with you about our agency's brand concept. We're a disrupter in the craft-media market."

"What time is the memorial for Kat on Friday?"

"Two o'clock, I believe."

"I'd like to pay my respects to her."

"Let's vis-á-vis afterward."

"I have the Fish Fry Gala that evening."

"How about later tonight? I'm in the reader's theater production, too."

"If there's time, Tim."

I wandered the tent to find Steven. So far, he was a no-show, but I felt confident in his safety, given the text from earlier. I moved toward a tall table in a corner. "Hey," I heard.

It was the donkey guy. "Don't you mean hee-haw?"

"It's me."

"Hello, me."

What was in the Puck's Fizz? Did Tim Gold slip a shot of sassy into it? Only a few sips, and I felt cheeky.

"Mel, it's me."

"Wooly?"

"Took you long enough. I stood next to you at the bar."

"I was avoiding you. Who wants to stand next to a stranger wearing a donkey head? People are weird these days."

"That's a good point."

"How's the Carrotini?"

"Can't drink it. I've got an eighteen-inch nose." He pawed the ground like a horse. "I'm working undercover. Thought I'd observe a few folks tonight, and it's best to avoid alcohol."

"Good idea."

"Gotta go. Oliver Roberts is headed this way. Keep the drink. Don't tell anyone it's me."

He disappeared into the crowd, as well as a guy wearing a donkey head can, but others were in costumes, too. I saw fairies, Oberon, and a few Pucks.

I sampled the carrot drink. Not bad. Carrot, then a zing of ginger and vodka.

Oliver stepped to my table. He wore The Bard costume again and carried a riding crop. "You look lovely this evening, Melanie. Who was that beast?"

"I don't know what you're talking about, Oliver."

He smiled, but the emotion didn't reach his eyes.

Why did Oliver seem angry?

Oliver asked, "I saw you speaking with someone—who was it?"

"Who's on first."

"Excuse me, what?"

"He's on second."

He smiled. Again, just his mouth. "And 'I don't know is on third.'"

I lifted the Fizz. "Correct."

He glanced at the drinks. I had two to pick from, the fizz and the carrot. "I'm glad you're enjoying yourself, Lady Mel. There will be coffee in the library's kitchen. See you in an hour?"

"Not if I see you first."

It was the drink talking, I swear. Tim Gold put something extra in mine. Besides, the theme of the event was potions and being silly.

Maybe I was acting a role, too?

Oliver harrumphed off, and I observed the activity in the tent from the corner, feeling like a fairy on a tree branch.

Tim Gold made and poured drinks like an expert. Perhaps he'd been a bartender in college or had belonged to a fraternity. His recent appearances at community events were suspect. Unless he, Eden, and Kat had planned to build their brand by becoming more visible, and the death of Kat was a plot twist none of them expected.

Unless one of them did it, of course.

Char Broadway entered the tent, laughing and towing Eden Hoff. If you had told me I'd see the queen of a New York magazine in a Wisconsin party tent, I'd say you had one too many Puck's Fizzes.

A crowd gathered near the ladies, and I recognized a few of my vendors. That group schemed against me. They'd sell as much as they could this week, the busiest week of the year, and then relocate to the new store using the intel they gathered from the Bell, Book & Anvil.

Kat Gold had been one of my vendors, too. But she was no longer with us.

Did a person in that group have something to do with it?

Pyramus and Thisbe dates back to the eighth century. It's the original Romeo and Juliet. Two kids are forbidden to be together because their parents are nuts. One mom thinks the other is plastic and fake. The dads battle over the size of their barbecue grills and the straightness of the mowed stripes in their backyards.

Well, maybe that isn't the exact storyline.

But it would be if it were written in modern day.

Shakespeare included the tale in *A Midsummer Night's Dream* as a play-within-a-play. He created a quirky bunch to play the roles, too. The cast performing the production is inept, and the tragic tale becomes a screwball comedy.

The young lovers end up dead, but it's pretty lively until the story gets to that point.

I stood in the library kitchen, script in hand. Oliver presented a cup on a tray. "Enjoy a coffee before we take the stage, Lady Mel."

My head felt woozy from the Fizz. I was glad to have the caffeine. "Thanks."

Tim Gold pressed against the kitchen counter, doing calf raises. "Gotta warm up before a production. I'm playing Moon."

"May want to stretch your arms, too," I said.

He smiled and lifted his hands. "Mel, you need to understand the vision that Eden and I have for the agency—"

"And Kat, too, I presume."

"Yeah, her, too. The craft business is huge. We're gonna control the network in the Midwest."

"How long have you known Eden?"

"Not long, but we clicked right away. She contacted me through my Chicago ad agency. Reached out because the magazine biz is collapsing, just between you and me. She had to come out here for fresh ideas. And a job, like, because she got fired." He bent over and touched his toes. "We're gonna make a great team."

Oliver handed him a lantern. "Timothy, you shall play the part of Moon, an important role. The young lovers rely on you for illumination. Thus, you must hold the light high. I hope your arm muscles are up to the task."

"I'll do my best, Ol."

"I shall be the master of ceremonies and play the part of Lion. A dual obligation, but I've done a bit of acting in my time." Oliver cleared his throat and practiced roaring. "Perhaps I need a cough drop."

We lacked two characters. Steven, who played my lover, Pyramus. And Wall, which was the barrier between us. No mention of that actor yet.

The door to the kitchen swung open. Steven breezed in, looking like the jolly green pirate. Wow, Cousin Lou must have been on a mint brownie sugar high when creating his costume. But it was good to see my friend in one piece.

Oliver scanned him. "You're expressing more of a St. Patty's vibe than necessary, Steven, but thank you for participating. Here is your script and plastic sword."

What was with Oliver's coldness toward my friend?

"Sorry I'm late," Steven said. "Had deliveries to make on the way. I'll take some of that coffee."

Oliver poured, then said, "The premise of this event is simple. Read your lines from the text. Act them out using your voice and gestures. The show is meant to be frivolous. The audience will reward your effort."

What did that mean? I didn't expect much of an audience. The fun, music, and drink were in the party tents, not the library.

How wrong I was.

Oh, what a tangled web is weaved when librarians practice to deceive.

We'd gathered in the children's section. There was a stage

with spotlights. Oliver stood at a microphone: "The part of Wall shall be played by Char Broadway."

Char walked on wearing a foam block on her head painted to look like a stone. (The block, not her head. Sometimes talent casting can be outstandingly accurate, no?) Tendrils of fake ivy trailed down that resembled leafy strings of hair.

She clasped her hands like a prizefighter, and the crowd roared.

The crowd, you ask? Who attends a bash at a library?

Other librarians, that's who—and they want their Shakespeare.

The cast sat on barstools, our scripts propped on stands. Lights blazed overhead, and we each had a microphone.

Char was in the middle due to her role as Wall. Her job was to hold her fingers up in a small circle; that was the hole through which Pyramus and I communicated.

Aside from our nutty parents, Wall was a problem. Pyramus and I lived on opposite sides, with only the hole to talk through.

I scanned the audience.

The librarian attendees treated the show like a medieval Rocky Horror Picture Show. I saw people dressed as Wall, Moon, Lion, and Puck. I also saw Bottom, the donkey-headed guy. I suspected it was Wooly.

Clearly, the crowd had pre-gamed in the party tents.

Eden Hoff stood in the back, looking amazed at the spectacle. My flabber was gassed, too, but there was no backing out.

Break a leg, as they say in the biz.

Oliver announced, "Welcome, all. It is my pleasure to present Pyramus and Thisbe, a lamentable comedy. Like the actors in *A Midsummer Night's Dream*, this cast is feebly skilled. We repent of this performance beforehand." He smiled. "Our rehearsal consisted of twenty minutes with the script. To paraphrase

Puck, if we offend thee, believe that you have only slumbered here—this was but a dream."

In other words, if we were horrible, the play didn't happen.

Not a bad way to manipulate an outcome.

Char had the first line. She squinted at her script. "Blast—I doth forgot my cheaters." The crowd roared. A guy in the front handed over his half-glasses. Char took them. "Thanks. Behold, this wall sees! Its two lovers whisper secretly through my generous hole."

Snickers and side-eyes while Char held her fingers in the air.

The audience followed. Most of the crowd held up their hands, digits forming a circle.

It was going to be a long night.

I was not prepared for the audience. If Lion roared, the group cried, "Well-roared, Lion!" If Moon raised his lantern, the reply was, "Well shone, Moon!"

And the ad-libs? Tim Gold started them, and he drove the production into the weeds. "'Tis a night black as coal," Tim declared. "To protect young lovers from lions, tigers, and bears—"

"Moon, we are not in Oz," Oliver-Lion interrupted. "That is a different production entirely. Stick to your script, Moon. Rawr!"

"Well-roared, Lion!" the crowd responded.

Tim lifted his lantern. "To protect the young lovers from this impotent lion, I shall light their paths as they approach Wall."

Oliver reddened at the insult. The crowd yelled, "Well shone, Moon!"

Steven-Pyramus said, "I approach Wall and do not see my lover. Where is Thisbe?"

"She's on the other side of Wall!" an audience member yelled.

Wall put up her fingers, as did the crowd. Steven looked through it. "I see no Thisbe. Curse thy stones, Wall!"

As you can imagine, colorful cursing followed. Wow, librarians have outstanding vocabularies! I saw Eden put her hands over her ears, which said a lot coming from someone who worked in the New York fashion scene.

When the cacophony died, I said, "Have you heard my moans—"

Loud groans. I feared someone gave birth.

"I hear my lover!" Steven declared. "To the chink!"

"Pyramus!" I cried.

"Thisbe, kiss me through this vile wall."

"Alas, I cannot—this wall is evil."

Not the line. But if the other characters and the audience could ad-lib, so could Thisbe.

Char glared at me. "Wall is not evil."

"It should be bulldozed," I said. "Where is my hammer of jack?"

That got a roar of frustration from Oliver. He guided us back to the script: "The two lovers leave Wall, promising to meet in the graveyard by the light of Moon."

Nothing happened. Someone yelled, "Hey, Moon—that's your cue!"

"Forgive me, Lion, your impotence." Tim raised the lantern. "Moon is present."

"You are present but not very bright," Oliver answered.

"Aye, but stiffer than you, Lion." Tim straightened his arm.

"Rawr!"

Tim asked, "Audience, have you ever heard a lion roar so … softly?"

"Softly roared, Lion!"

The crowd snickered. Char defended Oliver: "Lion is the king of the jungle! With enough strength to mount Wall."

"A wall with holes in it," I added.

"Well-insulted, Thisbe!"

Har, har.

The librarians seemed delighted we were off script. Probably because they knew Shakespeare's tragic ending: Thisbe bolts for the graveyard followed by Lion. Pyramus fears his lover will get eaten, so he kills himself. Thisbe returns, finds Pyramus dead, then falls on his sword.

It's a blood-soaked final scene. Arguably better, however. The two lovers could have ended up in therapy forever or lived in their parents' basements.

But this production became a crowd-sourced finale that detoured through the land of insults and sexual puns.

Typical Shakespeare, in other words.

In the end, Pyramus stabbed Lion, the two lovers eloped to Green Bay, and Wall seduced Moon.

Everyone lived happily ever after.

Except for Kat Gold.

To paraphrase footballers, the cast left its performance on the stage.

We gave the story our all. Even Char, who displayed a knack for comedic timing. After the curtain call, I congratulated her. And just when I thought we could coexist, she announced she was getting a restraining order.

I looked around. We were the only two actors in the kitchen. "Against whom?"

"You! You called me evil. That wasn't in the script!"

"Char, it was a play."

"And you kicked me out of your building today for no reason. I'm gonna keep you from coming near me. Crystal, too. I haven't forgotten you made her cry. Then, I'll sue you for everything, Mel Tower!"

Being an actor had gone to Char's stone head.

She marched out, ivy tendrils writhing behind her. They appeared to transform into snakes before my eyes, or was I seeing things?

Tim Gold and Oliver Roberts entered, both men looking agitated. I pressed against the wall in the kitchen, making like a mannequin. (Quite experienced in this regard, FYI.)

"Mr. Gold, you insulted me," Oliver seethed. "Your remarks went beyond the boundary of acceptable stagecraft."

"Calm down, Speilberg." Tim crossed to the coffeepot and poured himself a cup. "All the world's a stage, remember? They were jokes. The audience loved it. You should be thanking me."

Oliver grabbed his riding crop and raised it. Yikes. "I shall never again cast your untalented carcass in one of my productions, Timothy Gold. At best, you are an actor on the level of a plastic action figure. You are banished from this library's reader's theater forever."

Gold laughed. He grabbed the fake sword lying on the table. "En garde!"

"Out, Out, dark spot!" Oliver shouted.

I got the message and skedaddled.

I felt perturbed with Oliver. The librarian hadn't revealed that Char would be in the show until the last minute. He introduced her to us like pond water to a petri dish. I searched the tents for Wooly, but he was nowhere. Or everywhere. I saw donkey heads on all the partiers—or was I hallucinating?

I wandered from the tents toward my Saab, heard voices and stopped. Two lovers argued near me. Steven and Crystal Broadway were under the vestibule at the library entrance. I stood on the pavement, watching them nicker.

No, bicker. Their heads were normal.

I felt cold. No, hot.

Couldn't tell—oops, car. I shuffled out of the way. Why were my feet slow? The car guy honked, and I waved with my keys.

Where were my keys?

Ha, kidding—in my hand. I walked to my car. Where was it?

There, the Saab. What was on the wiper? Someone stuck a red clown nose on it—probably a real joker, LOL.

I climbed in. Where was the starty thing? I looked down between the seats. Not joking—that's where the ignition is, silly. (The Scandinavians were way ahead of everyone else about car safety. Look it up.)

I turned the key, pressed the clutch, and wiggled the stick. Neutral, then second gear. No, let's try fourth. Gets me home faster, hehe.

Shudder, clunk.

Oops. Guess not. Clutch, then starty thing again. What are all these knobs for? I turned a bunch. Headlights. Air—whoosh! Wipers. They swished across the windshield, and I tracked them. Made me dizzy. What's that?

That red thingy on the wiper swiped the glass. It was streaking—yuck! Every swoosh looked like brownish blood.

I shook my head. Bad idea. Felt like I'd stepped off a Tilt-A-Whirl.

I looked out the window toward the vestibule, where those people had been arguing. Who was it, again? Where'd they go?

I looked around. Dark parking lot. Woman alone. (Me, FYI.)

Blood on the windshield.

Lock. The. Doors.

I gasped. Max! I felt sooo discombobulated—but even in a

stupor, I thought immediately about Max. In an instant, I became a mother lion worried for her cub that was home alone.

Was Max safe?

I needed to get to my dog!

Nineteen —

pressed my cheek onto the cold tile. It felt good. Thick blankets covered my body. The chilly surface felt refreshing, like I dozed on ice harvested from a northern Wisconsin lake.

I heard the door open. "Hey, cowgirl, just checkin' on you. Need anything?"

"How did I get here, Lou?"

"Well, there are two scenarios: You either picked up Max from your place and drove straight to my ranch."

"Or?"

"Or, you drove home from the library, barfed, then called me from the bathroom."

"Then ... what?"

"Jason and I zipped into town and found you lookin' green. We grabbed you, Max, and that Tin Lizzie you drive, then convoyed back home."

"I'd like to believe I picked up Max and drove here under my own power."

"Fair enough."

"What was on my windshield?"

"Someone stuck that clown nose in somethin' disgusting, like half St. Bernard doo, half goose crap. Jason used the pressure washer to clean it off your car. Also changed out the wipers. Threw the nose in the burn pile and torched it. That thing was nasty. You want breakfast?"

"Where's Max?"

"Racing around outside in the puppy playground with his buddies. They're glad to see him."

"He needs to stay here until I get this thing solved. Until I find out who did it."

"Sure thing. You're stayin', too, cousin, FYI."

I didn't argue with her. I closed my eyes and felt the cold floor on my face.

Lou served me a bowl of soup and propped me in a chair in her living room. The space could have doubled as a Western Christmas holiday bazaar. The volume of her red and green decor rivaled my mall at peak season.

A fire blazed in the fireplace. Lou and Jason burned full-size oaks, it seemed. An evergreen the size of a sequoia flashed its lights in sync with Christmas music, a setlist that included "Grandma Got Run Over by a Reindeer" and Dolly and Kenny duets.

My cousin plopped across from me on the sofa—one of those enormous pit things that easily held the choir from church, the O.K. Chorale, and the group's organist and the instrument.

Okay, so maybe not the organ. But the rest was true.

I know because Lou sent the manufacturer a snapshot of the choir occupying the couch. They were a white-robed army.

The sofa maker replied by sending T-shirts that read, "Without couches, there is no rest. Without singing, there is no joy."

Lou wore the T-shirt. She studied me. "Nothin' like home-made chicken soup for a messed up gut. It's puttin' color back to your cheeks, Mel."

I spooned another mouthful. "It's delicious; thanks for making it."

"You want me to call Fern Bubble, you said? Give her an update? Cool. I'm like your assistant. Like Festus for Marshall Dillon."

"On second thought, I'll speak to her."

"No way. You eat that soup."

I spooned while she dialed. A little voice in my head screamed that the convo would not go the way I wanted.

"Hiya Fern, how's the horses? You got one with a bellyache, I heard." Lou winked at me while listening to the response. Uh, oh. "I have one with tummy troubles here, too. Can I borrow your nose tube and mineral oil? Gonna pump her full of grease to pass things through."

Cousin Lou has a colorful way of looking at recuperation.

My Max and Lou's dogs lapped water in the kitchen. Then the pack spilled into the living room. They roughhoused, then piled in front of the fireplace in a heap of snoozing fur.

I watched the canines while Lou spoke into her phone. "Here's the scoop, Fern: Last night, after Mel starred in the play— yeah, she was great, a real Mae West, I heard. Huh? Don't know. I'll ask." She looked at me. "Fern wants to know if Tim and Oliver fought on stage. Guess they got into it in the tents afterward."

I shook my head. "No, they were okay, but—"

"She said nope, the show was mostly peaceful, haha. Except

for 'Mae West Mel's' sexy boot scoot, of course." I grabbed a pillow and held it up. "Just kiddin'. Mel isn't sexy. Hold on. She's aimin' a pillow at me."

"Let me talk to her," I said.

Lou ignored me and continued. "Mel showed up here lookin' like a puppy that scarfed the cat's Fancy Feast. Yeah, pretty bad. I made a batch of sick chicken noodle. Great for a gal with a bellyache. The recipe? Here it is...."

She described the ingredients. Fern had a podcast called Bubbles and Fiber, and Lou was a popular guest. Her recipes and colloquialisms kept viewers on the edge of their barstools.

"Fern, this soup is so good it'll knock your relations off their publics."

Lou giggled and stared at me. Then, "A parasite in Mel's gut? I could de-worm her, I guess."

I lifted another pillow. "Let me talk to her."

"Gotta hurry up. Mel's gonna bean me with pillows, and I'll be in concussion protocol." Lou relayed—finally—that a clown nose had been stuck on my windshield wiper. "Not a big deal. I've got a stash of noses—who doesn't? Life is way too serious otherwise. But this nose was soaked in something gross. I would not want to see the clown attached to it, that's for sure."

Fern and Lou concluded I'd been slipped a mickey that made me sick.

Then, Lou said, "Fern, I gotta get her ready for the bake-off tonight. Mel's a judge. Good thing she's got four stomachs like everyone in Wisconsin. My neighbor is an EMT. I'll have him come check her out." Lou scribbled in the air like she was writing. "Note all this in your red book, Fern."

She hung up but went mute, quite unlike her. As Lou describes herself, she's never the quietest mouse in the tack room.

She pondered the logs in the ceiling as though counting them. Then she looked at the snoozing canines, probably counting them, too, because she fosters. The numbers of her pack change on the regular.

Lou walloped a pillow. "Here's the thing, Mel. You thought Steven was the killer's target, not Kat. Why, though? Everybody loves him; he's the curd to this county's cheese."

"Right, but he's not himself. I suspect—"

"Hold your horses, Ellie Mae; I'm not done. The Tool & Rye crowd bet on Char Broadway. If anybody would break the law around here, it'd be her. The woman is a bronco without a cause."

True. Char had a reputation.

Lou continued, "But killing someone is a stretch, even for Calamity Char. So—is your seatbelt buckled, Melanie Tower?"

I looked down. I wore a bathrobe with cowgirls on it, and its belt was a long red bandana. Close enough. "Yes."

"Fern and I think the killer was—is—after you."

"Fern's gonna tell the detective you got drugged," Lou said. "And Inga knows you're not coming into the mall today. I told her you met a cowboy last night, and you two were on a rendezvous today."

She pronounced it "rondez-voose." She handed me a snowmobile suit, hat, and mittens. "We got eighty acres of trails and a pack of dogs to guard you. Take a long walk. The cold air will clear your head."

Before stepping outside, I made a phone call to Hank Leigel. He was out for the day, his assistant said. But he was available tomorrow, Thursday. We settled on a time and place to "rondez-voose."

Then I headed down the snowy path with the dogs.

After an hour of walking, I felt like my old self again.

"Old" as in I'd aged twenty years in a week. The dogs loved me, though, and treated me as one of their own.

I didn't mind. It's when humans treat me like a dog that I mind.

Who would give this Fido her premature due? Seek an early shuffle-off of her mortal collar?

The sun warmed my face. Walking the trails on Lou and Jason's property was like strolling a folklore painting. I saw stands of white pines and snow-dusted restored prairie. I passed vintage farm implements—old wagons, a wooden plow—decorated with wreaths and red bows.

Max raced about, leaving the other dogs in his wake. Border collies are the race cars of the dog world.

I pondered Lou's words, boots crunching the ground. Lou and I agreed on things about half the time, and the topic usually involved baked goods. Sometimes vacation spots. Never fashion choices.

As for Fern, it was more like eighty percent. When it came to social media, I stood down. She took the lead for my business's online presence.

Did I agree with the ladies' suspicions? Was I the target and not Kat Gold?

A villain could have slipped something into my drink at the library party. I'd sampled several cocktails. Didn't finish them. I'd also nibbled appetizers in the tents. All prepared by the Tool & Rye, the signs said.

I'd sipped coffee in the kitchen, but so did everyone else. Occam's razor said I picked up a twenty-four-hour bug after attending four days of events involving buffets and shared airspace.

My suspicion about the murder of Kat Gold still included Tim Gold, Susan Victory, and Char Broadway—and Kat was the target.

I stopped to watch Max zoom among his doggy friends. They appeared slow, almost standing in place, like decoys. The scene inspired an idea. If I were the killer's target, the obvious answer was to become bait, to make myself a decoy.

To see if he—or she—tried again.

Twenty —

f I were to be a decoy, it would be named "Gold," as in gold, frankincense, and myrrh. I was a walk-on as a wise person in the nativity play, according to Lou.

I wore a glittery tunic and boots.

Lou looked me over. "You're a judge for the bake-off at the church. Before the contest, you're on stage. Want to wear a clown nose? Takes your Cleopatra vibe in a different direction."

I grimaced and looked for another pillow to toss. I looked like a desert sunset. "Steven is Frankincense? Who's Myrrh?"

"No idea. Jason will drive you in. I'm bringing ya home. My bake-off entries are ready—"

I held up a hand. "Don't tell me. Bake-off submissions are anonymous."

"You'll never guess mine."

"I bet I won't."

Total fib. Lou's entries will be the only ones with a Western theme. I'll judge them fair and square, like the others.

Lou rubbed my shoulders as though I was a prizefighter.

The stiff fabric of the tunic crinkled like foil. "You gonna be okay, champ? You've got the bake-off tonight, the community literature awards on Thursday, and then the Fish Fry Gala on Friday. You good with all that?"

"My royal duties end with Snowthanks on Saturday, right? Nothing after that—no surprises?"

My cousin widened her eyes and played dumb. "When have I surprised you with anything?"

Good thing I was a royal. We maintain composure at all times. Otherwise, there wouldn't have been enough pillows in Cleopatra's palace....

And so, it came to pass that I stood in the wings of the stage, about to step on, looking like a shiny french fry.

Steven looked resplendent as Frankincense. He wore a velvet jacket with crisscrossing white stripes and a fur hat. He looked like a cross between a Canadian Mountie and Santa.

And who was Myrrh, our third walk-on guest?

None other than Crystal Broadway.

She wore a luscious green robe with giant emerald stones. Even though the character she represented was embalming fluid, she embraced the role without complaint. While I stood there, pressed against the wall in the dark, I felt a vibe between Crystal and Steven.

It could have been stage jitters. I hoped they'd resolved the argument I'd witnessed in the library parking lot. As ill as I was, that moment had happened. I'd had no private time to speak with Crystal about her behavior on the night of the Cheese Ball and why she'd disappeared.

The backstage area was jammed with little ones costumed as

lambs, camels, donkeys, angels, and shepherds. Adorable. I don't have children, but I'd consider renting one if it came in costume.

The director gave us directions: "No cell phones, parents. Stand quietly, everyone. Wise men, wait for your cue."

Steven, Crystal, and I looked at each other.

It was quite a cue, believe me.

The director pointed at us, then gave a thumbs up. I walked out first. Steven and Crystal followed. One by one, we offered gifts to our Savior, then stepped to the back of the stage, our backs to the tall flats that depicted the night sky and a single, brilliant star.

There was a herald of trumpets from the orchestra pit. Fluffy cotton angels that looked suspiciously like the pretend sheep that soared over for every Mother's Day pageant flew above on wires.

For a second, I was reminded of a fellow who flew for a living. I hadn't heard from the pilot. No calls, nothing—Steven yelled, "Get down, everybody! Now!"

He grabbed me, then Crystal, and yanked us to the floor. I collapsed to my knees.

"Ouch!"

"Watch out!" Steven cried.

I felt a rush of air, then CRASH!

Darkness—a heavy flat fell. Others avalanched, wobbling and tipping.

"Stay down!" the director yelled from the wings. "Curtain!"

None of the children were hurt, thank God.

The flats were heavy but only painted canvas with wood

frames. The one over the wise peoples' heads landed on the pointy tip of the stable, so it hung there like a rectangular kite. The adults on stage caught the others, who held them aloft while the tykes crawled toward their parents.

The children giggled and acted as though it was an adventure. The mayor, who played Joseph, kept things light, joking that his name for next year's Mayor's Race should be "Falling Flat."

The set was recombobulated. The director addressed the audience: "Let this be a reminder of Psalm 46: Even though the earth gives way and mountains fall into the sea, we shall not fear. God is our ever-present help in trouble."

We finished the show, and the adults and children took bows. The wise people got a big cheer because we were closest to the debacle.

After we'd stepped offstage, the director asked, "Nice job. Any one of you need to see the school nurse?"

"We're fine," I said. "What caused the flats to go down?"

"Someone must have gotten in the space between the wall and the set. It could have been a crew member operating the wires for the angels. I don't know yet."

"Anybody else have access to it?"

"No, it's off-limits. See?"

He pointed to the back of the stage. I saw a heavy curtain, a cement block wall, and a gap between them. A sign said entry was forbidden, but there was no barrier.

Saints would obey, but not sinners.

Who sabotaged the set?

"C'mon, Mel," Steven said. "We've got a contest to judge."

The theme for this year's bake-off was angels versus devils. Contestants entered a light-flavored treat or something heavy, even sinfully rich. All entries must be named after a biblical or literary character.

The bakers' creative names of the desserts were part of the fun. And the charming cherubs who'd been on stage helped deliver treats to the judges.

We sat at a table in a Sunday school classroom. Aside from the soup earlier in the day, I'd eaten nothing. I felt safe sampling the entries. Cousin Lou was on duty in the kitchen, watching what was entered—and by whom.

She and a grinning lamb approached. Lou whispered in the lamb's ear. Then, "Daisy Buchanan Lemon Cupcakes!" the tiny gal trumpeted.

"I loved that novel," Crystal said.

"Daisy was a beautiful but unconscionable fool," Steven replied.

Huh?

The last book I saw Steven reading was *Catcher in the Wry*. And that's not a misspelling. Bob Uecker, a hilarious catcher for the Milwaukee Brewers, wrote it. Steven enjoyed sports biographies—but paraphrasing *The Great Gatsby*?

Knock me over with one of Lou's pillows.

Steven sampled the cakes. "Too sour for me."

"These are on the angel side of the entry form," Crystal said. "But that could be challenged, like, because of Daisy's materialistic character."

"Agreed," Steven said. "They shouldn't make the final group."

We marked our cards while another plate arrived. Lou announced, "All the Devils are Here Fruitcake. You guys okay with scorecards? Need any more?"

"We're good, thanks," I said.

Crystal was the first to sample the cake. "Decent flavor. But, like, dry."

"Not enough fruit," Steven added.

I gave Crystal credit. She had a discerning palate. And I was impressed by her literary knowledge and applying it to the desserts.

She clearly adored Steven. Who didn't? I felt relieved to see them get along. The tense posture I witnessed the previous evening had disappeared.

Between sips of water, we sampled Maya Angel-Food Cake, Moses' Sea-Foam Candy (red, of course), and Calamity Jane Chocolate Musket Pretzels with Texas Salt.

Cousin Lou made herself scarce when those appeared at our table.

Pyramus and Thisbe Cookies followed—chili-chocolate cookies so spicy they set our tongues on fire. "Anybody else want a glass of milk?" I asked.

Steven nodded vigorously. Crystal said, "Like, OMG, yes!"

I signaled for a timeout and headed to the kitchen. Lou was washing dishes. "What do ya need, Mel?"

"Three glasses of milk, please."

"Comin' right up."

I glanced at the hallway. No one was around. "Have you learned what caused the accident on stage?"

"Not yet. But you can bet your royal patoot I'll find out."

I watched Lou pour milk into glasses. "Did you see Char Broadway tonight?"

"Yeah, she was here. Tried to enter Char's Brownies. I told her they looked delicious, but she had to rename 'em. Gave suggestions: The Good, the Bad, and the Brownie. True Gritty Brownies. Anything other than her own name."

"When was this?"

"When you were on stage. Wow, that woman is stubborn.

She's part human, part wheel chock. She took her treats and left." Lou snapped her fingers. "Hey, if she was with me, she couldn't have been the person who kicked the flats down like a circus mule."

Correct.

Plus, Char would never have tipped the flat on her own daughter.

I walked back to the classroom with the milk on a tray, pondering who could have done it. I felt more comfortable around Crystal, knowing that her mother wasn't trying to kill me. Or Steven, if he was the target.

Char still may want to run my business into the ground. So what? I could compete with that.

It was the murder part that complicated things.

In the classroom, I handed glasses to Crystal and Steven. "Milk cocktails for everyone."

"Fantastic," Steven said.

Crystal looked toward the door. "Looks like the final desserts are coming in."

An angel delivered Noah's Art Cupcakes, treats with stunning animal decorations. "This could be our winner," Steven said.

Points were awarded, and we moved on to two chocolate desserts: Wormwood's Junior Tempter Truffles and River Styx Cake, a luscious chocolate sponge cake with a liquid-fudge center.

But in the end, it was a neck-and-neck finish between the Noah cupcakes and George Plimpton Paper Lion cut-outs.

My vote was the tiebreaker, and it went to the cookies. They were excellent. The recipe must have had sour cream in it, and the sugar frosting was a perfect complement to the tangy cookies.

Their shapes were works of art, too, with lions in magnificent poses.

All three of us adored the book *Paper Lion*. I was shocked that Crystal and Steven knew about the author's hilarious stint as an NFL quarterback.

We recorded the results, but then Lou entered the room with a pan of brownies. "Too late," Crystal said. "We, like, picked the winner."

"First prize is declared. I'm not eating dessert for a decade," Steven added.

Lou stepped straight to me. "Someone dropped these off in the kitchen when I was out for two seconds. Entry card says they're Rudolph's Red-Nosed Brownies."

A pan of brownies isn't usually a cause for concern.

Steven and Crystal left after I assured them it was a late entry. I stopped Lou from talking about the brownies until we entered the kitchen.

She stared at the pan on the counter. "Want me to call the police on 'em?"

"Which one of the young guys, Linus or Luce, is on tonight?"

"Not sure. But we can have one stop over and take a bite. See if there's somethin' screwy with 'em."

"We can't put an officer at risk like that."

"Okay, then we'll just tell him to tase 'em."

"What was written on this pan's entry card?"

"Just the name of the treats. No other info. Totally weird."

I bent over and sniffed, checking the brownies for a strange scent like burned almonds. Nothing unusual. Just chocolate and cherries. I did smell a metallic note, probably from the canned fruit. "There won't be fingerprints to use from the pan. We all handled it. And nothing dangerous is in them. This person doesn't want to hurt people at a church event."

"Yeah, probably wanted to freak ya out. Put a burr in your sock."

"I want to look around the stage."

"Lemme get the key. Auditorium is locked."

Lou pulled out a keyring the size of a watermelon.

I asked, "What place in town don't you have keys to?"

"When you volunteer a lot, you get lotsa keys."

Good news. If I needed to get in anywhere to investigate further, I could borrow a key. And it wouldn't be breaking and entering because I'd used a key.

That made it half-legal, right?

"Mel, change your clothes before we go wanderin' through the place," Lou ordered. "You're bright as a marquee. I wish you'd stop dressin' like a show pony."

She jumped back before I could strangle her.

Out of a gym bag, she pulled black leggings and a sweatshirt with motorcycles pulling a sleigh. It read, "Save a reindeer, ride a Harley."

She gave me the outfit. I changed, and then we trekked the hallways of the church.

I wandered the stage.

Lou stood in the wings. "Mel, have you talked to Steven about this? You still think some rascal could be after him?"

"No, and yes."

"You guys used to eat at the Tool & Rye. I haven't seen ya."

"We're both busy."

"How 'bout Rand? The bake-off was the one event he used to come to. Where's he tonight?"

I was hoping she'd forgotten that. "He's flying."

"Remember that time you guys entered the contest? Theme was chili that year. 'Wind Shear Chili' blew the judges right outta their seats."

I remembered. I smiled. "Maybe next time."

"No offense, Mel, but you two aren't meant to be. Rand likes to travel. You're the opposite. He's milk; you're vinegar."

"That makes buttermilk. It's not so bad."

"But he wants to fly into the wild blue yonder. You stay home. Sorry, but you're barn sour."

"Still on the sour theme, I see."

"You know I love ya. Just bein' honest."

I could have said the outfits she dressed me in didn't magically transform me into an extrovert, but I didn't want to get tased. Or have a six-shooter aimed at my feet.

She pointed to the flats. "The kids painted those. A teacher sketched the outline, then the students painted 'em."

I touched one of them. Thick canvas stretched over a wooden frame, triangle brackets at the base. They weren't tethered to the wall. Easy to tip if someone snuck behind them. The curtains would cloak whoever did it.

"Know what I think?" Lou said. "That sidewinder was sending you another message. Just like the red nose on the car and the brownies. He or she wants to scare ya."

"Could it have been the director? Maybe he crossed behind during the performance, knocked them, and didn't want to admit it."

"The guy is a pastor, Mel. You lived in a big city too long."

That was true. But thou shalt make a living. "I have a friend who acted in community theater. She said stage mishaps were common. It could have been a fluke."

Lou shook her head. "Nope. Add it up: A is for an accident on stage. B is for brownies. C is for Kat, who got pinned to death.

It equals somethin' spooky. Whatever's happenin' goes against what this place stands for. We can't let evil win."

My thoughts exactly. Though if I were to add something, I'd use numerals. And spell Kat's name correctly.

That's beside the point.

For once, my cousin and I were on the same script.

Twenty-One —

Dateline: Thursday morning, The L&J Ranch, Cinnamon Township, Wisconsin.

Conditions: Hurricane. Due to volatile moods, breakfasters should avoid Lou's kitchen.

Long story short: Via the Tool & Rye hotline, Lou got wind of Char Broadway's threat to get a restraining order against me.

I sat at the kitchen counter, listening to Lou fume.

"Whoever smelt it, dealt it! Char needs the restraining order. She pesters everybody." Lou threw up her hands. "I'm gonna throw a barbecue for you, Mel, and invite everybody except Char. I'll even invite Tim Gold and Eden Hoff. Char will drop that order faster than a politician holdin' a Bible." Lou paced her kitchen. "She'll die to show up."

Poor choice of words.

I wasn't going to mention it. Lou waved a cast iron pan in the air while she raved.

I attempted to calm the Tasmanian devil standing at the

sink. "It's nonsense, Lou. Let me handle it. Char is all bark and no bite."

"She's all frosted-tip hair and no brains. And I was nice to her last night. Maybe Char put that nose on your car and made those brownies because she's mad at you. Think about that?"

She slammed the pan onto the stove and stomped to the fridge. She yanked open the door with the power of a tow truck.

Jason built the place sturdy for a reason.

"Whaddya want for breakfast? I can make a lumberjack omelette. Or belly-buster ham 'n eggs. How 'bout it?"

"Just coffee and a hard-boiled egg."

"That's not enough—"

"I ate desserts for three hours last night, Lou. Cut me and I'll bleed frosting."

She relented after I promised to eat a big lunch.

Then Jason walked in.

A kitchen hath no fury like my cousin scorned. While questioning her husband about Steven, Lou stayed calm. But it was eye-of-a-hurricane calm.

Lou asked Jason if he knew what was happening with Steven—why he'd been secretive. (I'd wanted to inquire, too, but it wasn't my place to ask. I figured if Jason had an important revelation about his friend, he would come to his favorite relative on his own.)

"Where'd you last see or talk to Steven?" Lou asked.

"I didn't say I did," Jason replied, eye twitching. "I see him at bowling every Thursday. So do you, Lou."

He looked out the floor-to-ceiling windows that faced the backyard. The view was stunning. A hill sloped to a stand of white pines. Jason appeared to search for something, like he wanted Bigfoot to emerge from the trees to distract his wife from the line of questioning.

"What's. Goin'. On," Lou asked.

Not a question. She stared, pupils enlarged. One by one, the dogs arose from their slumber party in front of the fireplace. They padded about, panting and darting their eyes at one another.

Note: To read a room, watch how the animals behave in it.

"Don't gossip about this," Jason said. "It's not our business. Steven is a friend. Who he spends time with isn't for us to judge."

Lou gasped. "Is he seein' a Chicago Bears fan?"

Jason looked at me. "I hope this doesn't hurt your feelings, Mel. But I think Steven has a girlfriend."

The problem with quashing rumors is that if one protests too much, it has the opposite effect.

I shook my head. "Steven and I have never been more than friends. I'm in a relationship. End of story."

Lou looked at Jason. "You wanna tell her, or should I?"

"I'll do it—" he said.

"Hold on," I interrupted. "He and I became friends as soon as I moved back. I was remodeling a building. I needed one of everything; he delivered it. We have been just friends ever since."

"We know," Jason said. "And he's never really dated anyone since breaking up with his high school sweetheart. He's been like you, focused on making a living. He bought himself a nice house with a few acres. He's done good."

"But they're both a couple of workaholics," Lou interjected. "You see, Mel, that's why it would never go with Steven. It's okay that he's got someone. As long as she's not from Illinois."

"But I've never had a thing with Steven!"

Oops. I protested too much. Max came over and put his head

on my lap. I was sitting on a kitchen barstool, wishing I was in a real bar, away from people who thought I had a crush on my favorite deliveryman. "He and I are just friends. That's all we'll ever be."

"Sure, Mel," Lou said. "Lots of people have been sweet on each other, but nothin' ever happens, nor should it. But Jason, who's the gal? Pray to the ghost of Vince Lombardi that she's not from Illinois."

"It's Crystal Broadway. I think they're dating."

Lou stiff-armed us out the door. She loaded Jason down like a pack mule with food containers for his construction crew. I refused food but accepted the animal-print tracksuit she offered.

"I'll stop at my place and pick up some clothes," I said.

She shook her head. "There's plenty more where that suit came from. Do not go into your place alone. That nut with the brownies and red noses is still out there. You feelin' okay about Steven?"

I nodded. "If he's happy, I'm happy."

"Door's open if you want to talk. Couch, fireplace, cold Leinie's. You and the pilot okay? Still content in your dysfunction?"

"It's fine, Lou."

"I talked to Inga. Told her you'd be into your office later. Don't forget you got the Cinnamon Cinnies Awards tonight. You're their show pony; you gotta hand out the prizes. I'll bring your outfit by the mall. It's a doozy."

"How many more of these events?"

"Fish Fry Gala on Friday, then Snowthanks all day Saturday into Sunday. It's a twenty-four-hour shop-a-thon where all the bucks raised go to the food pantry. Sorry that you and Steven get most of the events. You guys are the youngest royals. The other ones do the day stuff because they don't drive in the dark."

"No problem," I said.

I told her I was driving into town. But as soon as I got out of sight, I took the road toward Lake Cinn.

The news about Steven didn't surprise me. I'd noticed a vibe between him and Crystal. I felt hurt he didn't confide in me about it, though.

How long the gossip stayed off the Tool & Rye hotline was anyone's guess. I adored the T&R and felt cinnamon roll withdrawal. But the idea of stopping in to be questioned about Kat Gold and my mall wasn't just off the table; the thought had fallen into a dark abyss.

Speaking of, I drove past the lake. Same frothy cauldron of doom, different day. I cruised by Tim Gold's place. Saw a generic sedan with out-of-state plates parked in the drive. Must be Eden's rental car. She either was staying with him or had shown up for a meeting.

Tim had said she was fired from her editor's job. But I'd heard a rumor from a model friend months ago that Eden had retired.

Did it matter which was true?

Not to me. My relationship with Eden had been all business. She'd booked me for jobs, treating me as another anonymous mannequin in her magazine's casting office. She'd always commented on my "commercial" look, saying I appeared too Midwestern.

Did I care? Nope.

A booking was a booking. If I was in the background of an advertisement or editorial, it never mattered. I did my job and got a check. Saved most of what I earned and now call the shots in my life.

I paid the price living in that detached emotional state. People like Eden had a lot to do with it. The good news is that I was emerging from the cocoon. But I'm involved in a plot twist I didn't see coming.

I smiled despite my apprehension.

The thought of Eden Hoff, a New York fashion maven, driving herself around the snowy Wisconsin countryside was beyond what I considered possible. "Does she even have a license?" I pondered aloud, watching the red-brick home get smaller in the rearview mirror. "How does she navigate? An assistant drives her, I bet."

Not my problem. Eden's predicament wasn't my photo shoot, not my flashbulbs. Or, as Lou would say, "Not my rodeo, not my clowns."

I followed the route around the lake, then continued toward Lily's Pond, the idyllic spot where Susan Victory lived.

I needed to speak with my friend.

Something told me Susan was involved in this mess.

"Oh—Mel? I wasn't expecting you!" Susan exclaimed.

I should say not. I tapped on the front door, and she opened it. She looked like Jessica Rabbit—sassy short hair, bright lipstick, clingy dress. "Susan? Wow, you look amazing."

"What time is it?" she asked.

"Time for you to confess. Who were you waiting for?"

She blushed, making her green eyes appear even brighter. "Come on in, Mel. Let's have a martini."

She stepped back, and I walked inside.

Susan didn't mix martinis. More like mar-TON-ees.

I watched her pour an alarming amount of booze into a glass pitcher and asked for a mini version. "Just a sip for me. I judged the bake-off last night. I'm still light-headed."

She sloshed a glass for herself, then waved toward a white china cabinet. "Pick whatever size glass you like. My bar is self-serve."

I paused to admire the cabinet; I'd always loved it. Susan had found a neglected hulk in a barn, hauled it home courtesy of Steven's delivery services, and then transformed the piece into a charming serving station.

She'd painted it, added mirrors to the back, and new glass to the front.

I stared at it. "Is this cabinet for sale, Susan?"

"Sure, of course. Everything, hic, in this place is for sale."

"It's time I updated my house. Decorate a little. This would fit in, I think."

She nearly fainted when I said that, but I blamed the booze.

✳

We sat in silence for a few minutes. Susan sipped her drink and checked her phone. I enjoyed the view. We were on the back porch, fire blazing, view amazing.

If I had a lake house, it would be like Susan's. A little cottage looking over a pond. Just big enough for me, Max, and an old cat. A charming veranda to entertain a few friends, too.

"In case you were wondering, I was not expecting Hank," Susan admitted.

"Do you want to chat about it?"

"Not really. The mystery man isn't coming, in any case."

"What can I do for you?"

She stood up. "I'm freezing. I need to change clothes. Then you can listen to what I have to say, hic, about Kat Gold."

I made a pot of coffee while Susan changed.

I carried the tray with the coffee, sugar, and creamer to the porch. I even added a bud vase with a red geranium from the bouquet on the kitchen counter.

Hospitality Mel was replacing austere Mel, and I liked it.

Susan returned wearing a cheetah-print tracksuit with a turquoise side stripe. "I thought we could twin. That's quite an outfit you're wearing."

I smiled, relieved to see her less stressed. "Coffee?"

"No, thanks." She raised her glass. "I'll dance with the one who brought me—unlike some people."

"I'm here to listen if you want to talk about him."

"Not today, but I do have a few things to say about Ms. Gold. She and I may not have gotten along, but we weren't enemies."

I poured myself a coffee. "You've never been the type to have enemies, Susan."

"Thank you for saying that." She glugged her martini. "I haven't been, that's true. It's why I asked Kat to have drinks with me at the yacht club a few times. I wanted to get to know her."

"That was kind of you."

"But she just kept rubbing it in my face, acting like she owned the guy, you know?"

Her statement ricocheted around the porch like a bullet. I watched Susan's features cloud over, reflecting the frustration she must have felt. "No one owns another person," I said. "You're smarter than that. I'm surprised you let it get to you."

"When she backed into my car that night and refused to acknowledge it, that was it. I was done with her."

"What does that mean? What did you do?"

"Tried to get her to admit it. She wouldn't, so I had it fixed. Never spoke to her again except when I saw her at the mall. You asked if I'd talk to her about selling jewelry. I helped her out of respect for you, but that was all."

I softly asked, "Do you know anyone who'd want to hurt her?"

"No."

I waited for her to say more, but she stood up and announced she wanted another martini.

I suggested a nap.

Susan agreed, fortunately, and I walked her into the bedroom, tucking her under a magnificent poinsettia quilt. I left for the kitchen, then returned. "Here's a glass of water and two aspirin."

She reached for the pills. "I didn't kill Kat, Mel. I swear on a stack of, hic, stuffed olives."

I smiled. "I believe you, my friend. But maybe you have information about who did?"

"No, I do not."

"Promise you won't drive today, okay? If you're coming to the awards tonight, call someone. Call me. Or Lou. Or Hank, even. He'll come get you if you need a ride."

"I don't know how I feel about Hank right now. But I won't drive, I promise. And the china cabinet is yours. Tell Steven to pick it up."

"Name your price, and I'll write a check."

"It won't be much, Mel. You've been wonderful to me."

I let myself out, making sure the front door was locked.

As I walked to my car, my phone pinged with a text from Hank.

Twenty-Two —

Hank asked me to meet him at a vacant building in town. I arrived before he did.

The place had a neglected appearance and gave an odd vibe. I stood alone, my back to the alley, squinting through the door's dirty glass into the space.

"Lady Mel, what are you doing here?"

"Oh—Oliver! You scared me. I'm waiting for Hank."

"What man would ask to meet you in an isolated spot? Is he not aware there's a miscreant on the loose?"

I looked up and down the alley. "It's one o'clock in the afternoon, Oliver. It's downtown Cinnamon. Shoppers are everywhere." I pointed to a group of ladies walking toward a car parked in the alley. "I think I'm safe."

"I shall stand with you until Attorney Leigel arrives, nonetheless."

We waited on the stoop, the November air breezy and sharp. It reminded me of the day Kat was killed. I shivered, and Oliver noticed. "Are you cold, Melanie? Would you like my jacket?"

"I'm f-fine, thanks. Hank's coming this way."

His office was only a few doors down, and he strolled up, jingling keys. "Mel, Oliver, nice to see you."

"Good afternoon, Mr. Leigel. I was passing through on my way to the library and spied this lady unaccompanied. I shall leave her in your capable hands. Good day, sir."

"Same to you, Oliver." Hank smiled at me. "Let's step inside, shall we, Mel?"

"Sure. I'd like to see the place."

I followed Hank inside. "Forgive the mess," he said. "It's been vacant for a while. I was pleased to get your inquiry about it."

He gave me the ten-cent tour, which lasted about nine minutes. "It's two stories. I've got an apartment upstairs with a long-term renter. This shop used to be the village hardware store. Still has the old shelves and original fixtures. I had a watch repair fellow in here, but he passed. I haven't done anything with the place since."

I examined the brick walls and touched the ancient counter with its glass case. I imagined containers of nails, screws, and shiny hinges inside. I smiled. "This was pre-big box era, clearly."

"So much local history in these walls. I think the place is as old as your mall."

"It will take a lot to rehab this. And, no offense, but do I smell a plumbing problem?"

"It's been closed up for a long time. It might."

I wandered, touching the rough brick, walking the floors that creaked with character. The shop wasn't large. But book-stores didn't need to be; the place was big enough for shelves, a fireplace, and a comfy reading spot for children's story hour.

Also, it needed a goodie shelf at dog's-eye level so Max and his friends could enjoy it.

I'd walked by the building a thousand times and meant to ask Hank about its availability. But I'd been busy with my mall.

No time like the present, as they say, even if a murderer was on the loose and I was a suspect in the saga. Timing was everything. "Is anyone else interested?"

"Ironically, I got a call from another party about it today. That's why I wanted to meet with you first. You and Sunny Days Restorations did a wonderful job with the mall. I hope you find this building suitable for another rehab project."

I looked at him and nodded. The place needed a lot of work. The village didn't have a bookstore, though, and I had a great relationship with Kevin and his crew.

I extended my hand toward the attorney. "Hank, I think we have ourselves a deal."

Hank needed paperwork from his office. "Be right back," he said.

While he was gone, I toured my new building. I loved it and was dedicated to bringing Ye Olde Bookshoppe to the village.

I was disappointed that I didn't act sooner, however.

It wasn't rocket science; there was only one vacant store in town. If there were to be a competitor to my mall, where would it be located?

Right where I stood.

I hadn't deduced the idea until two days ago. And thank goodness my competitors were of the big-picture mindset rather than worker-bee. Tim Gold was a talker. Eden Hoff was a delegator. Char Broadway, to use my cousin's vernacular, was all hat and no cattle. She wasn't the person to rely on for management responsibilities.

None of them acted on securing a physical location for their store. Or agency. Whatever it was they were creating.

Kat Gold may have been the person to do the legwork, but she was gone.

Hank returned with a stack of papers. We negotiated a bit, and he agreed to my terms. I signed on the dotted line and wrote an earnest money check.

"I'll get a building inspector through and a date for the closing," he said. "I know you'll preserve the integrity of this place and create something outstanding for the village."

"I appreciate that vote of confidence—"

The sound of fists pounding on the front window cut off my words. "Hey, let us in!"

I looked to see faces peering through the glass.

Tim, Eden, and Char had arrived to talk business, it seemed.

Tim Gold walked through the space holding up his hands. He resembled a movie director envisioning a scene. "Put a row of cubicles here. And maybe a foosball table in the front window? Gives the agency a chill vibe."

Eden brought along an assistant named Swan. He was a tall fellow with fiery green eyes and the bone structure of a Greek temple. He was such a perfect human specimen I wasn't sure if he was real or CGI when I first saw him.

Eden patted his arm while speaking to him. "Swan, see if you can reason with the seller. Find his price. After that, I'd like a mind-cleanse tea from that bakery down the street."

Tim Gold dropped his hands. "There's a limit to the budget, but we can top whatever the offer currently is—"

"What about my crafters?" Char whined. "Where will they go?"

"That's Phase Two of our vision," Tim said. "We'll put up a metal building on the outskirts of town. Bigger space and more parking access."

The scene was surreal, difficult to describe. It was like talking with Huey, Dewey, Screwy, and an onyx statue.

Tim attempted to "sell" me on the agency idea. "We're gonna scale this so fast, Mel. You're missing out on the ground-floor chance to make a killing. Let's go in together on this place, capisce?"

I shook my head. "No, thanks—"

"I'm getting a restraining order against you, Mel," Char interrupted. "And against Hank!"

Hank remained calm. He held the keys, after all. He attempted to calm the cowpokes whose cattle had been rustled. "Now, folks, let's be reasonable about this. Mr. Gold, if it's a business rental that you're after, I can help you find it, just not in this town. And Ms. Hoff and Mr. Swan, I'll buy you tea and blueberry scones. Ms. Broadway, don't you and I have a meeting about your rental on the lake?"

Tim reddened, Eden had blue circles below her eyes, and Char turned white. Standing shoulder to shoulder, they gazed forlornly at me as though I'd doused them with a hose.

In my defense, I said, "The place has plumbing problems, so there's that. Be glad you don't have to deal with it."

Hank turned to me. "Mel, you and I have things to discuss. Folks, please excuse us."

Upon buying the building, I made enemies, unfortunately.

From this point forward, Tim and Eden wouldn't be members

of my fan club. Char didn't qualify as an enemy; she was merely a pest. Swan wouldn't have an opinion. He was a detached deity observing silly mortals from a seat on Olympus.

After they'd left, Hank locked the front door and handed me a key. "Come and go as you please, Mel. I'm sorry I ignored this place. Things have been busy for me professionally and personally."

"I saw Susan earlier," I replied.

"How was she?"

"Under the weather. I put her to bed with two aspirin."

He shook his head. "We've been having troubles lately, sad to say."

"Anything I can do?"

"Just be her friend. We had many happy years together. It'll take time and counseling to work it out if she's willing."

"I'll put in a good word for you, Hank."

"Thank you, Mel." He looked at his watch. "It's almost four o'clock. Need me to walk you back to your mall?"

"I'm fine. It's only two blocks."

"Don't talk to strangers. As Oliver Roberts said, there's still a miscreant on the loose."

Twenty-Three —

Presenting myself as bait means I must be catchy, right? Bah dum bump.

In my upstairs bedroom, I stared in the mirror. Where does Lou get these outfits? The rodeo queen outlet?

Earlier, she'd dropped off a bronze-colored gown and a turquoise bandana. I looked like a glitzy, Western cinnamon stick.

My cousin ordered me not to return to my house, but I wandered from my office through the backyard anyway.

No worries about miscreants hiding in the bushes because I carried weapons of self-defense—a bottle of pepper spray and a gold bowling ball.

I'd had the spray. Lou gave me the ball. She constantly encouraged me to join her team, The Bowlin' Girls. (It sounds like The Golden Girls if you say it fast. Yes, their shirts, shoes, and balls are amber-colored.)

Lou claimed to have found a stray ball at a shelter that was my perfect finger size, and it needed a home.

To her amazement, I'd accepted it. "I'm not embracing my inner bowler yet," I'd told her, adding that I was exploring home decor and would display it as a conversation piece.

I packed a duffel with jeans and black cashmere sweaters. All vintage. When living in New York, I'd scooped up beautiful pieces on consignment before resale was a thing. I hadn't purchased new clothes in years.

That frugality was why I could invest in a new property. But the austere life also made me an emotional lone wolf. I'd isolated myself and worked too hard in a creative industry that, ironically, sought none from me, just a blank expression and a mannequin body shape.

I shook my head—that was a lot to unpack at five-thirty on a Thursday afternoon. What in the Eden Hoff was happening to me? Easy answer. Encountering the editor who'd been partly responsible for my reclusiveness triggered buried feelings.

I zipped the bag and stuck my fingers in the ball, carrying both down the steps. I placed the ball near the fireplace. Abstract living room art, maybe?

After pulling a shawl from the hall closet, I locked up and walked to the mall, duffel and pepper spray in hand.

Inga Honeythorne popped her head into my office. "I'm locking the place. Would you like me to close the shades?"

I looked out the window overlooking High Street. My office bulbs were slightly dimmed, so I could see the twinkly streetlamps and shoppers still wandering. "No, I'll do it before I leave."

"You're sure? People can see you." She gazed at my outfit. "They may think the awards are taking place at the mall and try to get in."

I laughed. "I'm leaving shortly, too. Are you going?"

"Yes, I'm up for a Sprinkle Award. So is Susan Victory. We've been artists so long they want to give us recognition, I think."

"Wow, lifetime achievement. Good for you."

"Thanks, dear. I'll see you at the Legion Hall. You're the only one in here; keep your phone handy."

She blew a kiss, then turned, her clogs echoing on the plank floor. The footsteps stopped after a few seconds. I heard the fire door slam.

The invitation to the party was on my desk. The Cinnamon Cinnies was sponsored by Wooly's paper, *The Cinnamon Roll*. It and the area's "foreign press," which included the regional shopper, a county tourism guide, and Lake Cinnamon's newsletter, *The Shore Line*, selected local winners in literature and arts.

I always donated. Many of my vendors were nominees. In the past, I'd purchased a table. Steven and I attended, along with a group from the mall. He was everyone's date on those evenings.

The Thompson twins adored him as much as I did.

I admit that when Steven and I met five years ago, when I was ordering one of everything, I sensed a vibe between us. Neither of us acted on it.

Okay, full confession: He delivered a dozen roses to my place after I'd been living here for a few months. He hadn't known about Rand, so I told him.

At that time, Steven said if we ever broke up, he'd like a chance.

I caught up on mall business and placed a call to Kevin Sunny about my new building project. He didn't answer. I left a message. The entire time I worked, the blinds were open, lights on.

Ne'er-do-well, be warned: This girl wasn't a sparkly rust-colored sitting duck—far from it. A quick tour through the first floor resulted in an arsenal of makeshift weapons for my office.

Near my desk were a hand-painted flowerpot, a giant whiskey bottle, and an iron skillet (learned that one from Lou). Granny from *The Beverly Hillbillies* couldn't have armed herself any better.

Those weapons would remain until further notice.

At about seven o'clock, I closed the blinds, shut everything off, and locked up. Pepper spray in hand, I exited the same route as Inga had earlier. Hung a right. Straight shot to the fire door leading to the storage area.

I put my hand on the door—it came toward me.

Who was coming in?

I backed up. "Who's there? Stop—I'll shoot."

"No—"

"Stop!"

Fern poked her head around the door, holding papers in front of her face. "It's me!"

"Fern? What the—"

"I'm d-dropping off the Snowthanks flyers."

I opened the door and stepped back. "Sorry—"

Fern patted her chest. "You ... scared me."

"A killer's on the loose. You shouldn't be coming here alone, after-hours."

"I-I can't breathe—"

"Fern, Fern! Are you okay?"

Fern had a mini asthma attack. I flipped on the lights, then parked her in the storage area. She dabbed her nose with a tissue. I retrieved water from the mini-fridge.

She sipped, then looked around. "Where am I?"

I felt her forehead. "What year is it? Who's the president?"

"It's 1994, and the person in the White House is a clown."

She was fine.

Fern looked around at the storage space. "Did Kevin do this?"

"Yes, it needed a refresh after what happened to Kat."

"G-good idea."

"Breathe deep."

After a minute of inhale-exhale, she reached into her briefcase and pulled out her red notebook. "Have Inga put the Snowthanks flyers around the building. And I have reminders for you."

We didn't have much time, so she kept it quick, giving a rundown of ideas for future social media posts.

When she finished, I asked, "What do you think about establishing a high school scholarship in Kat's name? Have students develop a creative brief about positive social media. You and Wooly could be judges. I'll talk to him about announcing the winner at the Cinnies every year."

"I love it!" She jotted it down. "I have personal opinions, but they don't appear online. And I've dealt with my share of bullies. We'll call it the Lemon Sunny Award."

I smiled. Other prizes were the Funfetti and the Mixed Nut, so her idea fit right in. "Glad you like it. Need a ride over?"

"No, I'm only staying for a bit. Take some photos, and then I've got posts to create. Wooly just emailed me the list of winners." She winked. "You're in for an unexpected treat."

I hustled back to my office to retrieve my crown and sash. I'd forgotten about them until Fern reminded me.

She said the law enforcement fellow had returned.

"Rats. I was hoping the lieutenant had other things to do besides tail me."

She shook her head. "Oh, I don't know where Lt. DuWayne is; I haven't heard from him."

"You told me he was out of town."

"Who?"

"Bruce DuWayne."

She stared at me. "No, I didn't."

Perhaps Fern was not fine, and the shock of our door encounter affected her memory. I pulled out my phone, then read her text from Tuesday night. "You wrote: 'The law enforcement fellow is out of town.'"

"No, I was talking about the other guy—the handsome sheriff I'm setting you up with."

"Not now, Fern."

"But—"

"I've got an awards show to attend. I'm their Carol Merrill, and the show can't go on without me."

Twenty-Four —

posed on stage, trophies topped with brass cinnamon rolls within arm's reach. Wooly stood at a podium near me, announcing winners.

The audience numbered about one hundred fifty, give or take. It included local writers, artists, and those who supported them.

Plenty of librarians, too. I felt sure because the group was as raucous as the reader's theater crowd. No costumes or stage-action pantomimes, but they cheered nominees as though they'd won a Hollywood award.

Spotlights mounted on temporary scaffolding blazed down on Wooly and me. The lights hung high in the air but felt inches away. My dress was the problem. The fabric felt like Mylar, and not a molecule of air could transcend its fibers.

Lou had swathed me in a personal sauna. The garment felt like military-grade sheet metal meant for insulation or galactic exploration.

But did I wilt? Or neglect my duties?

Not this former model. I'd worn spring frocks in Arctic temps and parkas in the desert. On stage in the Legion Hall ballroom, I performed my hostess duties without complaint, handing a Funfetti to a delightful elementary school writer and a Powdered Sugar to the author of a romance series.

Other prizes included a Glazer for a stained-glass artist and a Bear Claw for a wildlife painter.

The categories varied each year. Sometimes they repeated themselves; sometimes they didn't. Many were one-offs. I suspect they depended upon what Wooly's grandchildren preferred for breakfast.

But, even so, the Cinnies event always was a fantastic fundraiser for the arts community. And one of the prizes received the wildest response I'd ever seen; it nearly brought down the house.

The audience cheered so madly that the spotlights over Wooly and I bucked and swayed. I feared the lights would rip from their brackets.

Who was the winner?

I'm getting ahead of myself.

I'll rewind to the start of the evening.

At the front entrance of the Legion Hall, there was a red carpet and a step and repeat for photographs.

Crystal Broadway snapped pictures of those arriving.

Wooly showed up at the same time I did. We posed next to a giant, shiny replica of the trophies, and I blended in perfectly with the trophy. The effect was like camouflage. I felt relieved that the potential for a silly photo in the paper was thwarted.

We stepped into the historic lodge that looked like Paul Bunyan's weekend place, with oversized doors, a huge fireplace, and a polished wooden bar. Wooly guided me to an empty section of the pub. We stood close to the fireplace, which had a three-alarm going. (Unfortunately for me.)

Wooly ordered a brandy old-fashioned and offered to buy me a drink. "What can I get you, Mel?"

"Ice water, please."

We waited for our drinks, then he whispered, "I've got an update about working undercover at Midwinter's Night on Tuesday."

"Someone confessed? And you passed the intel to the authorities?" I raised my water glass. "Cheers to that."

"Not quite, but Lieutenant DuWayne was there disguised as a donkey, like me. Ran into him in the stacks. We both escaped to the back of the library to take our heads off and get some air."

"Wool, in different circumstances, that would be a hilarious sentence." I tugged at the neckline of my flameproof dress. "I understand."

"I questioned the guy. He wasn't forthcoming about much, but I got the vibe he hadn't made progress. Whoever killed Kat is either lucky or excellent at deception."

I told him about the falling stage flat at the bake-off on Wednesday night, finishing the recap with, "Thus, I've crossed Char Broadway off my list of suspects."

"Good to know." He glanced toward the dining room. "Are you hungry? I'm getting a plate from the buffet before we begin. Would you like one, too?"

"I'll make my own, thanks."

"See you on stage, Mel."

I lingered in the bar, glancing out the window, watching

Crystal take photographs of those arriving. Snowflakes wafted down, dancing playfully on the evening air.

Oliver Roberts stepped onto the red carpet with a woman I didn't know. They walked shoulder to shoulder, leaning toward one another. Her height matched his lanky frame, and they wore scarves with a patch that looked to be a stack of books.

They stopped to chat with those who showed up before them.

After a few minutes, Steven arrived. He pushed a dolly with boxes of awards stacked on it. Crystal stopped him for a photo. He posed with the hand cart and giant trophy, grinning broadly.

The image made me smile. I hoped that one made the newspaper's front page.

After taking the shot, Steven hugged Crystal. She leaned into him, showing off the picture on her camera. He put his arm around her while he looked at it. Their body language told me the tension between them had been resolved.

Attendees filtered into the hall, and the bar filled with thirsty patrons. The humanity heated the room. I felt like I was standing in a solar flare. I needed fresh air. Pushing against a side door, I walked around where Crystal was dismantling the photo set. "Hi, Crystal—"

"Oh—agh!"

"I snuck up on you. Sorry."

She rubbed her temples. "Wow, Mel, that scared me. I didn't hear you."

"Need help packing this stuff?"

"Yeah, like, sure."

I rolled up the step and repeat, a fabric backdrop with an event's name and other logos printed in a pattern. This one had images of cinnamon rolls, stars, and American flags. It doubled as the one used for the newspaper's Fourth of July picnic. Like me, Wooly watched his pennies.

"Crystal, you were upset at the Cheese Ball, but we never talked about it. Are you feeling better?"

"I'm good. That was, like, a big misunderstanding. Steven's okay about it now."

"It involved Steven?"

"Yeah, but I really don't wanna talk about it."

"Gotcha. But I'm worried about him."

"Why? He's doing okay now, I said."

"Are you aware of anyone who'd want to hurt him?"

She raised her eyebrows. "Hurt Steven? Gosh, no—who would do that?"

"The town's been weird lately."

She stopped packing her duffel. "Are you saying the person who hurt Kat could be after someone else? Like Steven?"

"Have you seen or heard anything unusual?"

I watched her ponder my question. Her cheeks were red from the cold, and she blew on her hands.

"No, but I'll let you know if I, like, think of anything."

"Thanks."

"Hey, Mel, I want to say one thing. I'm sorry about my mom. She can be, like, difficult sometimes."

"I appreciate that, Crystal. She and I will figure it out, whatever it is. Do you live with her at the lake?"

"Yeah, for now."

I finished helping her pack the gear, then walked inside, veering to the cloakroom.

I needed to sit somewhere in private and remove my boots. I had to pull the tape off the soles. It's an old modeling trick to keep scuffs from forming. The tape also muffles the sound of footsteps. Confession: I snuck up on Crystal while she was packing her bag so I could peek inside it.

I needed to see what she carried with her.

I was pulling on a boot when Tim Gold charged into the cloakroom carrying drinks. "Hey, Mel, glad to catch you. I saw ya outside." He handed me a glass. "Here, it's a French '75. You're gonna love it."

I set it on the little desk near me. "Thanks, Tim."

"Taste it. It's got champagne. You're a model. Less calories."

"Former model. Now I eat and drink what I want. Or not."

He smiled. The blue sport coat he wore enhanced his bright eyes. "Point taken. You really know what you're doin', don't you, Mel?"

"Right now, I'm pulling on my boots, Tim."

"I'd like to get to know you—outside of this place, this town. C'mon out to the lake. How's tomorrow for you?"

"You've got Kat's memorial service tomorrow."

"Not until two o'clock. Stop by before. We'll rap for a bit."

I tasted the drink. "Okay, Tim."

"Great, Mel. See you then."

If anyone believes I'd finish a drink given by Tim Gold, plus go to his home without backup, I have a lodge the size of the Brooklyn Bridge to sell.

I relished the chance to meet Gold at his home, though. If Tim instigated Kat's demise, I'd get a sense of it by speaking with him where he felt in control.

I picked up the coupe and sniffed the liquid. It smelled sweet and lemony. When I tasted it, it was delicious. But not for me at the moment.

I returned to the bar and placed the glass on the counter, then got a refill on the ice water.

I left a tip and stepped into the ballroom. Tables were set up, each one named for a type of doughnut.

The cheese royals had two: Custard Bismarck and Cheese-cake Kringle. I found my name next to Steven's. He stood across the room near the acres of buffet tables. Fans surrounded him—wait, Steven has fans?

I mean, the guy was popular, but I'd never seen him attract a crowd.

"Good evening, Lady Mel. You look lovely this evening. You're a cinnamon stick dipped in gold."

I felt like molten metal, that was for sure. "Hello, Oliver. Thank you."

"May I introduce you to someone? Lady Melanie Tower, please meet Ms. Foss Knickerbocker, librarian extraordinaire, walking encyclopedia, and delightful friend."

I shook her hand. Firm. She was my height and wore little makeup, proudly displaying wrinkles at her eyes.

Like me, she had shoulder-length brunette hair with a few grays interspersed. In fact, I could have swapped her scarf for my crown and sash, and she could have performed my duties for the evening. "It's nice to meet you, Ms. Knickerbocker."

"Call me Foss. It's a pleasure, Melanie."

"I love your scarf."

"Aren't they something?" Oliver interjected. "Mementoes from the online site Foss and I made acquaintance on, 'Dewey Belong Together?' We checked one another out, pardon the pun." He put an arm around her. "We hope to delete our profiles soon."

Her cheeks flushed. "I'd like that, Oliver."

"Congrats," I said. "You two look very happy."

Just then, Susan Victory spotted us. She wore a billowy

dress and silver jewelry that shined from across the room. Her earrings dangled like swords, and spiked bracelets on her wrist glinted in the light.

Weaving around the tables, she flowed toward us like a sorceress riding a carpet. The entire time she flew, her gaze rested on Oliver.

She arrived at the table, then circled him like a witch on a broom. "Oliver, I need a word with you," Susan hissed.

One guess as to the identity of Susan's mystery man, the guy she'd been waiting for this morning when I'd visited.

Hint: His initials were O.R.

Oliver apologized to Foss, then followed Susan toward the bar. Foss watched them leave, and then she turned to me. "How long have you known Oliver?"

"Since he arrived here. About a year and a half."

"Tell me about him."

"He likes books. And Shakespeare."

"Where did he live before coming to Cinnamon?"

I paused before answering. "The Middle Ages, maybe? Otherwise, I have no idea."

"Is he single? That's what he told me."

Again, I paused. "What do you think?"

Foss stared toward the bar. "It's been a pleasure to meet you, Melanie, but I need to powder my nose."

I watched Foss beetle to the bar, moving like a track star. I respected her decision. If it were me, I'd stand in the shadows to observe the parties while they spoke. Body language reveals much more than words, especially during confrontations.

I may have complained about my previous occupation—

hardly, if ever—but modeling proved the value of the adage "close one's mouth, keep one's eyes open."

When I'd been on set, I challenged myself to determine who held power. Often, it wasn't the person with the fancy job title. The makeup chair and the sidelines of a photo shoot, a shoot's shadows, were excellent points of observation.

Back to the Legion Hall's bar. What was happening in there?

Pulling out my phone, I texted Susan, telling her if she needed a friend, I was available. Hank Leigel came to my mind.

If he asked me to help work things out with Susan, I would.

Susan, Oliver, and Foss never returned from the bar. I assumed they left the building.

Steven approached the table with plates of food. He set one in front of me. "Brought you protein, Mel. If your blood sugar was like mine today, you need it."

"My mom taught me never to take food from strangers. Sorry."

He made a fist and stabbed his chest. "Cliché, Mel. Cliché."

"What's with the literary puns? Have you become Oliver Roberts, the librarian? Why are you surrounded by groupies?"

"First, let me apologize. I kept things from you, Mel, and I shouldn't have."

I heard his words but became distracted by the food. The only thing I'd eaten all day was a hardboiled egg. Seasoned roast chicken and a salad of greens, tomatoes, and cucumbers demanded my attention.

"No apologies until after I eat," I said.

"Fair enough, my dear," Steven replied.

Steven is a man of many talents. He's a bloodhound when it comes to addresses. Hold a package under his nose. With a few sniffs, he'll find its destination without reading any text.

He's a scratch mini-golfer. Decent at musical chairs. A steady hand at the egg-and-spoon race. He's an excellent bowler, too. But a prize-winning mystery book author? Knock me over with a candlestick in the conservatory, Mrs. Peacock.

Or, with a vintage door in the storage room, assailant un-known.

Steven and I did not get to discuss his revelation in detail. While I devoured the chicken and salad, he showed me the evening's program, pointing to the Mixed Nut, the award for best new mystery by a local writer. "That one's mine," he said. "I wrote it under a pseudonym."

"D.L. Varré is your pen name?"

"Yeah, that's me."

I shook my head. "That news is nuts, kind of."

"Yeah, it is. I think that's why Wooly called it the Mixed Nut. Attempting to write a novel drives one nuts." Steven sighed. "It's why you haven't seen me. I'm really sorry. I should have told you earlier."

"Yes, you should have."

From behind the podium, Wooly leaned into the mic and called my name. "Mel Tower, please come forward to start tonight's show."

"Gotta go, Steven, but I need your help tomorrow."

He didn't even ask about the job; he just agreed to assist.

I ate a last bite of chicken and then walked to the stage.

The news about Steven, plus my greenhouse dress, distracted me, and I messed up giving out awards.

I swapped the S'Mores (best book series) for the Hot Cross Bun (Christian fiction). The Key Lime Pie (won by a delightful octogenarian artist who crafted key chains) ended up in the hands of the Thompson twins.

"Our next prize goes to a man who's become invaluable to our community," Wooly announced. "Before there was the big online seller, our friend knew that residents of Cinnamon and the surrounding county needed things delivered—"

"We love you, Steven!" someone yelled.

"Yes, we certainly do," Wooly agreed. The crowd applauded, and he waited for it to subside. "Seeing Steven's yellow van around town is like seeing Santa every day. To paraphrase the post office, 'Neither bad roads nor frozen windshield wipers, nor overheated brakes nor nighttime hours kept Steven Delavan from the swift completion of his appointed rounds.'"

"Yeah, but tell us about his book!"

Wooly chuckled. "I'm getting to it, Crystal. Oliver Roberts alerted me to the popularity of an indie-published book at the library. *Package of Remorse* was one of the most popular titles in the place this fall, but no one knew who wrote it. With a tip from a friend, the foreign press committee and I discovered who it was. Steven Delavan, also known this week as Prince Mild Brick, come up and get your prize!"

He approached the stage. My heart warmed for him, and it wasn't due to the dress. Even though Steven kept the news from me, I felt delighted by his accomplishment.

As he walked toward me, smiling, I looked past his shoulder and saw a man leaning against the back wall of the ballroom.

The fellow looked familiar.

I'd seen him before—but where?

The event ended with Inga Honeythorne and Susan Victory receiving a Sprinkle Award, a lifetime achievement prize for "sprinkling positivity and encouragement" for years over the Cinnamon arts community.

Susan didn't appear, so Inga accepted it on her friend's behalf. The applause was the loudest of the evening. Great for her. But I kept my gaze on those stage lights. Not only were they hot, but they wobbled like an Alberta clipper was blowing in from Canada.

I had horrible visions of Kat and what she went through in my storage room. It actually gave me shivers, despite the discomfort of the overhead lamps.

I needed a drink.

After the event ended, I headed to the bar and took a seat. The bartender approached. "What can I get you, Mel?"

"I'd like a mind-cleanse tea, please."

She laughed. "Sorry. Those are exclusive to the Tool & Rye."

"Then make it a mind-cleanse ice water."

"Coming right up."

Wooly took the spot next to me, setting his phone on the bar. "Wonderful job, Mel. You're hired for next year, too."

I dabbed my brow. "Great. But tell the foreign press I move to hold it out in the cool air and under the light of the moon."

"I'll put in the word. But it may only result in lowering the air conditioning, just so you're aware."

The bartender placed the water in front of me. Wooly ordered a pop.

"Let me guess, Wool," I said, "the tip about Steven being the mystery author came from Crystal Broadway."

He nodded while saying, "I don't reveal my sources."

I winked. "Gotcha. And the name D.L. Varré is a take on the word 'delivery,' as well as the author John le Carré."

"You're an excellent detective, Mel. Just as I knew you would be. Have you read Steven's book?"

I shook my head. "Oliver Roberts put me on the waiting list. I've been so busy I forgot to ask my status."

"The backstory is that Steven and Crystal are in a writing group that meets at the library," Wooly confessed. "The members were impressed with his work and encouraged him to publish it. I hear he was upset about being discovered but seems to have gotten over it."

"An award helps. Does he have plans for a sequel?"

"No idea. I hope he writes another one; he's talented. I've always preferred short-form writing because long-form can be mental torture." Wooly's phone pinged with an image. He looked at it, then held it toward me. "Nice picture of us with the trophy."

Indeed, it was. I blended in nicely, and Wool had a big smile. "Send that to me, please."

"Sure, and I'll log it into the Mel Tower modeling archives."

Bless his heart. Wooly had collected my modeling images over the years. Who else would have? My parents were gone and Cousin Lou didn't have time to archived my work.

Wooly compiled a record just as he'd done for other local figures of note.

"Thanks, Wool. I don't know who will want that archive. But I appreciate that you've kept it all this time."

"My pleasure, Mel. It's the newspaper's due diligence, I believe."

"Speaking of diligence, did you notice undercover police working the room?"

"No, but I saw one who was not undercover. The tall guy standing at the back."

"Who was he?"

"He's assisting in the sheriff's office until a new one is

appointed. Been back and forth from the Northwoods a few times. I hear he's asked about you."

I cringed.

That was not a good sign.

Twenty-Five —

After the awards, I found something in the cloakroom of the Legion Hall that made me sweat worse than the dress. I raced home with it, and Steven followed.

In my kitchen, he and I stared at a ribbon. It snaked over itself in a pile of frayed red satin, about twenty inches long, an inch wide.

To an observer, it would appear to be a shred from a long-ago party held at the hall.

To me, it was another warning.

"You found this in the cloakroom tonight?" Steven asked.

I shook my head. "I didn't find it. It found me. It was tied to the hanger my shawl was on, and I think it showed up after I hung it there."

"You're sure the ribbon wasn't on the hanger first, and your coat covered it?"

"I didn't wear a coat—" I yanked the black shawl from my shoulders, "because this dress is asbestos."

He touched my sleeve. "Feels bulletproof. Where'd you get it?"

"Where do you think?"

"Dumb question. Sorry."

I moved to the stove, then fired up the burner under the teapot. "Can you make cocoa? I've got to change out of this thing."

"Sure, but wait just a sec." He wrapped me in a hug. "Thanks for agreeing to talk tonight. I know you're upset with me."

"No, I'm happy for you. You won a Mixed Nut."

"The name sure fits."

"It's almost as painful as childbearing, I hear."

He laughed. "You got that right."

"Do you remember where the cocoa is?"

"Of course, Mel. Go change out of that fire extinguisher. We'll figure out the mystery of the red ribbon."

I left him in charge of the water, cocoa, and whipped cream.

Then I stomped upstairs.

My home's vibe felt peculiar.

I jumped when the floorboards creaked. Behind every crooked-hanging door (my house is an ancient, federal-style brick box), I feared a boogeyman.

Or a red-nosed menace, to be more accurate.

I changed and zipped back downstairs.

Steven was parked in the living room with cocoa. "Is it okay if I make a fire? That outfit won't make you melt?"

I wore a cashmere sweater and matching pants. Had them for ages. "Go ahead. My temperature is back to normal."

While he knelt by the hearth, I explained about finding the nose on my windshield at the library and the shock of seeing the cherry-topped brownies.

"You should have told me at the bake-off," Steven admonished. "I suspected something was up the way you and Lou acted."

"And you should have mentioned your book," I snapped.

He winged crumpled newspaper into the fire. "I'm sorry, Mel. Writing was an experiment. I joined the library group cuz I needed something to challenge myself. I never thought I'd be any good at it. Then it got submitted to the library and the committee."

The pained expression on his face made me wince. "I'm glad you tried something new, Steven. That's what matters."

"If it helps, I'm writing a sequel. You can be one of my betas."

"What's that?"

"I keep you on speed dial. You read my drafts. If I want to quit, you bring first aid, a martini, or a puppy. You're like a writer's St. Bernard."

"But I'm your friend. I'd do that anyway."

He smiled. "Yeah, I know."

"It sounds like Crystal helped. She was the person who submitted—"

"Back to that ribbon," he interrupted. "You're sure it was tied on the hanger after you hung the shawl?"

"Almost positive."

"Who saw you in the cloakroom? Who knew which hanger was yours?"

"Wooly Gallagher. Crystal Broadway. Half the attendees saw me arrive. But the person who matters is Tim Gold."

I told him about our conversation in the cloakroom. "Tim saw me re-hang my shawl. I'd been outside helping Crystal."

"So Tim is your number-one suspect?"

"Yes. And tomorrow—or later today—you're helping me. I'm talking with him before the memorial for Kat."

"Oh?"

"You're going to run surveillance while I'm in his house."

Steven stared at me. "Now you're the one who's nuts."

"Yeah, probably. But I need to know if Tim did it."

Steven dozed on the floor in front of the fire. I slept on the couch.

It felt like old times.

Five years ago, when I moved in, we'd had nights like it. Usually after a Crazy Eights card game marathon and spiked hot cocoas.

Not this time, however.

Just conversation about what evil lurked in our beloved village until neither of us could keep our eyes open.

I slept like a baby—one affected by colic. My mind felt positioned at the proverbial fork in the road. Impossibly, it traveled both.

On one fork, my life, well-being, and fellow citizens were plagued by an unsolved murder.

On the other fork, I teetered like a foal on freshly unfolded legs walking a new pasture.

An emotional wilderness beckoned, one of unexpressed, unexplored feelings. I saw Captain Rand's face and heard myself say, "I need more." Next, I was in Susan Victory's kitchen, buying a cabinet.

Where had this spirit emerged?

Under closed lids, visions flashed. I saw Susan on her porch drinking martinis. Then, she was floating on a carpet in the Legion Hall, a crazed look in her eye.

Next, I was in my living room staring at Rand's suitcase. Impossibly, the case sprouted wings and flew out my front door. But just as impossibly, red ribbons blew in. They twisted and danced in the air around me, then snaked themselves into a mound on my kitchen counter.

Wooly arrived wearing a red nose. Tim Gold followed; he wore a nose, too. But he didn't enter my home.

He remained in the doorway.

Suddenly, with superhuman strength, he yanked the door from its hinges and moved toward me with it, arms extended. I saw it above me—it hovered over my body like a tank, an assault weapon. "No—stop!" I cried.

I felt a hand on my shoulder. "Mel? Mel!"

"H-huh?"

"Wake up."

"Steven?"

"Yeah, it sounds like you had a bad—"

Glass shattered. "Watch out!" I yelled. With the sweep of an arm, I linebackered Steven down, then rolled from the couch on top of him.

Something—a ball, a rock, a projectile—pinged the fireplace. It ricocheted into a lamp, smashing it—hey, that was my only one! It fell, landing on the rug with a thud.

"What the heck was that?" Steven asked.

In the early morning light, staring at the object on the floor, I saw a stone. The fire flickered on it, reflecting its colors. I saw gray and red mottles on a rock about three inches big, give or take its irregular shape.

Someone pitched it through a window into my house.

Officer Linus—remember him? He was the young fellow who questioned me the morning of Kat's death.

He showed up with pastries and coffee from the Tool &

Rye. "I was there when Steven's call came in. Help yourself. You both okay?"

"We're fine, Linus. But someone in town isn't," Steven answered.

They stepped from the kitchen to the front door, examining its broken sidelight. The stone had shattered it, then peened to the fireplace. From there, it smashed the lamp and hit the carpet.

I didn't care about the lamp or rug. Both were secondhand finds from the thrift store. Easily replaced. While the two men discussed the speed and trajectory of the stone, I knelt and peered at it.

It remained on the floor where it landed.

I took a picture of it with my phone. A quick search on my device revealed the projectile happened to be the Wisconsin state rock. Not that important.

Its name was, however.

Red granite.

Whoever sent a mini-missile into my house on an early Friday morning stuck with a theme.

Kevin Sunny's voice rang out. "Hey, folks. Someone call for plywood?"

"Hi, Kev," Lou called from the kitchen. "C'mon in. Have some breakfast first."

Small towns. Between word-of-mouth and the police scanner, half the Tool & Rye morning audience arrived at my place with provisions.

The first person after Linus was Cousin Lou.

She brought a pan of baked French toast and pounds of bacon, then set out a spread on the counter with paper plates and napkins. "You got an army comin', Mel. People are upset about this. I'm glad you texted me last night, sayin' you were here with Steven, but you're not stayin' here again until we find whoever is responsible."

After Lou, Inga Honeythorne came with folding chairs from my building's workroom. "Thank goodness you're safe, Mel. The mall isn't scheduled to open for an hour, but I won't do it until I get the okay from you."

Vendors who'd been at the T&R, and the Thompson twins, showed up. They had positive words for everybody and framed needle art for my walls. "God's mercy is fresh and new every morning," they cooed like elderly doves. "These pictures are for you, Melanie. Make your life a masterpiece; you only get one canvas, my dear."

"Lady Mel! I walked over as soon I heard the distressing news. Pray not a hair was harmed on your lovely head."

Oliver Roberts. He wrapped me in a hug and smelled of fresh air, I noticed. "Thanks, Oliver. I'm fine."

He kissed the twins' cheeks. "And my two favorite teenagers! How delightful to see you this morning. If you'll excuse me, I'll put these rolls in the kitchen."

He delivered a giant pan of cinnamon rolls to Lou. She gestured with a spatula, running the meal service as though she was the loadmaster and we were in a combat situation.

Both half-time police officers, Linus and Luce, stood near her, holding plates. Lou piled on the food while giving them orders: "You two get on the horn to that lieutenant. Tell him Mel had nothin' to do with Kat's death. How could she pitch a rock into her own house if she's sound asleep on the couch with Steven?"

All eyes in the place—and it was a considerable number— gazed at me. I began, "Steven wasn't with me; he was on the floor—"

"Hey, everybody! This food is gettin' cold. Who needs a plate?" Lou called out.

I looked at Steven. He leaned by the front door, half of his body inside my house, half out, watching Kevin measure the sidelight. Steven didn't hear Lou's comment; I was certain. He would have corrected her like I tried to do.

It had begun to snow. I saw white flakes swirl through the open door. Cold air blew in, too, but given the people in the room, the fireplace, and all the stove's burners set on "blistering summer"—Lou likes to serve food hot—the room felt stuffy.

I'd never had so many people in my home at once. The humanity felt claustrophobic, and I stepped toward the cool air of the foyer. As I moved toward it, I saw a shoe step over the threshold. It was a dress shoe, a man's size.

A uniformed leg and overcoat followed, then a pilot's cap.

Captain Rand Cunningham, in full uniform, nearly slammed into me. He spread his arms. "Mel, thank goodness you're okay," he said.

Lou handed Rand a plate. "Here ya are, Captain. Eat up. You know what they say about airline food: It's too 'plane,' hehe."

He smiled. "Thank you, Lou. I appreciate that."

"How long's your layover this time—or are ya on a weather delay?"

He looked at me. I sat across from him at the kitchen table. "I'm here as long as necessary to keep Mel safe. If I have to cancel my trip tomorrow, I will."

"Oh, no worries about that. She's stayin' at my place. Well, except for last night when she was here with Steven. But otherwise, I'll keep her locked down like an airfield after a crash. Ah, pardon my words."

"We'll take things from here, Lou," I said.

"Kitchen's clean, everybody's cleared out, and the window's boarded over. Lock up and head out to my house later, Mel. You need your outfit for the Fish Fry Gala tonight."

"Got it."

"Everything cool between you kids? I kinda sense turbulence—"

I shook my head. "It's fine. I'll see you later, Lou."

"Aye, aye. But I left the 'seatbelts fastened' sign on just in case."

My cousin clattered out, overloaded with pans and utensils.

"Mel, I'm sorry for dropping in. I wanted to talk face-to-face. But I drove up and saw the squad car and the people. I thought something terrible happened. What did the police say about the broken window?"

"The speculation is that it could have been a vehicle driving by that kicked up a rock. The snowplows push objects into the road. Car tires have been known to spin out and throw them."

He nodded. "That happens; we've all had cracked windshields. I've encountered incidents on runways involving airplanes no one would believe."

"Or, somebody deliberately aimed a projectile into my house. If they had a major league arm, it could have been pitched. Or, they used a baseball bat or a slingshot."

"I see."

"I want to clarify something about Steven—"

Rand shook his head. "Let me guess, his on-time stats are better than mine; that's why you left me."

"Of course not—"

"It's a joke, Mel." He covered my hand with his. "Somewhere along the line, we forgot to laugh together. I don't know why it happened, but I miss you. I'm like an aircraft without wings. A terminal without security."

"A service desk without a line of irate passengers."

He smiled. "That's the spirit. Things are strange between us right now. After a little while, after we've both had some space, I hope we can work things out."

Rand had attended college on a baseball scholarship. Had an arm like a missile launcher. He used to throw the ball for Sadie, my old collie, and the thing would land in the next week.

I did not suspect that Rand threw the rock. I doubted he spied another man's van in my driveway, then careened a small boulder through my window in the early morning. It wasn't his nature to do anything like that.

I did suspect Crystal Broadway, however.

Neither she nor Char attended the impromptu village get-together at my place. Char wouldn't have because she had a re-straining order against me in her mind. She'd know that showing up in my home would violate it, right?

Don't answer that.

But Crystal may have misunderstood the situation. She may have gotten angry at seeing Steven staying over and used a bat or slingshot to wing a rock at my house.

But where does the red granite part fit in? Was it a coin-cidence? Or was the person who menaced me sending another warning?

I didn't mention my concern to Rand.

After I assured him I would be safe, he departed for Chicago. He waited while I showered, packed a bag, and locked the house. Then I drove the two hundred yards to the mall; he followed in his car.

I parked and waved at him. He smiled and saluted like he'd just been given the all-clear for take-off.

It was only ten o'clock, but I felt exhausted.

Twenty-Six —

Inga stuck her head into my office. With her powdery curls, half-glasses, and red sweater, she looked like Mrs. Claus. She narrowed her twinkly eyes in concern. "That was quite a commotion this morning, Mel. Feeling okay?"

"No, I'm not."

"Any further news about who broke your window?"

"Someone who owns a slingshot or a baseball bat. Do we have a vendor who fits that description?"

She shook her head. "Not that I know of."

"Well, if one applies for membership, the application is denied."

I felt punchy. Lack of sleep and a special-delivery rock made my head spin. "Do you mind holding down the fort? I've got a meeting at Fern's farm, and then I'm going to the memorial service at the yacht club this afternoon."

"I didn't know you had a meeting—"

"It's last-minute."

"Sure, Mel. I'll see you at the gala. Drive carefully today. The forecast calls for snow."

I made sure my phone was charged, then headed out to the Saab.

I cruised the alley behind the High Street businesses, passing my new place. That's what I was speaking to Fern about. I slammed on the brakes when I came to the back door of the Tool & Rye.

I felt exhausted, as I mentioned. A long day loomed: Fern's place, the meeting at Tim Gold's, the memorial for Kat, then the gala. All the while, I needed to be on my toes, leaving a trail of crumbs for Cinnamon's red menace but not letting them catch me.

A sweet, chocolatey Wiscocoa called my name.

I'd dodged my favorite bakery-hardware store all week because I didn't want to discuss what happened. But since its regulars camped at my place this morning and filled up on the gossip, there was no longer a need to avoid it.

I parked by the "Bakery parking only. All others will be toast" sign and got out. Suddenly, the sky darkened. Snow still drifted from the clouds, but the flakes swirled in odd patterns as though a mass affected its flow.

"Ms. Tower."

I looked up. Either the brick building spoke or a man in uniform did. He was quite a specimen, too. Age fifty or so. Tall and solid. Jaw like a stone monument.

I'd seen him before. Mount Rushmore, maybe?

No, he was the fellow from the party last night. The guy who held up the back wall of the ballroom.

"O-officer," I croaked.

He tipped his hat. Silverbelly-felt covered by a weather protector. I saw snowflakes land on the clear plastic, but they singed away as though touching a broiler.

I'm not one to judge appearances; I understand how deceiving they are. But this fellow, if he were a blacksmith, could light his forge without tinder, as Cousin Lou would say.

I felt disarmed, weak. Maybe it was the uniform. The officer wore gray trousers, a shirt that matched his ice-blue eyes, and a vest with a badge.

But Captain Rand wore a uniform, and it didn't impress me. Wait, who was Rand again?

Sorry. That was horribly shallow.

Something about the lawman standing before me, who shielded me from the falling snow, weakened my knees. My heart felt lassoed, and I hadn't even seen a rope.

Get it together, Mel.

"Ms. Tower, I'm Sheriff Cole Lawrence. We have a mutual friend, Fern Bubble. She's told me a lot about you."

Fern and I stood in her pasture. She insisted on a walking meeting despite the snowfall.

"I'm glad you met Cole, finally," she said.

"I'm not—I could barely speak. And I looked pathetic, like one of your rescues. He said that's how you know me. You rescued me, fixed me up in your barn, and got me back on my feet."

"No, he did not. You're kidding."

"Maybe not, yeah. But we talked for, like, two seconds, Fern, then I fled. I felt dumbstruck."

I coughed, the wind choking my words. Tulip had been following us. I patted her massive neck, clearing my throat. "Why didn't you tell me Sheriff Lawrence was an action figure?

He's bigger than Tulip. I stopped at the Tool & Rye for a hot drink and didn't even get in the door. It's like I was locked in Sheriff Cole's gaze."

She grinned. "I've never seen you like this, Mel."

"I'm overreacting from exhaustion. And from being stalked by Kat's killer—who also wants me dead for some reason. I'll get over it as soon as I solve this thing."

"He's a wonderful man, Mel—"

"I'm sure, but not now, Fern." I stopped to cough again. "B-being a suspect in a murder is a bit overwhelming. And there are new developments."

I explained about finding the dirty piece of red satin in the cloakroom. "And today, I'm going to Tim Gold's place. We're having a t-talk."

"Not alone, I hope."

"Steven is h-helping me."

She touched my cheek. "You're freezing. Let's head into my office, Mel. I'll make something to warm you up."

Fern made cocoa while I shivered in a chair. She handed me a mug. "Here, Mel. Drink this. I'll turn up the heat, too."

"I b-bought a china cabinet from Susan Victory."

"That's excellent! You've got a picture on the living room mantle and now a nice piece of furniture. You're changing, my friend. I've got so many ideas for your place—"

"And a building."

"Excuse me?" She felt my forehead and waved her fingers in front of my eyes. "How many do you see? Should I take you to urgent care?"

"I see a hand that needs to take notes. Where's your little book? Write this down."

"Okay, Mel. But I'm getting concerned."

I took a long pull of cocoa. Sweet chocolate and spiced cinnamon hit my throat, then traveled down to my tummy, warming it like an internal blanket. "The vacant place on High Street ... I bought it."

"Excuse me? I thought Hank Leigel owned it."

"He did. Sold it to me. Now my craft-mall 'competitors' can't have it. Tim Gold, Eden Hoff, and Char Broadway may have talked about stealing vendors and opening another place, but no one thought to secure the only vacant store on High Street."

Fern stepped quickly to her desk and took a seat. She picked up a pen and scribbled in her red bible. "That's genius, Mel. How can I help?"

"Cinnamon needs a bookstore. And I need your expertise to develop its name and market the place. Can you handle another account?"

She nodded, her salt-and-pepper curls bouncing enthusiastically. "Absolutely. I'd love to work with a bookstore client. Welcome aboard again, Mel."

"Authors need all the brick-and-mortar exposure they can get, according to Steven."

"Oh, this is going to be fun! I'll brainstorm, then we'll meet next week—"

"One more thing. If she isn't trying to kill me, I want to hire Crystal Broadway to run it."

The hot drink provided a shot of energy.

But Steven's intel about running surveillance at Tim Gold's house drained me again.

We met in the lay-by above the lake. The gravel area where,

when I'd done the ride-along with Steven earlier in the week, I tried to walk Max, and the tempest-like wind almost tipped me top over teakettle.

I'd parked the Saab and hopped in Steven's van. Sitting in the passenger side, I felt the vehicle shudder as another tempest blew up the hill from Lake Insane.

"I checked out both houses next to Tim's place," Steven said. "They're vacant. Owners have gone south for the season."

"Can you use their driveways? Park in one of them and keep an eye out?"

"If the owners were home, I could. Stop in and sort packages, you know. Chat with them for a while. But the places aren't even plowed out."

"What about across the lake? Can you sit over there and watch?"

"Too far. And it's a nature area. There's no road or any way into it."

"Do you think the police are watching Gold's house?"

"I saw squads patrolling a week ago, right after Kat was found. Nothing lately."

He drummed his fingers on the steering wheel. He wore cargo pants and a thick flannel shirt. He had a new name badge, I noticed. The picture showed the same wild-haired, smiling Steven, but his descriptor pronouns were "au/thor." My guess was Crystal suggested it. I sensed the young gal had a natural talent for promotion.

"Why are you so nervous, Steven?"

"Sorry, Mel. I don't work well with other people. I've figured that out. That's why I drive all day—alone."

"Let me guess: when you're driving and thinking is when you get your best writing done."

"Yep, for sure."

"I get it. I worked solo for a long time. Modeling sets are filled with people, but there's a lot of standing and thinking. May I ask you something?"

He nodded. "Shoot."

"It's about Crystal. I don't want to offend you, and if you two have a thing going—"

"I didn't know how to tell you, Mel. She and I have talked a lot. She's the one who submitted my mystery manuscript to the awards. At first, I was embarrassed, but it turned out okay."

"I don't want to offend you, but I'm wondering who threw the rock this morning. Could it have been Crystal? Would she have gotten upset at seeing your van in my driveway and done something foolish?"

His face reddened. "I asked her, Mel. She swears she didn't do it."

"You believe her?"

"Yeah, I do. I also confirmed that you and I are friends. Only friends. Despite rumors she's heard. We live in a small town. People talk. You've got a long-term thing with Rand. I'm single. Nothin' more needs to be said."

I didn't correct him about the change in my relationship status. Heck, I didn't even know what was happening. Talk about a mystery.

Nor did I remind Steven of his statement five years ago that he'd "like a chance if I were single."

If Steven and Crystal were happy together, that was all that mattered.

Twenty-Seven —

My toxic trait was a tendency to act as a lone wolf. But I've reconsidered. It's believing I could solve a murder by watching someone's body language.

Tim Gold's sweeping gestures revealed that he felt like a king in his home on Lake Cinn. Looking out the picture window at the water, he reached his arms skyward and yawned. "Love this view. I stretch every hour while I work. Gotta keep the blood movin', you know?"

Was he serious? Blood was red. And I'd been taunted by red-colored widgets for a week.

Tim Gold was playing mind games, and I hadn't been in his house for fifteen minutes.

In my pocket were pepper spray and my cell phone, its line open to Steven. He'd parked on the road a few doors down, as close as he could get to Gold's place.

"Glad you stopped, Mel. What can I get you to drink?"

I looked out at Lake Sea of Troubles. The angry-looking cauldron turned me off of water, that was for sure. "Hot tea, please."

"Two rye chais, comin' up."

"I can do without the whiskey."

He moved to the bar. The living area of the tri-level was open, with seating in front of large windows that overlooked a patio, then the lake beyond. A side table showed off pictures of the Gold family, Kat and Tim among them. "That's a nice shot of you and Kat," I said.

"Yeah, she was cool. We didn't work out but still got along. I'm proud of that."

"How long were you married?"

"Couple years. Both of us had priors, if you know what I mean. No kids. Just couldn't keep our synergy goin'."

"She was living here when she passed?"

"Splitting time between my house and her folks' place in Chicago. I was helping her get, ah, get that business goin'. One like yours, you know. One that could complement yours, I mean. Not a competitor, exactly. I want you to know that."

Liar.

I thought about making a citizen's arrest. The guy had to know I didn't believe him.

But just because Tim fibbed about a business didn't mean he was a killer. And I had no idea about how he pushed a door onto his ex-wife.

I took a deep breath. He brought the tea over in white mugs inscribed with black text. I read aloud, "Good agencies are built on trust."

"Yeah, there's a typo on 'em. These mugs were experiments for the new biz. Gotta brand-build with merch." He nodded toward the couches. "Please, sit down."

"I'd like to ask a few questions about Kat."

"Sure. I got Q and A for you, too. I love trading intel. Game on."

I sipped the tea. He'd added booze even though I'd asked him not to.

Okay, Tim.

Game on.

Tim held his mug in the air. "I'm not angry that you bought that building, Mel. Bold move. Toast."

I pointed to the typo on my mug. "Here's to BUILD-ings."

"Good one." He flashed his teeth. "About Eden and Char, those agency 'partners,'" he used air quotes, "we're only in the seed stage. Nothin' in writing. I likely won't move forward with those two."

"Oh?"

"Char isn't reliable. And Eden, I don't know very well. We have different ideas about company culture, I think. I'm more laid back. That woman is intense." He leaned forward, hands on knees. "What's your take?"

"Well, Tim, you know what they say in fashion: one day you're in; the next day you're in the Midwest, trying to start a new agency."

He laughed. "Yeah, it's funny. People comin' here after thinking the Big Apple was the only place to work. What was it like living there?"

I tipped my head toward the churning water. The snow fell harder, and the lake appeared even more volatile. "Sort of like that."

"Ha, ha. I like you, Mel. If you're looking for a consultant, I can be had. I'm not cheap, but I'll give you a good price for my services. I can fundraise for the new venture. What are you gonna do with that building? Tech company? Sandwich franchise? I may have a cash infusion soon, too, if you need start-up capital. No one risks their own green these days."

"A cash infusion?"

"Just some policies that are comin' due."

"I'll keep that in mind." I placed my mug on a side table. "If you'll excuse me, I need to get back to the mall."

He glanced at his watch. "Memorial's in a couple hours. You still coming?"

"Oh, I wouldn't miss it, Tim."

"I'll walk you out."

I stood and stepped toward the front door, keeping my distance. I shoved a hand in my pocket, clutching the pepper spray in case he came too close.

Trailing behind, he said, "Wait, Mel, you didn't ask anything about Kat. What was it you wanted to know? I've already talked to the police, but I'll answer your questions, too."

I didn't respond until I was safely outside on the front stoop and knew Steven saw me from his vantage point on the hill. "Sorry, Tim, I'm running late. Let's reconnect at the memorial."

"Let me know about that deal, okay? It's on the table but not forever," Tim said.

He slammed the door violently, and I jumped. The whole house shuddered. Had he meant to do that? Maybe it was some weird lake-effect venturi that yanked the handle out of his hands.

Or, maybe he said too much and realized he couldn't take it back.

I looked toward the road but didn't see Steven's van.

Where had he gone?

Just as I revved the engine in my car, Steven pulled in behind me, trapping my vehicle in Gold's driveway.

I watched the rearview mirror. He waved toward the house, then got out of his van. He jogged toward me while holding an oversized cardboard envelope.

I figured Steven was pretending he had a delivery for me and "found" my car at random while making his rounds. I powered down the window. Snowflakes blew in.

"Hiya, Mel. What are you doing in lake country? Got a delivery for ya."

He winked and handed me the envelope. Then he trotted back to his van. I glanced at the note on the white cardboard: CELL WOULDN'T WORK. COULDN'T HEAR ANYTHING. DROVE AROUND TRYING TO FIND A SIGNAL. CALL LATER.

He backed out and sped away. I headed in the opposite direction.

In the mirror, I watched Tim's house. The snow clouded the view, but it appeared he emerged from the garage and drove off, following Steven, heading toward the yacht club.

He hadn't fallen for our ruse. I was sure of it. If Tim was the mastermind behind the demise of his wife, and he sent red-themed nastygrams to intimidate me from investigating, he saw through our pantomime in his driveway.

I pulled into the gravel lay-by. The snow was accumulating, and the ground was bumpy. I tried to call Steven.

No answer.

I sent a text telling him that Gold was on the road and to watch his rear. I also texted Lou, who'd be driving to the club for the bartender gig. "Keep an eye out for Steven," I wrote. "And let me know when Tim Gold gets to the club. See you soon, ~M."

Then I headed back to town.

My theory had holes, but Tim Gold was my number-one

suspect. "I should have put money in the pool," I said to my reflection in the rearview. "The last I heard, Tim was still in the lead."

I cruised toward the mall. The gentle snowfall and twinkle lights on the streetlamps soothed my spirit. I couldn't wait for this investigation to be over, so my little burg could return to being a quaint, touristy spot untouched by evil.

I parked and hustled into my office. The evidence—the ribbon and the chunk of red granite—was in the safe. The dirty rubber nose had been burned. I packed the evidence to give to Bruce DuWayne, who I figured would be at Kat's memorial.

Time to connect with the lieutenant in charge and wrap this thing up.

I felt awful for Kat but relieved that the person who hurt her may soon be apprehended. Tim confessed to me that he was getting a "cash infusion." A life insurance policy, or policies, on Kat, most likely. Money or passion are motives, friends. And if Kat had a mystery boyfriend that created tension or jealousy, Tim had a double incentive to hurt his ex-wife.

How did he do it? I didn't know yet. But he appeared to be a talker. He easily let it slip that he had insurance payments forthcoming. What else would he reveal if I befriended him?

Perhaps I should pretend to consider his investment in my new business.

I would still need to present myself as bait. Not appealing. But between my hyperawareness, cell phone, and pepper spray, I could do it.

I waved to Inga, then stepped back out to my car and zipped over snowy roads toward the yacht club.

Just as I pulled into the yacht club lot, a speeding station wagon careened across the road. "Yikes!" I cried, jerking the Saab's wheel. My car skidded sideways, barely avoiding a collision.

The driver of the wagon, Susan Victory, slammed on her brakes. But the area was slick with fresh snow, and her car kept going—not good.

I watched her slide toward the creek, the waterway used for the Mayor's Race, the one that emptied into the lake.

Killing the Saab's engine, I jumped out. "Susan, turn! Susan!"

She cranked her car to the right. The thing poofed into a snowbank like a freight train hitting a pile of feathers. It looked like a snow bomb went off. I was temporarily blinded by a fluffy, white curtain.

I shielded my face for a few seconds, then saw the wagon's headlights. The wipers still slashed back and forth. I saw Susan; she was bawling.

"Are you okay?" I called out.

Powering down her window, she yelled, "I n-need to talk to you! Please, Mel, c-come here!"

I opened the passenger door. "I need the keys, Susan."

"W-what do you mean?"

"Turn the car off. Give me the keys."

She wiped her face with her coat sleeve. "Don't act crazy."

"Okay, then I'm not getting in."

"Mel—wait!"

"The keys, Susan. I mean it."

She shut off the wagon and handed me the jewels. I'd seen alarming behavior from Susan during the last week. She could drive off with me in her car; I took no chances. "Have you been drinking?" I asked.

"No."

Yes. I could smell it. "What happened?"

"It's Hank. He doesn't understand."

"Hank does understand. And he wants to work things out with you."

"No, he doesn't!"

"Don't yell at me. I'm your friend. I'm here to help."

"I'm not yelling!"

"Susan, there's a parking lot full of snow out there. You're going to get a face full if you don't stop."

Was I being harsh? Yes. But I'd seen enough from her, and I knew her secret. "Does Hank know about your affair with Oliver Roberts? Did you tell him?"

"What? No!"

"You should. Hank wants to work it out. And Oliver isn't Prince Charming, Susan. He's not the person you think." I looked in the glove compartment for tissues. Scored a full box. "Here."

She blew out a wad, then said, "He wouldn't understand."

"Susan, I don't mean to be short with you, but you're reminding me of me. No woman is an island. Don't be stubborn. Hank told me he loves you, no matter what. He'll forgive you."

That statement sent her into near-convulsions. "I don't believe it. How could he?"

"Because that's what love means. You put up with the rotten stuff—the difficulty and the pain and the crap. That's the reality of loving someone. Passion is easy. It's every other part of a relationship that's hard."

"Oh, Mel—I have something to tell you."

I shivered. It was how Susan said it; the timbre of her voice changed. Like she sobered up immediately, and whatever she needed to reveal affected my life, my soul. "What is it, Susan?"

She used another wad of tissues before answering. Then, "Mel, I stole your garage code, and I gave it to Kat."

"Oh, Susan—you didn't."

"I did. We were in a meeting in the workshop in the mall. I snooped in Fern Bubble's red notebook. The code is written on the inside cover. I'm so sorry, Mel."

Twenty-Eight —

I called Hank, who showed up within minutes. He moved Susan's vehicle to a remote spot in the lot, then buckled her into the passenger seat of his Volvo.

"I'll take things from here, Mel," he said. "I'll call you soon."

I stood under the canopy at the club's entry, watching them drive away, snowflakes drifting from the sky. Something about Susan's confession didn't sit right with me.

Why would she give my entry code to Kat?

I'd asked her, but she didn't elaborate, just cried into a clump of tissues.

Thump! One of the massive wooden doors, carved with sea creatures holding umbrella drinks, bumped me from behind.

"Excuse me. Hello, Ms. Tower," Swan, Eden's assistant, said. "I'm waiting for Ms. Hoff."

Just then, a limo the size of a school bus pulled under the canopy. Swan glided toward the vehicle's rear door.

The fellow didn't walk, I noticed. More like drifted. He held himself like a ballroom dancer, chin high, shoulders wide. And he made no sound while his legs conveyed his body across the ground; he was a master of silent movement.

Eden stepped from the car. She saw me but didn't acknowledge my presence.

"Hello, Eden," I said.

She ignored me. Swan floated to the club's double doors and opened one for her. He held it for me, too.

"Thank you," I told him.

The man smiled. "My pleasure, Ms. Tower."

The nickname for the yacht club is Cirrhosis by the Sea.

I entered to find the bar open, the glasses sparkling, the shelves stocked. A fire blazed in the hearth, and a Christmas tree decorated with nautical ornaments—little sailboats, jumping muskies, smiley starfish—stood in a corner.

Cousin Lou stood behind the bar. She wore a green cowgirl blouse that showed off her red curls. "How 'bout a cinnamon coffee? Quite a party in the lot. Saw it through the window. Gimme your coat."

"Thanks, Lou."

She hung my coat in the foyer and then charged back to the bar. "Susan okay? She did some stunt drivin' out there. Her wagon almost ended up in the creek. Just about called the tow truck."

"She's safe with Hank."

"You're lookin' a little wound up, like a filly who needs to run." Lou placed a glass mug in front of me. "Here, have a sip. Everything good with Captain Rand? You two break up?"

I shook my head. "I don't want to talk about it."

"I knew it! There was somethin' off with you guys this morning."

I thumped the bar. A few patrons looked over. "Do not tell anyone, Louella Jingle. I mean it. It's my business. No one needs to know."

"Okay, okay. But Fern Bubble told me she knows a sheriff—"

"Lou, I mean it. People could get hurt. Not a word."

She leaned forward. "Does this have somethin' to do with Kat?"

"No, it's just personal, and I want to keep it that way. But speaking of Kat, did you discover who pushed the flat down when the Wise Men were on stage Wednesday night? Did you find out anything?"

"Sorry, nope. Nothin'. It's like it didn't happen."

"Keep an eye on Tim Gold today."

"You think he did it? Makes sense. The pool money still says it's him."

I felt a whoosh of cold air as a group stepped inside. The service didn't start for another hour, but the crowd was turning up for the pregame food and drink. Signs on the bar called the event "Hors d'oeuvres and Kind Words for Kat Gold."

Lou said, "Look for strangers. Undercover police always turn up for the funerals of victims. They're probably in the parking lot takin' pictures of license plates. Gonna look up whoever doesn't belong. I've seen enough detective shows to know."

"Thanks for the tip," I said. "Eyes open, mouth closed, re-member."

"That's almost impossible for me, Mel. But I'll do it for you. We gotta get this thing solved."

Lou's willingness to listen was surprising.

I wasn't used to being in charge of our relationship. Perhaps things were changing in several areas of my life, not just with Rand and my wall decor.

I sat at the bar, sipping the warm coffee, watching people arrive. So far, no Tim Gold.

But Oliver Roberts and Foss Knickerbocker came in. Oliver hung their coats, then escorted Foss toward me. She wore a stunning blue velvet dress. Oliver wore what I would describe as modern Shakespeare: a puffy white shirt, vest, and black slacks.

Lou said, "Howdy, you two. Thanks for comin' out in honor of Kat."

"Thank you, Louella. Mr. Gold and I have our differences, but I felt it important to pay respects to Kat. May I introduce Ms. Foss Knickerbocker." He picked up my hand and kissed it. "Lady Mel, it's delightful to see you. I hope you are well after the incident this morning."

"I'm fine, thanks."

"What can I get ya?" Lou asked. "How 'bout a signature cocktail?"

"Excuse me, but the memorial has a specialty drink?" Oliver inquired. "Most unusual for a funeral service, is it not?"

"Not for a celebration of life like this. I'm tryin' to keep things light. That's what Mr. Gold wants. He said to keep things loose. And take car keys so nobody has too much and then drives. I know—I'll commandeer Eden Hoff's limo and bus everybody home in it."

Oliver smiled. "A grand idea. Louella, you never cease to amaze me with your innovative thinking. We'll take two champagne cocktails, please. Lady Mel, may I offer one to you, as well? My treat."

"No, thanks." I lifted my mug. "Coffee for now."

"I shall bring one in a few minutes, then."

"Excuse me. I need to powder my nose," I said.

The bar began to feel crowded. I stepped into the dining area to search for Lt. Bruce DuWayne. My thought was DuWayne would attend this event, even if undercover officers also wandered about. He needed to hear my theory about Tim Gold.

In the large room, I saw round tables set with linens, silver utensils, and crystal stemware. A stage was set up with a podium, mic, and speakers. A bouquet of red roses shaped into a heart was next to the podium, and a framed picture of Kat hung on the wall behind the stage.

Wow, Tim went all out to make it look like he mourned his ex-wife.

I heard his voice. There was a smaller bar in this room. He stood near it with a crowd around him. I recognized them as lake folks—the mayor and his wife and a few of my vendors. I noted who the vendors were; it was the same group who'd gathered in the tents at the library event.

I assumed they were the artists and crafters who wanted to leave with Kat. I'd assist them with that. They'd soon get notifications that their booth leases at The Bell, Book & Anvil wouldn't be renewed.

Eden and Swan were in the group, too. Did she know that Tim tossed her under the bus earlier today? That he was willing to cut her loose and make a deal with me about my new business venture?

I sensed someone at my shoulder. "Good afternoon, Ms. Tower," Bruce DuWayne said. "I hope you're all right after the incident this morning. The officers who attended told me what happened."

"I need to talk to you."

"Here—now?"

"Yes."

I towed him down a hallway between the pub and the dining area, the same one where I'd had the claustrophobic encounter with Tim, Eden, and Char during the Mayor's Race. There were meeting rooms off that corridor where we could converse in private.

I pushed open the first door that was unlocked.

Clearly, Tim Gold had been in there before us.

The room was a small conference space with a whiteboard, a table, and a few chairs. No windows. An open briefcase with the initials "T.E.G." inscribed on it rested on the table.

A speech for Kat's service lay next to the case. But inside it, plain as one on a face, was a red clown nose. I pointed to it. "That's a problem, Lieutenant."

"Excuse me?"

"Fern Bubble informed you about what happened to me, right? The nose on my car at the Midwinter's Night at the Library? It was disgusting, filthy. Since then, I've been menaced by other things, always red, including a red granite rock this morning."

"She and I have been in contact. But are you saying this proves Mr. Gold's guilt?"

"I don't know how much time we have, Lieutenant. Tim could come back for this speech at any second. But earlier today, he basically told me he had a life insurance policy on Kat. He was expecting a 'cash infusion.' He proposed going into business together." I looked toward the door. "I think he's been trying to intimidate me from investigating Kat's death. And now, he's trying to bribe me with an offer of investment."

I paused to take a breath. I felt light-headed. There wasn't much air in the small space. DuWayne seemed unimpressed. He maintained a poker face, his features unchanged. Again, I suspected there was a kindly grandfather behind the façade of a detective.

But I couldn't let my guard down. I had been one of his suspects, after all.

A terrible thought crossed my mind. Maybe he thought I planted the red clues on myself to throw off suspicion!

I feared our conversation was a mistake.

"I'll take that champagne cocktail," I told Oliver Roberts.

We were in the dining room. I was sitting with Oliver, Foss, the Thompson twins, and Steven, who arrived after I finished speaking with the lieutenant.

"Of course. Right away, Lady Mel," Oliver replied. "Back in a jiff."

He tossed his napkin on his chair, then scurried for the pub. We'd been nibbling hors d'oeuvres for half an hour, waiting for Tim to begin his speech.

I felt miserable. Like I'd stuck my foot in the punchbowl. Lieutenant DuWayne had not been impressed with my revelation. To me, the clues fit: Tim Gold's motive was money, and he saw an opportunity when Kat declared she wanted to open a shop like mine. Then Susan gave Kat the door codes.

Why did Kat sneak inside my business on that fateful night? I wasn't sure. Perhaps she wanted to glimpse my financial records. But that's just a theory; I had no proof.

Tim Gold seized his chance on that Wednesday evening over a week ago. Knowing I'd be a suspect, he killed his ex-wife in my shop. I looked around the room. DuWayne wasn't anywhere in sight. Why couldn't he understand my theory about the crime?

On stage, Tim tapped the mic. "Hello, everyone. Thanks for coming. Kat would dig that you're here. She's up in the clouds, probably taking pictures of all of us, posting on heaven's social media. I'm really going to miss her."

A stemmed flute appeared next to my plate. I heard a voice whisper, "Drink up, Lady Mel. And I have a second one on order for you. Please try to relax. You look so worried."

"Thanks, Oliver."

I reached for the glass.

If someone had said Kat's memorial service would end with a square dance and a limo ride, I wouldn't have believed it. But it's Wisconsin. We can turn any event into a tailgate party.

Tim Gold departed after giving a touching speech about his ex. Then he turned us loose in the bar for cake and coffee. "Enjoy, everybody. It's all on me! On behalf of Kat, please stay and have fun."

Lou was ready for us. A giant sheet cake with "We love you, Kat" was on the counter with plates and forks next to it.

A polka trio had set up in a corner. As we entered, the musicians played "All of Me" in a moving tribute. A few enlarged images of Kat hung on the walls.

I felt bewitched, almost like I had a surreal experience. I couldn't figure out why Bruce DuWayne had been so dismissive. Another bubbly drink appeared in front of me. Lou nodded toward two young men standing near the band. "Undercover police," she whispered.

"How do you know? Did they tell you?"

"Yeah, Mel, but keep it quiet—shhh. This intel is need-to-know only."

I glanced at the men, who appeared to be in their twenties. One was blond, the other dark-haired. Both stood stiffly as though they felt out of place.

"They're brand new at it; I spotted 'em right away," Lou continued. "Said they were locals but couldn't pronounce Oconomowoc or Mukwonago. They didn't even know where Minocqua was. I was on to 'em pretty quick. I told 'em I'd keep their secret safe. Gave 'em tips about blendin' in, you know. They'll be at the fish fry tonight, too, so be nice."

Swan approached the bar. Lou said, "Hiya Swan. I gotta ask a question. Are you wearing wheelies on your shoes like the kids do? How come you glide everywhere?"

He giggled. I loved seeing him break his cool. "Ms. Lou, in a former life, before I became an executive assistant, I was a dancer. I guess it shows?"

"You betcha it does! Polka? Or two-step?"

And so, it came to pass, and the floor was cleared. The Do-si-do and hootin' and hollerin' were on. The accordion player turned out to be an expert caller, and everybody who remained in the bar took a spin around the square, Eden Hoff included.

I had mixed feelings about seeing her enjoy herself. She smiled and clapped, hitching up her long frock. She even removed her dark glasses.

Eden Hoff—or Eden "Hoofer" as Lou referred to her—had made my life miserable in New York City. Every encounter with her reinforced that I didn't belong in her world. Every conversation made me retreat more into myself.

Eden Hoff and "fashionistas" like her were why I'd discon-nected from my emotions. Hearing you are "too commercial" and "too Midwestern" repeatedly affects an eighteen-year-old.

And here she was, enjoying the very spirit and place she'd criticized, and now she wanted to work among us. In a business competing with mine, no less!

She and I bumped hips on a "promenade home." Well, we didn't bump, exactly. I might have pushed her.

She was fine, just stumbled a little.

Lou intervened, "Don't let our new friends, Starsky and Hutch, see ya pushing people, Mel. Time for you to head out."

She stuffed me into Eden's limo and told the driver Lou knew from the school bus route to take me out to the ranch. "Get an hour's rest," she told me. "Then get ready for the gala. Your dress is in the guest room closet."

Twenty-Nine —

Lou said the dress was in the guest room closet, but she
erred.

It was in the guest room.

The layers of tulle and ruffles took up the entire space. It had
to come from a kit like those for replica cars. I looked like a gold,
souped-up version of Glinda of Oz.

"You should arrive in a floating bubble," Inga Honeythorne
said, watching me ascend the stairs in Lou's living room. Inga
had been dispatched to pick me up because Lou was running late
at the yacht club.

"How was the memorial for Kat?" she asked.

"It was a nice tribute," I said. "Still a tragedy to lose her. And
to not know who did it makes it even worse."

"I penned a card for her family. I'll send it to her address in
Chicago."

"I'd love to read it, Inga. You always create such beautiful
things."

She placed a document on the coffee table. White card

stock covered with tissue. I sat on the couch to read it but was swallowed by layers of tulle. Inga placed it in my hands, and I read it while pushing my arms against the mounds of fabric:

She is beyond time, beyond pain,
Fear she will n'er feel.
To God she belonged, not us.
God's will is not ours.
His ways are hidden from mortal eyes.
But strength, He provides,
If we surrender.
Step, child, under His mighty wing.
Give to Him grief.
Give to Him tears.
Give to Him pain.
He comforts us in loss,
To Him, Kat was gain.

It's lovely, Inga," I said. "I'm sure her family will appreciate it."

"I did my best. How do you comfort someone in terrible circumstances?"

Indeed, Inga's hand-penned creations were angels of mercy. As she says, when there's nothing else and the world has gone to ruin, people can still give compassion to others.

I studied the black script. Time after time, I'd seen shoppers stop at Inga's booth, select a card, and weep. She slid the note into a protective sleeve.

"Inga, I don't mean to bring up a painful memory, but has

anything else occurred to you? Are you aware of any observations about finding Kat?" I hiccuped. "Excuse me."

She hesitated, her blue eyes twinkling. "No, nothing that comes to mind. Why?"

"I can't figure out why she'd be in my place. What was she after?"

"I have no idea. But, there was one thing, now that I think about it. It's what Kat wore. Seeing you in that gold dress made me think of it. You're wearing a neutral color. It's jazzed up, but it's the same palette. Kat wore neutrals. Always. She said it made a similar—what's the word? About how those influencer people want to look?"

"Uniform? Cohesive?"

"Cohesive! She said neutrals were the cohesive color for her Pinwheel feed. I overheard her teaching a class one evening."

"How does, hic, that connect with what you found?"

She closed her eyes. "I'll never forget seeing her. Well, parts of her. Most of her was under that awful door. But she was splayed out. I could see an arm and a leg. Her thigh was—"

"What is it? What are you saying, Inga?"

"Kat wore a red dress. I'd never seen her wear such a bright color. Had you?"

I thought about her question. "No, Kat always wore neutrals. Browns. Sepia tones."

"I know. Why would she wear a red dress, Mel?"

Inga loaded me and the dress into the back of her SUV. We headed to the gala on pillowy roads. Snow still fell from the sky, and the effect was magical.

Through the vehicle's sunroof, I saw a blue-black sky and

clouds tossed out snow like popcorn. "I feel like a Wisconsin Cinderella, hic," I said.

"Are you feeling okay, Mel?"

"Yes, of course. Why?"

"You don't seem like yourself."

"Just tired, Inga. I'm ready for my reign as a cheese royal to be over—oh, no! I forgot my crown and sash!"

"I have them here in the front seat. Lou sent me a text and reminded me to grab them."

We cruised toward the location of the gala, The Promenade Deck.

About twenty years ago, a village engineer genius proposed twenty acres near the Cinnamon High School be developed as a senior living complex. A private investor who adored cruising came forward to create The Promenade Deck, a cruise ship experience on land for those fifty-five and over.

The place had fancy dining, endless activities, a pool, and a gym. Many residents stayed young at heart by volunteering at the high school.

It was a natural fit that The Promenade hosted the Fish Fry Gala.

Inga turned into the driveway leading to the palatial building. Evergreens trimmed with twinkle lights lined the winding road. White-arrow signs pointing toward the "ship" offered a narration of what was to come: "Departures, this way" was followed by "Sail tonight!" and "Casino, karaoke, and disco."

Lest cruisers fear going hungry, the last bulletin addressed the problem: "Buffet, Formal Dining, and Captain's Table."

The place made getting older sound fun. Who needs modeling and its aversion to aging?

I should mention the signs were not flimsy plastic. They were permanent wooden ones, refreshed each year by the high school wood shop. Wooly Gallagher faithfully reported the news every fall in the paper.

We waited in a line of cars, then drove under a canopy at the entrance. Gray-haired footmen escorted attendees inside. A silver fox opened my door. "Welcome to The Promenade, madam. We cruise the tri-county area. We'll be departing in approximately one hour. May I escort you up the plank?"

"Yes, as long as a bayonet and a blindfold aren't involved."

He laughed. "Certainly not. That is a stunning dress you are wearing, madam."

Reaching over from the front seat, Inga passed him a bag. "Here is her crown and sash, sir. Please make sure she wears them."

"I was told to expect royal passengers! We have minstrels and fanfare for your arrival."

"No, please—"

He snapped his fingers. "Attention, please!"

A group of senior troubadours strode over and began a jazzy adaptation of "Dancing Queen." The canopy amplified the sound, so everyone in the tri-county area heard them, I was certain.

Oliver Roberts and Foss Knickerbocker walked over. "Welcome aboard, Lady Mel. May I escort our Cheese Princess inside, Captain?"

"Certainly, sir," he said.

Oliver looked into the SUV. "Thank you, Ms. Inga. I will take care of her."

She waved and drove off. Through the minstrels we walked. I recognized a few of the players from the Cheese Ball. Not one of them appeared younger than seventy, but they played with the energy of a teenage garage band.

"I've often wanted musicians to serenade my best customers at the library," Oliver said. "I'd have them for both of you ladies every time you arrived."

Crystal Broadway stopped us at a step and repeat for a photograph. She assisted a professional photographer whose camera was as large as his head. Oliver handed Crystal the cloth bag with the crown and sash. "Would you please help Lady Mel?"

I donned the royal accessories, then was ordered to pose. Like a reflex, I weighted a back leg, cocked my hips sideways, and relaxed my face. But in my head, I had a flashback: I heard Eden Hoff yelling at me, and I grimaced just as the camera flashed.

I wrecked the shot; I knew it before the photographer checked his camera. "Let's take another one, folks," he said.

"Smile, Mel," Crystal said.

I shook my head. The movement made me feel tipsy. "Sorry, everybody."

We repeated the scene, and I took a deep breath, flaring my nose and loosening my jaw. *CLICK!* "Much better," the camera-man said.

Oliver patted my arm. "What a magical moment. Do you know that's our first photograph together, Lady Mel?"

He leaned over and kissed me on the cheek.

We stepped into an atrium. Twinkle lights hung from the glass ceiling, along with flashing stars and a sleigh pulled by reindeer.

A stunning Christmas tree dominated the space, its ornaments created by the senior residents and the high school art students.

Wooly and Cozette Gallagher stood near it, admiring the colorful globes. I laughed, thinking about those giant balls at the bowling alley. Had they really dangled overhead? Was there really a bowling ball tree? And those giant penguins at the entrance—how silly!

The memory made me giggle. Oliver patted my arm. "Lady Mel, I love seeing you smile. You were so pensive earlier today."

"I'm tired, Oliver. Exhausted. It's been a long week. I'm ready to hang up my crown and sash, go home, and put my feet up. Think about a vacation."

"I understand. You two ladies wait here. I'll get us glasses of Christmas punch."

I saw his white dinner jacket fade into the crowd. I had trouble following where he went; so many people were arriving.

I refocused on Wooly and the tree. I wanted to talk to him but didn't have the energy to wander over. Maybe I should try to float like Glinda. I wished I had a bubble transportation device.

I felt my legs wobble. Foss grabbed my arm. "Are you okay, Mel?"

"I'd like to sit down, please."

The poofy dress made sitting a problem.

I ended up on a tall stool, my back propped against the wall, guarded by a six-foot nutcracker. Fern Bubble, the night's cruise director, came over to check on me. "Is this fellow your date, Mel?"

I smiled. "I feel like my head's been cracked open, that's for sure."

She felt my forehead. "Shall I call the medics? We have a sickbay on this ship." She looked down at the clipboard she carried. "I can get you seen right away."

"I'm fine. Just tipsy from the champagne this afternoon. And tired. I'm ready for this to be over."

"I understand. Me, too."

"I had a talk with the lieutenant at the memorial. He doesn't believe my theory. I think Tim Gold did it for insurance money."

Fern frowned. "Why do you think that?"

I gave her the same spiel I told DuWayne and got her up to speed about the rock and Inga's revelation about the red dress. "I mean, I want to redo my house, Fern, and I need your help. But absolutely no red decor, please." I grabbed the nutcracker's arm. "Did we leave port? Is this ship moving?"

"I'm calling a medic—"

"I'm kidding, Fern."

"You're sure?"

"Iceberg—look out!"

She sighed. "Can I get you anything?"

Steven approached with a tray. He looked resplendent in a white dinner jacket and bowtie.

"My prince is here," I said. "But thanks, Fern."

"I'll check on you later."

"Hot tea for the princess?" Steven set the tray on a table near me. He pulled a packet of crackers out of the pocket of his jacket. "I hear you're feeling seasick."

"How did you know? Thanks for the restorative."

"Sorry about earlier today. I messed up our surveillance job. Now you know why I operate alone. Too much pressure, otherwise."

"I hear most writers are loners."

He smiled. "Sort of like retired fashion models."

"I'm working on that." I noticed Crystal standing at the bar, watching us talk. "I may head home early, Steven. I hope that doesn't spoil your evening."

"Do you need a ride?"

"Absolutely not. There's a dinghy leaving for shore every hour. And if that doesn't work, I'm sure Lou has a buckboard for me. I'm all set. You enjoy yourself."

"Aye, aye, Captain. Drink your tea. By the way, you look gorgeous."

"Thanks. You do, too."

I reached for the mug.

Sipping the warm tea, I observed the people in the atrium.

Tim Gold stood near Eden Hoff. The sight of her made me angry.

It was good I felt incapacitated, or there could have been another square dance injury in the editor's future.

Lou trotted over, the pink fringe of her dress swaying. "I'm herdin' the royals into the Grand Salon. We got the grand march, then the fish fry. I'm gonna auction off a seat next to you for charity—"

"Nope, sorry. Mr. Nutcracker already won the seat next to me. No dance, no auction. This royal is abdicating."

"But—"

"I had too much champagne at the memorial, Lou. And I'm wiped out. Time for me to head back to the ranch."

"But you'll miss the fried cod and potato pancakes. We've got the dance afterward—"

I removed the crown and sash. "Give these to Crystal Broadway. Let her take my place tonight."

"You sure, Mel? It's not like you to jump ship. I'm gonna have one couple who doesn't match their pictures on the wall. Or in the program."

I smiled. "No one will notice. Tonight, I'm a castaway. We can start solving this mystery anew tomorrow when Snowthanks starts."

"Yeah, that's twenty-four hours of shoppin'. Gonna be a big day."

"Exactly."

"Want me to walk ya out?"

"No, but you can help me up. Take my arms and pull."

Together, we got me on my feet. She pointed me toward the lobby. "The senior bus will run ya home. Tell Herbert I said thanks. See ya at the ranch."

I felt like a salmon swimming upstream.

The crowd flowed toward the Grand Salon while I pushed toward the exit. The cumbersome dress didn't help. People stepped on it, knocking me sideways, and I began feeling like I was in a foosball game.

Wooly saw me, fortunately, and towed me out of the waves of humanity.

We stood in a corridor off the atrium. "You're headed in the wrong direction, Mel."

"I'm departing the ship early. Time for this Cinderella to turn back into a parlormaid."

He laughed. "I think that dress is ballast. You may need to stay docked to let the crowd move past."

"But my chariot turns back into a pumpkin in a couple minutes."

Cozette stuck her head in the hallway. "Wooly, we're needed at the newspaper's table in the Grand Salon. They're taking photos of the groups."

Photos—that was it!

Cozette's remark triggered a memory. "Wooly, at my surprise party, when we were in Lou's barn, where did those modeling pictures come from? Did Lou get them from you and have them blown up—"

"Come on, dear," Cozette repeated. "We need to be in the salon."

Wooly patted my arm. "We'll chat later, Mel. I'll catch up with you tomorrow."

He turned to walk with his wife. I hitched up the dress, then started down the corridor. Straight ahead, then a right. From what I remembered, it was a passage to the foyer. A figure popped around the corner in front of me. Who was that?

"Hello, Mel."

"Ah—"

"Why are you alone?"

I backed up, got caught in the dress, and went down! I crashed to the tile floor. It stung. I hit my elbow. "Ow!"

"Let me help you, dear."

I saw long arms reaching for me. He wore gloves and a frightening expression. He looked crazed, like someone possessed.

"NO!" I screamed. "HELP!"

"Yelling isn't ladylike, Mel."

Hands over my mouth—a heavy weight—his body on top of me. I couldn't breathe!

I squirmed. "HEL—"

"BE QUIET, MEL."

SLAM! A knock to my temple. "OW!"

"Thou shalt not speak!"

Another knock to my head.

I groaned.

My world went black.

Thirty —

I heard the slap of windshield wipers.
Christmas music played. I felt sick to my stomach. My head
ached. I tried to move my arms—ouch! Elbow. Hurt. I remembered falling—and a man with gloves.

I was in a vehicle, my hands tied, my eyes covered. I lay flat
on a seat, still wearing the dress; I felt the scratchy fabric with
my hands.

"That concludes our tour of Cinnamon's downtown, Lady
Mel. You cannot see it due to your blindfold, I'm aware—"

"Let me see. I want to ... see the view."

"I beg your pardon?"

"It's not fair. Let me see—"

"Nice try, but I shall not release you until we arrive at our
destination."

I heard the vehicle groan and squeak. It was probably the
library bus that Oliver had used to chauffeur people to and from
parties this week.

He'd gotten me into it somehow. Probably told people he was taking me home.

I coughed. "Why … are you doing this?"

"Isn't it obvious? Because I can."

"I c-can't b-breathe—"

The van swerved.

I spooked him; he must have looked back to see if I was dying. "Help … me."

Another swerve. "Hold on, Lady Mel. We are almost at our destination. Then our photo shoot will begin."

The van accelerated. I felt it rock side to side. Please don't crash this heap. Icy roads, old vehicle.

Holy smokes.

I felt the brakes lock. We were sliding.

Oliver kept the jalopy on the road.

The engine growled as the vehicle swayed and spun. Then it stopped, still idling. He got out. *Whoosh*—cold air blew in. After a few seconds, I heard him climb in, then bang the driver's door shut.

We drove a few feet. He killed the engine. "We have arrived."

"C-can't b-breathe…."

"Hold on, Lady Mel. I am coming to your rescue."

I still wore heels. If he gets near, I'm kicking like a mule. "Untie m-me." I felt hands near my face. I'll bite him. Come closer, Oliver.

He loosened the blindfold, then snatched it off. "Lady Mel, please exit."

"No."

"We've arrived at our hidden abode. One I purchased just for this occasion."

I blinked. Yep, I was inside the delivery van. "I hope you get your money back."

"Please do not be upset. You will enjoy this shoot. I promise."

"I haven't enjoyed a photo shoot since '87, Oliver. My thirteenth birthday party."

"Please do not be stubborn. It is time."

I coughed again to keep up the ruse I couldn't breathe. I tensed my muscles. "C-come closer. Untie me."

He didn't fall for it. "Mel, you must exit. I have hair, makeup, lights, and a set ready for us."

I thought fast. All of those things could be weapons. I slowly climbed out of the van, hands still tied.

Let the shoot begin.

How many photographers does it take to change a lightbulb?

Just one. And the universe revolves around him.

Old joke from my modeling days. Still applied.

Oliver strutted around the photo shoot "set." From my seat in front of a makeup mirror, I saw a backdrop, lights, and a tripod. He'd ordered me to a chair, then tied my arms with a bed sheet.

My elbow still hurt. "You're nuts, Oliver."

"Nonsense, Melanie. I have prepared for this for a long time. I'm relieved we finally have our moment."

"Where's Foss?"

"Who?"

"Don't play games. Please tell me you didn't hurt her."

"Will you cooperate if I tell you?"

"Where is she?"

"I sent her home from the gala. I needed to assist you, Melanie."

I looked around. We were in an old barn. I saw slip stalls

and a hay pulley hanging from a rope above us. Someone had converted the barn into a garage. The library bus sat in front of the sliding door.

Oliver had set up a fabric backdrop, a camera on a tripod, and a makeup station. I sat in front of a mirror surrounded by lights.

"Lady Mel, it's time for your close-up. Please prepare."

I shook my head. "I have a headache."

"It's time to prepare!"

"I have a headache!"

He charged toward me, his arm raised. Was he going to hit me?

"Models can't shoot with marks on their face, Oliver!" I yelled.

"The images we create will be superior, no matter what."

"What's the creative brief?"

"I beg your pardon?"

"How can I do this without seeing the creative brief?"

He pondered my comment. Good, it bought time.

Oliver must have been drugging me. That's why I'd been so foggy after the champagne. Had he put something in the tea I'd had at the gala, too?

I watched his eyes. His pupils were dilated. He was on something. He'd always given me such an odd vibe.

Now I knew why.

"How can I interpret your vision if I don't know the direction of this?" I protested. "Models always have input about what they're shooting."

Total lie. Models' opinions are equivalent to novelists and the movie adaptations of their books.

Oliver strutted in front of me. "We will create my vision of a lover waiting for her beau to return from war. You shall wear lingerie."

I noticed a rack of clothes. Feather boas and lacy things. Such a cliché. "That's not unique, Oliver. Why don't we use this dress I'm wearing?"

"Hush. I have studied your work for a long time. Do you know where I lived? New York City. I became aware of you then and have a trove of your images. Supplemented by Wooly's archive at the paper."

I looked at posters leaning against a wall. They looked familiar. "Did you supply the pictures for my birthday party?"

"I did. You are welcome."

I knew I should have asked earlier. I didn't think anything of it at the party. Just assumed Wooly produced the images. What was I going to do now? I thought about the attitudes I'd seen on sets. Not from me, of course. I'd been the model who'd always been Midwest Nice.

The only way out of this would be to fight my way out.

"When do hair and makeup arrive?" I demanded. "I need help getting ready, Oliver."

He sniffed. Definitely was on drugs. "They're not coming."

I rolled my eyes. "Did they cancel again?"

"Ah, yes, they did." He smirked. "I shall have them killed."

"It will be difficult to work in these conditions."

"You can do it, Lady Mel. The industry was most awful to you, kicking you out as you matured. When you came into your true beauty."

"You heard?"

"I have followed you for years. I'm your biggest fan. We shall create stunning images together for the rest of our days. After this, my next action will be against Eden Hoff. Her demise will be positively Shakespearean."

That gave me an idea.

✳

I'd never had a diva moment in my entire modeling career. Better late than never, right?

"You need to untie me," I ordered.

"I intended to photograph you in bondage."

"But your premise is that I'm waiting for my love to return from war. Am I tied up for years?" I shook my head. "No editor would accept it. Amateur mistake. The concept is off."

"But I am your soldier. The analogy is that you're waiting for me."

"You mean metaphor, Oliver. The audience won't get it. And an editor will think it's dumb." His face turned red; I shook his confidence. "Release me to make this work. I have to do my makeup and hair."

"You're a natural beauty. You need neither."

I sighed. "Then why do you have the mirror and lights? You want us to be taken seriously. We have to do this right."

I saw marbles rolling around in the three-ring circus of his brain. He looked down at the table. There were foundation, powders, and brushes. It looked like they had been used. I suspected he'd experimented on himself.

Watching him, I estimated his position on the crazy-to-genius scale. (Another skill gained from working in a creative industry.) Some people are visionaries; some are purely nuts. Oliver was about medium-high. Definitely crazy, moderately intelligent.

He untied me.

If I were keeping score, I'd say I won the first round.

✳

Thirty-One —

"The pros use natural light, especially for a shoot like this." I shook my head in disappointment.

"This shoot will be magnificent."

"Then we need to do it right! I've been on thousands of sets! How many have you been on, Oliver?"

"More than you ... in my head."

"The pros prefer natural light."

He looked around. There was a row of windows along the wall of the little barn. All draped by black curtains. The walls shuddered from the wind.

It was cold out, probably approaching dawn.

I pointed to the corner by the sliding front doors. "Angles are always best. You need to move the set to that corner. We'll use those windows at right angles to one another. And pull back those curtains."

"Very well," he said. "Please assist."

I shook my head. "No way—this is a union set. Models don't touch the equipment."

I leaned toward the mirror, powdering my nose. I still wore the huge dress. I'll be darned if I put anything else on for that maniac.

I applied mascara while eyeballing the interior of the space. In the dim light, I saw snow shovels and ice picks leaning against the wall near the doors. A bucket of road salt, too.

I didn't see my purse or cell phone. He'd taken those. Probably in the van.

Oliver moved to the corner, then pulled back the curtains. The light streamed in at a low angle. I saw a black camera bag near the tripod.

He hadn't left his car keys or cell phone in sight.

"What are you staring at?" he demanded.

"The set. It's an old chair and an ugly rug. None of the props are period appropriate. How do I work with that crap? Where are the flowers? Or a pillow, even? Do you have a prop room? Who owns this dump?"

"I do. I've only just purchased it from Hank Leigel. I became enamored of the building's charm. You and I will make history here. It was time to make my move. It appeared you were becoming close to Steven Delavan. I like the fellow, but he's beneath you. I have waited a long time for this, Lady Mel."

Score! I knew the building. I'd seen it in Hank's "Sold" listings when I bought my new place. It was on the gravel road that extended from the lay-by near the lake. The barn was at least a mile down from the lay-by. There were few homes on the road. Most likely those residents had gone south for the winter.

Breaking free would be harder than I thought.

I stood up from the makeup table. "Where's the candy bar?"

Oliver stopped setting up the lights. "That's absurd, Melanie.

You stayed away from drugs. That is why you are well-preserved for your age."

True. But it angered me that a weirdo who was high on something lectured me about drug use. "A career among librarians made you an expert in party behaviors?"

"You observed us during the Midwinter's night event. Librarians are neither restrictive nor repressed. We express ourselves in a healthy way."

The nerve of this guy. I glanced above the barn door. That hay pulley gave me an idea. "I need to stretch before we start. And we need to do a light test."

"We do not. This set is superb. Excellent idea about the window angles. Please change your clothing."

"I stretch beforehand, and I test. Take it or leave it."

I moved toward the door, wrestling with the dress as best I could. He charged toward me, blocking my way. "Where do you think you're going?"

"I need fresh air."

The barn was drafty, and outside temps were about forty degrees. Any idiot would understand the air was already fresh.

"Very well," he said. "You can't get away from me in that dress. I am faster and stronger than you."

"Why would I run if I'm reviving a career stolen from me, Oliver? Eden Hoff is the bad guy, not me. What took you so long to come to my rescue?"

That surprised him.

He raised his eyebrows. "I-I had to find you. I followed you in the city, but then you disappeared. I moved here as soon as I could—"

"And brought me to this dump? Why didn't you tell me your idea sooner?"

A camera hung from his neck. It was an old thing. Film, not

digital. He reached into a trouser pocket, pulled out a vial of something, and dabbed his tongue with it.

I pushed further. "What did Kat Gold have to do with our vision? Why did you hurt her?"

"Who?"

"Do not play games with me."

"Kat was beautiful but lacked astuteness."

"You killed her for that?"

"We dated a few times. She became enamored of me. She discovered my passion for you and threatened to tell you."

"But why kill her in my building?"

"Why not? It was a simple matter of slipping her the codes and telling her I'd meet her there. Gravity did the rest. And it brought you and me closer together."

"You had an affair with Susan Victory, too?"

"I am appealing to women. I cannot hide my light under a bushel."

"Did you get the door codes from Susan?"

"Indeed, I did."

I shivered. "I think I need a drink."

"That, m'lady, I can provide."

You know you're in a Wisconsin version of *The Twilight Zone* when the guy who's kidnapped you serves cheese curds.

Oliver pulled a folding table from the van and set up a buffet of curds, strawberries, water, and champagne.

I sat in the makeup chair. "Where are the straws? I can't drink out of a bottle after my lipstick is on."

"Ah—"

"Steel straws. No plastic."

He pointed at the table, his hands shaking. "I have ice and a bottle of bubbly in a silver bucket. See?"

"It's not open."

"I thought we would celebrate after—"

"You thought wrong. Open it! Do I have to think for both of us?"

He fumbled with the wrapping on the bottle. His motor skills seemed to be deteriorating. The adrenaline was wearing off. I'll bet he was exhausted after not sleeping, too.

Fortunately, my adrenaline had kicked in. I've never been kidnapped by a stalker before. Perhaps it's part of the experience. I swished quickly to the table. I yanked the bottle away and gave it a shake. Ouch, elbow. I twisted off the wire cage. He ducked at the last second, so the cork zephyred past his ear and shattered a set light.

"Oops," I said.

"That light ... we need it."

"No, we don't."

"But you just said—"

"Stop being a drama queen, Oliver. This is a professional set." Gaslighting was easy once you got the hang of it. "Clean up the broken glass. Union rules."

He squinted at the mess but didn't move.

"Time is money, Oliver. Get going—stop. I need a glass for the champagne."

Back in my modeling days, I'd protected people who'd been targets of verbal abuse. I'd never been an instigator. It was a fascinating power trip. The more confused Oliver behaved, the more I wanted to destroy him.

✳

Oliver stooped by the camera. "I shall require a moment to prepare. Please get into position."

"Where's the wind machine?"

"I beg your pardon?"

I swished to the large sliding door. Yanking with my good arm, I said, "This. Needs. To. Be. Open."

"Stop right there! No farther."

"But that's barely enough. The wind needs to blow to give my hair movement." I stomped my feet. "Fine."

I selected a shovel that leaned against the wall. "I'll clean up the glass by the broken light. Time is money, Oliver. How are we ever going to produce content consistently?"

Moving to the corner, I scraped the glass into a pile with the shovel. Then I leaned on it, using it as a prop. "Don't use the tripod, Oliver. Move in, shoot lower. You have to make up for the broken light."

He looked down, fiddling with the camera around his neck. "I must focus—"

"Which of us has experience? Shoot lower!"

"You need to change clothing."

"Test poses first! On your knees, Oliver!"

"I beg your pardon—"

"On your knees!"

He actually did it.

I'd never had such power at a photo shoot.

All those years of being silent—being told that I didn't belong, that I was too "working class"—manifested in the strength to break this man.

In my mind, I pushed through boundaries I'd had for years. Feelings of never being good enough. Fear that my career had been a mistake, a matter of luck.

But Mel, you didn't chase what you couldn't become. You accepted what you were—and made it a success. You didn't hurt people for the sake of an image. You didn't abuse your body. Be proud of that.

I watched Oliver fumble with his camera. His face had paled, and his shoulders drooped. He appeared exhausted, like the guilt of his actions weighed on his mind. I almost felt sorry for him. Oliver Roberts had been obsessed with a woman who didn't exist, with images in a magazine. Or a brochure. Or a poster.

But he'd killed Kat Gold over it.

My compassion had limits.

People like Oliver believed the camera mattered more than human beings.

That perversion made him kill a woman and kidnap another.

The thought overwhelmed me. Between knowing what he'd done and feeling powerful—like I was transitioning from my prior life and into a new one—I stepped toward him. "What do you mean I'm not good enough, Oliver?"

He looked up from the camera. "I never said such a thing—"

"I am not moving to the back of the set this time." I gripped the shovel. "I'm staying right here. At the front. Where a woman like me deserves to be."

He wobbled. "Step back. You're threatening—"

"Darn right, I am!"

Quick as a cat, I snatched up the shovel and smashed it down. Clang! Right on his head!

The reverb shot through my hands and arms—that hurt!

Down Oliver crashed. "Ow—"

He still held the camera. Held it up to protect his head. I stomped on it—Clunk!

It broke something. His nose. Teeth. He clutched his face and rolled. I smashed him once again with the shovel, then swiped at the light tripods. Crash!

Glass shattered all over him.

I grabbed the skirt of the dress, racing to the open door. It was light out, but the clouds were low; it could snow any second.

I saw a snowy road and tall pines but no houses within view. I turned. Could I use the van? Where were its keys?

Oliver lay inert—but for how long?

I swished to the van, knocking over the table. The glasses and ice bucket smashed to the floor—so much broken glass!

Yanking open the van door, I climbed inside. The keys were in the ignition!

I slammed closed the door; the dress caught in it. I looked at Oliver. He was moving. I cranked the ignition and threw the vehicle into reverse. Pressed the gas. Please go, please go.

Oliver pulled himself to his hands and knees.

The vehicle flew backward and swerved as it backed out. Smash! It broke one of the sliding doors.

I steadied the wheel to keep from plowing into a snowbank. I threw it into drive, and the tires spun on the slick ground. Would Oliver get to me before I could drive away?

Lock the doors!

I pressed the gas, but the vehicle wouldn't move!

Oliver was getting up.

Please, van. GO!

I felt the tires gain purchase; the van lurched. I steered from the barn, slipping and sliding toward the road.

I gripped the wheel, trying not to press the gas too hard and fishtail into a ditch. If the van stopped, I had no way to run, not in the dress, not in the snow.

Please, Lord, don't let that happen!

Thirty-Two —

"**T**urn this h-heater to b-broil," I chattered.

"You're okay, Mel. It's okay."

Steven held me to his chest, rocking me. We sat on a box in the back of his van.

"Ow. W-watch the elbow," I cautioned.

I'd driven to the lay-by above Lake Cinnamon and gotten stuck. I jumped out and stood in the road, waving the folds and tulle of the dress in that insane lake wind to flag down a car.

Steven had been looking for me for hours, he'd said, since early Saturday morning when Lou got home from the gala and sounded the alarm that I wasn't at the ranch.

Steven grabbed a moving blanket, one of those quilted, insulated things, and pulled it around us. "You're a ballgown-shaped icicle," he said. "But you're gonna be okay, Mel. I'm here. You're safe."

"Thank G-God," I answered.

Every hospital room should come with a dog—a smart one with an advanced degree in greetings.

Mine did.

Max burst through the door and leaped onto the bed. Lou followed, carrying a pink cardboard box.

She set it on the counter. "I was gonna jump on ya, too, but Max is better at it." She pointed at the box. "Brought bakery in for the nurses. Want ya to get good care. Your pooch misses ya. He wanted to visit."

I wrapped my arms around him. The elbow still felt sore. I patted Max's head. "I won't be in here much longer. You and I will be in our backyard again soon, big fella."

"How ya feelin'?"

"Fine."

She cupped her mouth with her hands. "No, Mel. How are you feeling? Like, for real."

I smiled. "Like I was a suspect in a murder. Then knocked unconscious in a hallway. Then kidnapped by a maniac."

Lou rubbed her hands. "Now we're talkin'. You're busting out of your shell as we speak. Go on."

I looked at Max. He wagged his tail. "Oliver was drugging me. He put something in the champagne at the yacht club. That's why I felt so woozy. I suspect he did it to me at the library event, too."

She nodded. "He jumped ya in that hallway. Then lied and told Wooly he'd get ya home. What a weirdo." She looked at the chart at the foot of my bed. "They're keeping ya in for shock treatment, I hear?"

I shook my head. "No—I was in shock, Lou. They didn't put electrodes on my temples and zap me."

"Oops. I told everybody at the Tool & Rye that you had shock treatment. May need to correct that when ya get out."

I hugged Max, relishing the sight of his warm eyes and the feel of his beautiful, thick fur.

He was all the treatment I needed.

My next visitor was Wooly Gallagher.

It was great to see him. I teared up, even. My emotions felt like they were written on the sleeves of my hospital gown.

It's like I was test-driving them.

He carried a poinsettia. "From me, Cozette, and everyone at the paper," he said, then rearranged the bouquets on the windowsill to make space for the plant. "You have quite a flower collection, Mel. Lots of well-wishers."

I wiped my eyes with a tissue. "I hope everybody knows I survived. I'm not sure what Lou's told people."

"I didn't write your obit. Your friends will figure it out."

I laughed, and it hurt. I ached everywhere. The doctors said it was due to the trauma of the whole thing. "Glad to hear it."

"Lieutenant DuWayne said Oliver stalked you. No one knew."

"I should have known at my birthday party. I assumed you supplied the old modeling pictures. But Oliver did, apparently. I missed that clue."

"Kat knew he was off his rocker. That's why he killed her."

I shook my head. "Oliver thought I was getting too close to Steven. That's what made him act, finally. The jealousy drove him crazy. How's Foss Knickerbocker? Is she okay?"

"She returned to Illinois. Glad she didn't become a victim, too."

"I fell for Oliver's act. He gave me a strange vibe, but I had no idea he was obsessed with me." I shrugged. "I had a fan during my career. Who knew?"

"He's behind bars now. Charged with murder, kidnapping—everything the authorities could think of."

My phone dinged with a message. "Could you please read that? I'm too tired."

"Sure thing." He reached for it. "It's from Rand. He heard about what happened and is landing in Chicago. Then he's on his way up here. Should I reply?"

"Tell him he doesn't have to; I'll call him when I'm out of here."

"Sure thing."

"Thanks, Wool. I appreciate it."

Crystal Broadway appeared in my new building after I was released from the hospital.

She always had a unique fashion sense, I thought.

She wore a velvet pantsuit with jingle bell earrings. "Hi, Mel. I hope you don't mind, like, if I stop by. I heard this was your new place."

"Come in, Crystal. How do you like it?"

She gazed around the interior. Faded wallpaper hung from the walls in strips, and the floor had scuffs. "It might, like, need work?"

I laughed. "Don't we all?"

"What are you gonna do in here?"

"Picture this: rows of wooden library shelves, a fireplace with chairs and a rug in the corner, and racks of handmade greeting cards."

"Inga Honeythorne could make those! I love it," Crystal said. "And replace the wallpaper with something really fun."

"Would you like some tea?"

"Yeah, but want me to make it? I heard you had, like, shock treatments."

I shook my head. "I did not, but thanks for asking."

I stepped to the scarred service counter and pressed buttons on the coffee machine I'd brought from the mall. Hot water began flowing into a mug.

"So, what is this place gonna be exactly, Mel?"

"I've considered a few ideas. Kevin Sunny is doing the renovation. What would you think about a bookstore?"

"Really?"

It delighted me to hear the enthusiasm in her voice. I turned toward her. "Yes, and I'd like your help if you're willing."

"Wow, Mel—yeah!"

I stayed with Fern Bubble because Kevin Sunny had to replace the sidelight glass in my door.

You know how that goes.

A small job leads to other house projects. My boxy, federal-style fixer-upper finally got its facelift—the first floor, at least.

I budget my pennies.

The second level can wait.

It felt fantastic to be near the horses. Max loved it. He and I took over the evening barn chores. It was Winston Churchill who said, "There's something about the outside of a horse that's good for the inside of a girl."

I couldn't agree more.

Tulip got carrots and a grooming every night. Took forever. Grooming a draft horse isn't like washing a car; it's like scrubbing the car wash building.

Did I mind puttering in the barn until the wee hours?

Not in the least.

It should be what doctors prescribe (and what insurance includes) to recover from trauma. Fern said she'd love to have us as regular visitors, even after we returned home. Max barked his head off when she said it. Done deal.

Fern, Susan Victory, and I developed a social media scholarship in Kat Gold's name for the high school marketing department. The "Gold Croissant" will go to a student considering a career in social media who displays layers of "empathy, truth, and leadership" online. It's the Golden Rule: Treat others as you want to be treated.

The first one will be awarded next year at the Cinnamon Cinnies. I'm nominated to present it. We'll see. It should be a group thing.

To nurture my newly discovered inner decorator, Fern and Susan took me on shopping excursions to antique places, thrift stores, and home decor shops. My place will look lived in, not a campsite where a woman is just existing. I took a decorating quiz. Apparently, my style is Homebody Chic meets Emotional Disconnect.

Just kidding.

According to Susan, it's Ralph Lauren meets Northwoods cottage. "It's clean, classic lines, yet cozy with warm colors and lots of light. It's you, Mel," she said.

My fireplace mantle now has more than one picture. Mom and Dad are up there in a place of honor.

I miss them so.

I never spoke with anybody about the shock of losing them when I was young.

Memories of my parents come up while I'm grooming Tulip. Another famous person once wrote, "A horse's neck can absorb a lot of tears." Wow, is that true.

Speaking of truth, Susan and I had a long talk. She was not honest about stealing the door codes to my storage space off the loading dock. Yes, she did snoop in Fern's notebook and write them down. But she slipped them to Oliver, not Kat.

Had I known that detail, I would have suspected Oliver immediately.

He manipulated Susan into it. Just as he manipulated Kat into entering my building. It took soul-searching to forgive Susan, but she and I are cool now.

She agreed to see a therapist. She and Hank are trying to work things out. I support them as long as they're both happy.

On the relationship front, the pilot and I have kept in touch, but I need space.

To best describe it, he and I are in a holding pattern.

I also made vacation reservations for next summer, only a few months away. I'm taking a respite for the first time in about twenty-five years.

I was in my office one afternoon, talking with Inga Honeythorne, gripping a voucher in my paw. "Inga, I'm taking time off."

"That's wonderful, Mel—finally!"

We discussed dates. She would operate the mall while Max and I were gone. We settled on a few weeks in the summer.

"We are you headed?" Inga asked.

I looked at the coupon. It was the one I'd won at VIP Bowling. "Up north. Copper Falls. Something is drawing me there. I sense a new adventure awaits."

Note to Reader

Dear Friend,

Thank you for reading my debut mystery novel, *Model Suspect*. I was thrilled to write it and sincerely hope you enjoyed it. I write books for readers who want to laugh and escape, if only for a little while. When I moved into my fixer-upper home with a beautiful backyard, it immediately inspired me to write a mystery. The yard led me to create Cinnamon, Wisconsin—a cozy, touristy small town—and the story's main character, Mel Tower.

I'd love you to join me in the Backyard on Instagram: @ thebackyardmodel. It's a lovely, peaceful spot; I share the yard's beauty, wildlife, and book updates with readers. If social media isn't for you, please visit my website and join my email community! www.tksheffieldwrites.com. This is where you'll find information on my new books: *Pontoon*: romance, boats, and bad business in the Wisconsin Northwoods, and *The Infinity Thieves*: a Bonnie Law novella.

Take care,
T.K. Sheffield

Inga's Shortbreads

Inga likes her shortbread cookies light and tender. She sprinkles them with colored sugar crystals depending upon the season: Red and green for Christmas, pastels for Easter, orange for Halloween. She prefers making them in fingers, but rounds and molds are excellent, too. Baking time for different shapes varies.

Preheat oven to 325 degrees.

- 4 sticks (2 cups) unsalted, grated butter or cut into pats*
- 1 cup brown sugar (note: alternatives are 1/2 cup white granulated sugar, 1/2 cup powdered sugar)
- 1 TB vanilla
- 1/2 tsp. salt
- 4 cups flour (note: can use half rice flour, too)

In a mixer, combine the butter, sugar, and vanilla. Mix on high until fluffy and light in color (up to 4-5 minutes, depending upon speed of mixer.) Add salt to flour, then add flour gradually to dough in mixer. If it combines in a clump, don't add all the flour! Don't overwork the dough.

Chill until firm (about 30 minutes), then roll out to about 3/4 inch thickness on wax paper dusted with powdered sugar. Add more powdered sugar if it gets sticky.

Cut into fingers (1x3 inch strips), then place in rows on an ungreased, parchment-lined baking sheet. Prick dough with fork.

Bake 325 for 18-22 minutes. (Or more, depending upon thickness of shortbread and the oven.) Keep an eye on it!**

Sprinkle with granulated sugar immediately after removing from oven. Let cool in pan for a few minutes, then move to a wire rack to cool further.

*Use good butter. Inga loves Westby organic butter and the locally made butters available at Pearce's Farm Stand in Walworth, Wisconsin. Use close-to-room-temp butter with just enough chill to grate or cut into pats. (Plan ahead and remove butter from fridge before making.)

** Keep an eye on it! Watch the edges. It should be the color of a summer sunrise—very pale gold.

Tips:
 - Prick the dough in neat rows to allow the dough to rise while baking.
 - To create a more buttery flavor, freeze in a freezer container with a lid (not a plastic bag), then thaw.

January 6 is National Shortbread Day.

Enjoy!

Biography

Author Tracey "TK" Sheffield, MA, lives in Wisconsin and writes about her home state from her heart. She's an author, educator, and over-50 model, and she pens mysteries and romantic comedies for readers who want to laugh, escape, and enjoy stories served with fried cheese curds or that sweet, Midwest-only treat, frozen custard.

Tracey has been a horse lover since reading *A Filly for Joan* by C.W. Anderson as a child. She grew up in Madison, Wisconsin—a problem for an outdoor-loving, horse-crazy girl—and quickly moved to the country. She has degrees from UW-Madison and Mount Mary University, and when she's not writing, she's sharing her beautiful backyard on Instagram.

Tracey is co-secretary of the Wisconsin chapter of Sisters in Crime and a member of the events committee for the Wisconsin Writers Association.

In book one of The Backyard Model Mysteries, *Model Suspect*, a retired model uses her skill at spotting "posers" to solve murders in her touristy Wisconsin town. The manuscript was nominated for a 2023 RWA Daphne du Maurier mainstream mystery award.

For news about upcoming books, events, giveaways, and writing tips, please subscribe to Tracey's newsletter, Bubbles & Fiber, on her website, tksheffieldwrites.com.